Break The Chain
Part 1: Hustle Game Too Hard

D1484229

Damian L. Johnson

Cadmus Publishing
www.cadmuspublishing.com

Elements of Peace Co.

Other books to come

Break The Chain Series:

Also check out book one of my fantasy series called Elementals, Rise the Hell Fire Storm. Find it at amazon.com or Barnes and Noble.

Other books to come

Elemental Series:

Table of Contents

Part 1:

Hustle Game Too Hard

INTRO: A HOOD LEGEND

January 4, 1989. Money Lane, Texas.

It was dark in the house and my big bro Daren said he didn't know why. At the time big bro was only eleven, but still he knew something was wrong because not even a hallway light was on.

Our father, Kenneth, known as Kay in the hood, stood at the window with an all-black hoodie over his head with is AK on his shoulder. When big bro would tell me this story it always reminds me of that Malcolm X movie. Like history replay's itself over and over.

Our father K sold dope in the hood of westside Money Lane to get this house. It made us feel good to have something as a family even though it was in the hood, and we was still poor. Somehow my father made it look good and he was always happy. My father put the house in my mother's name because at the time she had off and on jobs and her check income was just enough to squeeze by. Ma said my father would say, "the man don't really care what goes on in the hood as long as you make it look good."

Big bro also said my father will forever be a hood legend. A surgeon with the AK, I mean cold. Hence his nickname Kay. I was only six or so at the time, so I don't remember much about that night, but Daren does. He tells me the story every now and then. Truth be told sometimes he relives it like a nightmare.

Kay stood in the living room window with his AK aimed. Every time he would hear a car approaching he would peel back the blinds to watch the street by the dim streetlight. Ma, Daren and me sat hidden behind the long couch as if it was going to protect us should slugs start flying. Daren said I was crying because ma was crying, but her tears fell silently while I screamed like a newborn.

My father tensed up then relaxed with a deep breath, his AK ready and on aim out the window. Down the street he could see a grey crown vic on the creep. Kay was just about to let the AK go but the crown vic sped off with a loud SKIRRT, then bent the corner.

My father's voice was strong yet calm as he spoke. "BAE." When my mother didn't answer Kay yelled, "REA!"

My mother jumped speaking through tears, "What Kay?"

"Go get the money form the closet and go out the back to ya mama's."

"You said you wasn't gon kill no body Kay!" Korita cried.

"Don't tell me what I said, do what I say Rea!"

My father's anger made me cry harder util my mother picked me up and held me tight. I stopped crying as my mother ran to Kay. She kissed him pleading, "I love you; we need you. Please don't go back to prison!"

Kay nodded slightly with his attention still watching the streets. "GO REA!"

"Kay, I got a bad feeling about-".

My father shouted over my mother, "Now is not the time, GO REA!"

Ma could only shake her tears away as she grabbed Daren's hand, taking us to the back room. Ma took us to the closet telling us to lay down and play hide-n-seek. Then she was gone.

If Riverside thank legendary K done went soft, they playin with death. Lord knows death is one of God's most trusted, needed soldier's, Kay thought to himself. Seconds later he spotted the grey Crown Vic hit the block again, slowly approaching. When the Crown Vic slowed to a stop in front of the house, the back window rolled down exposing a Tech-9 Kay let the AK spit through the house window with no hesitation. The Crown Vic sped off as the Tech-9 bust back with reckless aim. Kay cleared the glass from the window with AK then hopped out thinking, I must have got a good shot in because the Crown Vic crashed into the neighbor's fence across the street. I marched to the Crown Vic ready to light it up if I saw the slightest movement. I glanced back when I heard my boy's and Korita come out of the house.

TAT TAT TAT TAT TAT – it seemed like I felt it before I heard it. Hot lead entered my chest and at that moment felt so unreal to be. All I could think about was what my father used to say. If you live by the sword, then you die by it. Now that's its my time I can't cry about it. But in this moment, it hurts to leave. . . When my body hit the ground, I saw a blurred vision of a wounded person hop out the back of the car and take off running.

With me being eleven you would think it was strange that I didn't cry. To be honest I didn't know what to think or feel because I've seen dead bodies before. I heard gunshots on many many nights that it soon became my bedtime story. But this was real, and it's different when it's your flesh and blood, your father's body dead in the street. I stood frozen on the porch watching my father's killer get away and all I could think was my father is really gone.

My lil bro Kasey followed my mother to my father's side in the street. My mother dropped to her knees in my father's blood, crying, holding my father. . . She looked up to heaven crying, asking why? This went on for hours until the cops finally came. I'll never forget that night. It haunts me, but also drives me to play the game right. Now I hate cops for not giving a damn.

Rich, one of my father's friends came and hid the AK before the cops came. When he saw my face all he could say was, "You gotta break the chain, youngsta, ya fathers hustle game was too hard."

CHAPTER 1

HUSTLE GAME TOO HARD

10 years later . . .

Daren forced himself out of bed at his usual time (late afternoon). The first thing he did was turn the TV on.

"Gang violence is at an all-time high in Money Lane. This city stared off as a peaceful community, but now . . ."

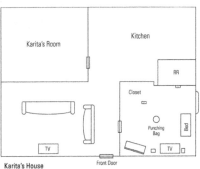

Daren smacked his lips, turned the TV off then hit the switch on the radio. His favorite song bone things n harmony played loud from the speakers. "It's the thuggish ruggish bone," Daren sang along as he did ten sets of thirty pushups between hitting the punching bag. After his daily forty-five minute workout he jumped in the shower, mentally preparing for the day.

After his shower he entered his closet thinking what to wear. He put outfits together in his mind from his collection of kick's, fitted hats and name brand clothes. He had plenty of jay's, air forces and Nikes lined up on his side of the closet wall. Daren's side of the closet was nothing compared to Kasey's. it was Daren's unspoken rule to make sure Kasey was good with their absence of a father. Daren threw on some black polo jeans that were pressed from the cleaners, a pair of red jay's and a grey and red polo shirt. After he got dressed he sat at the edge of his bed wiping down his jays just for the hell of it. When he looked up his mother was standing in the door, a hand on her hip looking like the strong, beautiful black woman life molder her to be.

Daren turned the music down, checking his self out in the dresser's mirror. He brushed his waves to perfection adding a little bit of blue magic to make them shine. He could see Korita staring at him through the mirror, so he asked, "Wha's good ma, you lookin good today. You goin out or something?"

"Don't what's up ma me!" Korita shot back, crossing her arms. The evil eyes she gave Daren let Daren know where this was going so he just listened.

"Umm Humm, dope slangin, gang bangin just like ya father."

"I'm not bangin ma, for real!"

"Tell that to somebody else. Boy I'm ya mama . . . Do you honestly think yo shit don't stank? . . . Huh!"

"No ma," Daren replied, shaking his head.

Korita joined Daren at the dresser, giving him that concerned look only a mother can give. She'd been overlooking Daren's actions for so long but now she felt the need to let her oldest son know how she felt. "Walking around like you're untouchable, in and out at all times of the night. Disappearing for days at a time. You betta not be havin no guns and drugs in my house Daren!" . .

"Alright ma, damn! Why you naggin?"

"Alright ma my ass! You know Kasey worships the ground you walk on. He wants to do everything you do. I just-" Korita paused then continued with a stressful sigh, "I just want a better life for my kids than this shit."

"Ok I see now. You need some money. That's why you naggin."

Daren made eye contact with his mother through the mirror trying to read her. Korita snapped with a sudden explosive anger, "I don't wan you damn drug money! You know what? I'm through talkin to you! Go get your brother from school so he don't get into no shit." As Korita stormed out of his room he shouted, "Love you ma." But all Daren could hear was the front door slam.

Daren crept to his room's door and quietly closed it after making sure Korita was outside. Next, he went to his bed and moved the bunk bed to the side. Daren located a loose wooden floorboard with this foot, gave it some of his weight until the floorboard raised slightly. Once he was able to pull the board up his stash was exposed. Daren had $31,000 in cash, a triple zip-locked pound of dro, half an ounce of work, a scale, his weed tray, a 9 with a regular clip and extended clip, some baggies, a box of grape swisher sweets. Last was Daren's' prized possession, an AK-47 with a banana clip and a few boxes of bullets.

Daren counted out a thousand dollars then pocketed the money. He listened making sure his mother didn't come back in the house as he rolled a blunt of sour diesel. After he finished rolling up he stuck the blunt in his pocket while making sure to put the gar gut's in a paper. Daren balled the paper up and put it in his pocket as well thinking; I know ma be on my trail. I just gotta work clean like I been doin. He snatched his Glock, his extended clip. Popped the clip in and hid the strap behind his back. Finally, Daren quietly put the floorboard back then moved the bunk bed back in its place.

Daren left his room feeling like his mother needed a man in her life, but it wasn't his place to bring it up, so he didn't. When Daren walked out the front door his mother sat in her porch chair smoking the last of her cigarette. Korita watched her oldest child count out $500 and hand it to her. She didn't move forcing Daren to explain, "Take the money ma, you need to pay the gas, lights, water and we need some food." Daren forced the money in Korita's hand with a soft kiss on her cheek, "Ma can I take the car?"

Korita responded with a sassy, "Hell no! You don't have nobody's driver's license and you had my car smelling like weed the other night. I don't smoke in my car what makes you think you can?"

Daren walked out of the yard not trying to argue with his mother. He headed West to shake her, but she followed him and stood in the middle of the yard still nagging, "Boy, where you think you goin? Kasey's school is that way!" she pointed in the opposite direction with concern for Kasey. For the last month Kasey's been coming home later than usual. Daren had to find him a few times getting blowed with a few of his friends in bandos in the Fairway Apartments. Ever since Kasey got shot at after a fight Korita made it a top priority to make sure Kasey came straight home after school.

Daren yelled back, "com on ma, I know you don't think Ima walk. I headed to Smoke Joes house to get a ride."

Korita took a few steps yelling, "Oh okay, tell Joe my car jerking every time I pull off."

"Alright, ma, anything else?" Daren asked sounding a little annoyed. "Yea, smart ass, tell Joe I need to run some errands which means you need to come right back and watch the house till I get back."

"Okay ma," Daren shouted. Korita wanted to tell Daren to please be careful, but he was already a few houses down.

Daren glanced back checking for his mother. When he didn't see her he tossed the crumbled paper of gar guts to the curb while pulling his Motorola phone from his pocket. He called his connect and Rich answered on the first ring.

"Pockets lookin young. I need to swang through!"

Rich's voice was deep, but he was playa in his own way. "Coo as a fan young blood. You know where we at."

"I'm bringin lil bro if it's coo."

"Y'all good in my book. What we lookin at for the mean time?"

Daren did some quick calculations in his head then told Rich, "Probably like 120 if the price tag still the same."

"Pull up family, it's all love. You know that."

"No doubt, gimme like twenty minutes Rich."

Daren ended the call just as he got to Joe's house. Joe's house was four houses down from Daren's and it was always the same every time Daren walked into Joe's yard. Raggedy dismantled cars and a few trucks were in the front and back yard like Joe ran the hood mechanic shop. Joe's red lack was the first car in the driveway, catching Daren's eye. Daren opened Joe's gate, walked down the side of the driveway making sure not to step on any oil spots. He found Joe working on a car behind the lack, leaning in the open hood of the car with his body half-way in. Daren stood by Joe looking in trying to find out just what Joe's dirty old ass was doing.

"Look-out Smoka Joe! Let me holla at-chu real quick," Daren shouted. Joe pulled his body out of the car so fast with a wide smile at the sound of Daren's voice. Joe was fifty-three years old, but you would never tell from the way Joe was always amped up.

Joe faced Daren talking a hundred miles an hour, "How you doin D? Is everything ok wit-chu. How's little brother. Is Korita alright?"

Daren emotionless eye contact with Joe turned Joe's smile to a frown.

"Tell me why you sold me that car for ma that's full of problems."

Joe shook his head rapidly as he stressed, "Naw D, you know I wouldn't do bad business wit-chu. What's wrong with it?"

"Ma says its jerkin every time she pull off." Joe thought for a moment then already knew what to do so they both could benefit. "The motor mounts must need to be changed. It's no big deal D. Motor mounts wear down over time. I'll go to the junk yard on the east side, strip some mounts and put'em on fo ya. Just bless my game."

Daren pulled his blunt from his pocket, straightened it then lit it. All the while he gave Joe the you must think I'm stupid look.

On the exhale Daren asked, "Why you tryin to play me fam?"

Joe looked down with a goofy grin explaining, "You know I need to wake up D. Don't be like that. When I finish this car ima spend some big money with-chu. I just need you to look out fa me D."

Daren took a few puffs fighting the urge to cough. "I need a wip for tonight." Daren glanced back at the lack of indication it was time for his and Joe's regular routine. Joe's eyes lit up because he knew it was about to go down.

"I got-chu D! Just get me a six-pack of O.E and nice slab of work an you can push the lac till tomorrow night. On top of that I'll still fix your mother's car."

"Bet, make it quick I'm in a rush." Joe found the keys in the toolbox next to him in a jittery action. He tossed them to Daren with the quickness.

"How long you gon be D? To get the work I mean."

"About forty-five minutes or so. I gotta take care of some shit first. Oh yea, come by later tonight to fix ma's car. She said something about she gotta run some errands."

"You got it D, I'll be waitin." Daren shook his head at Joe's sudden sad demeanor as he hopped in the lac. He wished he could show Joe how less of a man being a smoker made him. But it was what it was.

Daren parked the lac in the long line of cars in front of Park Village High School. He waited until he saw Kasey cross the street to the Sonic with a couple of his friends. Daren got out of the car and yelled, "Kasey!" while flagging his younger brother down. Kasey dropped his head wishing he could chill just once. He was really getting tired of Korita's naggin and strict rules. Daren hopped back in the lac, turning the car on for some AC.

A minute later Kasey jumped in the front seat rubbing his hands together. "Big bro, I'm old enough to drive now! Please let me drive the lac."

"Sorry lil bro, I can't let you push the lac but happy early b-day." Daren handed Kasey $400 as he pulled off. Kasey watched Daren light half a blunt with wide eyes. His mouth watered from the smell of hydroponic buds. Kasey sang and danced while reaching for the blunt, "Gon n let me hit dat!"

"Nope, not till you talk to ma first. You know she be trippen on me if she see you blowed."

"Big bro, I'm gettin tired of ma! Why she won't let me do me?"

"Because she love you. don't let her put you in a bad mood bro bro. I want you to put on your best shit for tonight! Get ready for a birthday night so live."

When they got home Kasey ran inside to his and Daren's closet. He stood in deep thought about what to wear. "I hope big bro put me in the doe with some hoes. I'm about to be 17 so I gotta be playa," Kasey thought.

His final decision was a Chicago Bulls fitted and jersey, denim jeans and some all black suede #4 jay's. Next he brushed his wavy hair a few times before he put his hat on.

"Hurry up Kasey! We gotta go and I need to show you somethin real quick!" Daren shouted from the room. When Kasey walked into their room he could only stop in front of the bed and say "DAMMMMN BRO, that's all yours?"

Daren continued pulling money out of his stash in a rush. "It's really both ours. I don't cherish this shit bro. Plus, if something happens to me it'll be yours. That's why I'm showing you the stash."

Kasey's face turned sour forcing him to ask, "Why would something happen to you?"

Daren gave Kasey a serious stare while explaining, "The game good to me right now but shit can go downhill fast. Ma can't keep a job that's worth it and I refuse to let us starve. With no other choice I gotta ride for the fam."

"So you gone tell ma to let me ride tonight?" Kasey asked feeling turnt.

"I got to. You're 17 now so I figured why not." Kasey grabbed the AK out of the stash asking, "this was dad's right?"

Daren continued bagging money allowing the silence to confirm a hurtful truth. After a few minutes Daren said, "I guess I gotta teach you how to shoot. But we gon start off small." Daren pulled the Glock 9 from behind his back, showing it to Kasey. Kasey set the AK on the bed then grabbed the Glock while whispering, "UOOO this is nice."

"Be careful bro! Glocks don't have safety's and it's loaded."

Kasey gave a deadly smile stating, "I know a lil somethin big bro!"

Daren watched Kasey take the extended clip out and pull the slide back. A bullet fell out of the chamber and hit the wooden floor with a clank and roll. Kasey bent to pick the bullet up, but Daren stopped him. "Wait bro! Number one rule, never touch a bullet with your bare hands."

"How come?"

"I see you don't know as much as you should. Bare hands leave fingerprints and fingerprints get you caught."

"Fa-show, fashow big bro," Kasey replied while picking up, cleaning and forcing the bullet back into the clip with his shirt. Kasey watched Daren put a latex glove on his right hand. Kasey didn't understand why Daren didn't touch the slab of work as he cut off a nice piece, weighted it on the digital scale then bagged the work. " Why you don't touch the work big bro?"

"So crack doesn't get in my pores. I've seen nigga's handled work with their bare hands, even hold work in their mouths to hide it from laws. In the end they end up dope fiends from exposure."

"Dat's why you didn't put the work on the scale without a baggie huh?"

"Exactly lil bro, I'm happy you do know a lil something because ima need you to have my back tonight."

"Why? What's finna happen? We finna ride on some nigga's?"

"Nothin like that bro. I'm bout to cop some pounds, move some shit and I'm taking pop's AK just to be safe."

"You don't trust ya man's or something?" Kasey asked with great interest.

"I do, but I never copped with all my bread before. Plus the number one rule in this game is ain't no such thing as friends. Even family will cross you if they can. Remember that lil bro."

"Who taught you the game?"

"O.G Rich gave me a lil sauce, but I learned mostly from bumping my head. I took a few losses from jackers, I used to run out of bandos in the Manor that were used for traps. I crashed a few of my cars as soon as I copped'em. But I've grown wise now and my hustle game too hard. Fa real bro, I could lock shit down in Money Lane if I wanted. But I'm just chillin."

Daren put the work in his pocket in deep contemplation. Kasey watched Daren put the 30,000 in his duffle bag then stuff the AK in as well. Kasey stood with a open mouth watching Daren bolt to the closet and return with three more duffle bags. "You hold the money, watch n learn. Now let's bounce. We gotta hurry before ma gets back. And put the clip back in the 9 and put it behind you back. Be careful." Kasey did what Daren said, happily following his big brother outside.

When they hopped in the lac and pulled off all Kasey could think was; this is so turnt. . . I shoulda been turned seventeen a long time ago! Den big bro woulda been let me ride.

Daren pulled up and waved Joe down. Joe moved with the quickness, leaning in the passenger window when Kasey rolled it down.

"What-chu got fa me D? an ima fix ya mother's car too D! Just tell her to drop it off whenever she can." Daren pulled Joes work from his pocket but held it in a dangle. "Ma's goin through some shit. Just go over there and fix it when you see her home later. Don't take her money when she try to pay you either. I gave you a lil more than two fifty packs."

"Ima knock it out D!" Kasey held his laugh when Joe grabbed the slab of work with a cheesy smile. Joe bolted inside as Daren pulled off, hand on the wheel. "Tha's crazy big bro, why you bless his game when he a crack head. Den you paid him all that money for ma's wip."

"Because he's still a human being even though he's a dope fiend. Then you gotta realize professional shops might charge anywhere from $900 to $1500 for shit like that. On da coo I'm the one that got over. But his addition makes his mind weak."

"Hell yea, I didn't think about it like dat."

Rich's house was around the corner and the corner house of Oak Ride. Daren parked by the curb because two cars were in the driveway. The Buick was Rich's, but Daren didn't know who's the other car was. Daren and Kasey gathered the bags then quickly hopped out of the lac . . There were maybe eleven or twelve people on the porch who each had a red flag somewhere, dressed in black and red. Kasey noticed the guns they held out in the open and got nervous. Kasey followed closely behind Daren through the yard. When the homies threw Big B's at Daren and Kasey acknowledging their presence Kasey threw the B back to show love. Daren pulled Kasey in the house telling him, "Come on bro," because Kasey was about to start up a conversation while accepting a blunt that was offered to him.

Once they got inside, they noticed a middle-aged heavy-set but stocky Hispanic man sitting at the round table in the corner of the living room watching TV. He sat by himself, and Kasey wondered why. Rich sat in the middle of the living room on a long black leather couch in front of a coffee table.

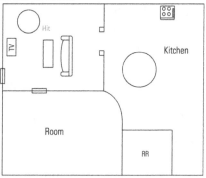

"Come sit wit-cha O.G.," Rich directed with open arms. . Daren pulled two chairs from the table, sitting them at the coffee table across from Rich. Rich leaned over the coffee table demanding, "Hit this befo it hit-chu." Rich's hand was out waiting for Kasey or Daren to lock B's with him.

"Come on now Rich, you know we straight." Daren explained.

Rich looked at Kasey causing Kasey to try and lock B's with him, but Daren held Kasey in his seat. Rich began talking hysterically, moving his hands and spitting as he spoke with a deep passion for his way of life.

"Legendary K was a O.G in the hood. My brotha from anotha motha. It's only right, law that his boys get down with the set."

"We just tryin to eat Rich," Daren explained.

"Oh yeah. Tell me why y'all always flamed up along with half of Oak Ride?"

Kasey proudly stated, "Red was dad's favorite color!"

Daren slapped his forehead mumbling, "Please be quiet Kasey."

Rich continued his rant, "Yo fatha was born into this way of life! That's why red was his favorite color. Oak Ride is bloody just like Riverside is clued up. I want you to know young dough that your fatha did thangs. . . Put in work, undastand me. . . On the strength of that I look out fa y'all. When y'all was hungry I'm the one Korita called for groceries back in the day. So y'all been eatin befo you knew you was eatin." Rich paused to let his words sink in.

"Is that the only reason you look out fa me?" Daren asked, with his bag of money ready.

"Humph, well. . . Ya hustle game too hard to not you play." Rich smiled with a long pause, showing off his gold teeth. Kasey rubbed his hands together feeling turnt for no reason. He liked Rich's vibe and the way he carried his self. Rich cleaned his gold designer frames with a chuckle. "You know I gotta give you hard time young dough. How much bread you tryin to invest."

"It's the same price tag?"

"Ahh, most likely with the numbers you putting up." Rich cleared the table as Daren and Kasey began taking money out of the bag and stacking it on the table. "Lookin good amigo," Rich said to the Hispanic man. The Hispanic man nodded with little interest, deep into whatever he was watching.

Kasey took in the man's casual wear and thick gold chain with a gold dragon medallion. When the Hispanic man locked eyes with Kasey, Kasey quickly turned his head back forward. Daren sat there already running scenarios in his head on who to hit licks on and who to bless. Once the money was piled on the table Rich shouted, "Vicky, Janice! Bring 120 out real quick!"

Five minutes later two fine women came out of the kitchen each pulling two baskets of thirty pounds to the table. Vicky resembled a high yellow Aaliah with golden champagne colored eyes. Janice was a sexy chocolate who had a body so right God probably had trouble getting a permit to build her perfection.

"Hey Daren," Vicky sang with a voice as sweet as heaven.

Janice tied her long black real hair in a ponytail exclaiming, "He must be Kasey! Vicky he is going to be so cute when he get older."

"Y'all gone on back to the kitchen." Rich ordered. Janice and Vicky left the living room laughing and talking close together like bad bitches would. Daren began weighing pounds while checking out the quality of the bud. Once Daren was almost done he glanced up at Rich to find him watching him.

"You not gon count the money Rich?"

"Naw, I trust you. If it's short I'll cover but you always on point. Now get on. Rich spoke in a trusting fatherly manner that made Kasey want to come over more often. But Kasey knew that Korita would never let that happen.

Back at the house Daren and Kasey sat in their room waiting for their mother to come home. Daren hit the punching bag softly, so he didn't break a sweat. Kasey sat on the bottom bunk wondering what the plan was for tonight. Daren saw Kasey's bored face and began thinking out loud, "I need to make a call to all my pound movers. My phone so live that the rest will fall in place." Kasey grabbed Daren's phone from the bed, "I'll do it."

"Alright, umm if a P is before a name they a pound custo. If it's a S before a name it's a sack custo and I don't move for less than $40 unless I'm at a party or something."

"Ima just tell everybody we on with some flame. Is that coo?"

Daren nodded suddenly stopping his combinations, remembering Kasey's other gift. "Get out the way real quick lil bro." Kasey stood to the side making calls while Daren pulled the floorboard up opening the stash. Kasey watched Daren weigh out a zip of dro, bag it then toss the zip to him. Kasey ended a call and took a long whiff. "Thanks big bro. Since my b-day really tomorrow do I get more stuff?"

"Be happy for what you got bro. Some people don't get shit for they birthday but being thankful for another day of life." Daren made sure to zip lock all three bags that his pound of dro was in so the strong odor wouldn't escape. Daren put the wooden board and bed back and joined Kasey on the bed. Kasey made a few more call's then asked, "I wonder what's taking ma so long. I ain't tryina spend my b-day eve here bored."

"She probably stopped by GG's, you know how she and grama get. They most likely gon cook you something tomorrow." Kasey didn't like the sound of that, so he continued looking through Daren's phone. "Big bro I know some of these people."

"Yep, you probably gon know the rest by the end of the night. Need to knows. Rick is a white boy I used to go to school with. He a hoe but he'll but pounds for 450 if it's some fire. So don't rob 'em. Kel, I met him at the strip club one night. His parents got a ranch just out of the city. He claims we went to school together too, but after freshman year he started going to school in Adams Hill to not have to come to the hood no mo. I don't remember him, but he buys 20 – 30 pounds every time I turn up. Sharena, she's a fine ass stripper from Paradise. She good for a few pounds. Her mom got a house in Riverside and all they do is sell sacks. They make a killin because it be dry over there. I can't forget about Mike and T, they sell pounds, but they don't get a plug. They end up bringing me a lot of bread and they tax on top of what I charge. I never meet they custos but I ain't trippen. Plus, I know they powder heads and be on some dope fiend shit."

"What kinda dope fiend shit?" Kasey asked.

"Shit like digging in they custos pounds, takin a sack here and there. It's fucked up but that's how the game go when you don't got yo own plug."

"And you coo wit dem jucin nigga's when you could be makin more bread."

"It's less hastle on my end bro. I'd break my neck tryin to serve everyone in Money Lane. Plus I got a live set up where I trap. Check me out. Johnnyboy and Aron kinda like my potna's/ workers. I say that because they move a lot of shit for me and I give'em little or nothin. You see, they bar heads so what I do give'em is a blessing in they eyes. . . You gon meet'em at the party tonight. . . Oh, I can't forget about Shella. She's a white girl. One of them skater rocker chicks who got a lot of friends who buy QP's for $110 and HP's for $215. I got more pound custos but those are the major ones. A lot of the niggas I fuck wit get they bread and fuck it off so I don't depend on them too much. When I trow these parties I spend $250 on each pound with a goal to make at least $380 =$400 a brick."

Daren stopped talking when he heard Korita's car pull into the driveway. A minute later the front door slammed. Korita yelled "Kasey! Come get the groceries out the back seat!"

"Kay ma!" Kasey yelled back.

Daren laughed to himself because he knew this was Korita's way for Kasey to check in with her.

Daren joined Korita in the kitchen to help her put the groceries up. When Korita saw Daren dressed up she asked, "Where y'all think y'all goin?"

Kasey brought the last few bags of food in with his eyes on the bag of green grapes. Kasey sat the bags on the counter and began savagely attacking the grapes until Korita snatched the bag from him. "Uh uh, if you hungry I'll make you something to eat! Actin like you don't got no damn since."

Daren asked, "Ma I was wonderin if Kasey could come with me to my homegirl Niesha's tonight. She's throwin a party and tomorrow is Kasey B-day."

"Uh uh, Kasey too young to be hangin with you and yo friends."

"She got some young homegirls ma."

"Yea ma, why you always actin like dat ma. I'm seventeen now. I'm about to go crazy from bored-izm," Kasey pleaded.

"Ima watch him ma. You got my word," Daren added. .

Against Korita's motherly judgement she said, "fine, be back by one."

"Come on ma, at least give me till three. This ain't teen club night."

"Two Daren, now get outa my face." Kasey ran out of the kitchen so fast to get his dro then slide outside. Daren calmly kissed his mother on the cheek with a thanks ma. "Do you need some more money?" Daren pulled his last $100 out of his pockets but Kortia huffed, "boy if you don't get outa here. . Before I change my mind." Daren left the money on the counter with a mission to run it up on his mind.

The moment Daren pulled off Kasey turned the music up. 2 Pac's song That's Just The Way It Is had Joe's bull shit ten's knocken. Daren turned the music down with a shake of his head. "Bro, we ridin with over a hundred bricks in the trunk. You strapped; I'm strapped. We already in a lac! Beatin down Money Lane is just askin for racial profilen."

"What-chu mean big bro?"

"Law's will pull us over just because. Knowin Joe this lac probably stolen an hot den a bitch. Until I can get my own shit we need to attract less attention as possible."

"Hell yea, you right big bro I'm trippen. I'm just tryin to turn up fa my b-day."

Daren drove down Money Lane with caution, watching his surroundings. He had the AK on the floor of the driver's seat, just in case. Daren glanced down in his lap to see that his phone was ringing off the hook just from the fifteen people Kasey was able to call.

"Ima turn you up tonight lil bro. Don't think I'm getting on yo ass for no reason I'm just tryin to put you on G. . . But let me finish tellin you about how I move bricks so clean. I learned long time ago that posted on the block with Rich and nem or posted up in hot spots bring bull shit in general. So I started trappin out a my home girl mama crib. Her mama know I move on some do somethin for me I do somethin for you unspoken agreement. Really she a hustler herself and a major part of my operation. Her daughter fine as aged wine. She remind me of a half black and Columbian stallion. We went to Park Village High School together and we coo as a fan. She got a gang of fine ass home girls that be havin a nigga like damn. She the one who hooked me up with my side chick Crissa."

"You gon put me in the doe wit her big bro? I feel like I need a older female to show me wha's up!"

"Naw, I think she and Johnnyboy got some shit goin on on the low because he always over there."

"Dang tha's cold. How you end up trappen over there anyway?"

"About a year ago me and Johnnyboy were in and out, in and out of her crib makin hella plays. It was a Friday night just like this one and my phone was stack back up after I crashed my 5.0 I copped from Joe. I was sick cause I put so much money into that car. But anyway, I called myself trying to be respectful by hittin my licks in the streets. When me and Johnnyboy got back to Nancy's she called me to the kitchen. She was frying pork chops and main mac n cheese with some greens that smelled so good that my stomach growled.

"You stayin fa dinner child?" she asked.

"If its ok with you I will. I haven't had time to grab nothin to eat."

"Why would I ask if it wasn't ok? . . Hum honey." She dopped some hot golden chops o the napkin then motioned for me to get one. When I did she asked, "What I really want to know is what you're in and out of my house sellin, don't lie either." I couldn't even lie if I wanted to from the way I would bring bags of bricks in Niesha's room to break shit down. Before I could answer she confessed, "I'm asking because I used to hustle myself. Just so you know if you get caught with some shit comin outa here you'll be bringin my house heat."

I knew I was dead wrong, so I apologized, "My bad Nancy, I'll fall back. I thought Niesha gamed you up already."

"She did but she didn't tell me you'd be doin as much as you're doing. All I'm saying is find a better way to conduct business."

"How when Niesha and Johnnyboy be havin constant parties and traffic of their own. I thought I was being respectful by-"

Nancy stopped me with a sassy, "Honey, the only reason my daughter and JohnJohn got anything goin is because of you. Use their parties as a cover. Break your shit down in the garage so people don't be in your mix. Look out for the house when you can, and we shouldn't have a problem because we don't sleep with anything major in the house."

Daren pulled into Riverside then pulled the AK close so that it was on the right side of his leg. "But yea, since then my hustle game been too hard as Rich be sayin. But I'm really movin slow boogie if you ask me."

Kasey noticed how Daren got serious when he pulled into Riverside. He watched the houses, people and kids as he kept it moving. Kasey remembered the many stories Daren would tell him at night about Riverside and Oak Ride beefing. But here they were, strapped and in the wrong hood about to get they trap on.

CHAPTER 2

TRAPPIN AT THE SPOT

Daren eased the lac into Nancy's driveway still on alert. Before he could stop Nancy opened the garage so Daren could pull in. Once Daren parked, Nancy pulled the garage down and locked it. She waited for Daren at the door that led into the kitchen. Daren hopped out the lac feeling like he was safe. Kasey followed right behind him smiling, happy to be in the mix. Daren gave Nancy a motherly hug.

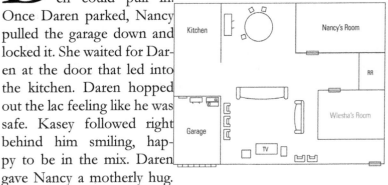

"They say African queens held the keys to eternal youth. With you getting younger and younger every time I see you I can only think you found the secret."

"Cut it out young man, I'm too old for you," Nancy joked. She looked Kasey up and down speaking with extra emphasis with her hand on her chest.

"You must be young Kasey! My have I heard so much about-chu!"

"Good or bad?" Kasey asked with a frown, looking up at Daren.

"I'll never tell," Nancy winked with a laugh. Kasey loosened up a little realizing that Nancy was one of those playa t-jones just like Daren said she was. She wore a sunflower dress and brown sandals with a light sheen of makeup. Her skin was smooth and light brown. From the looks of it you'd never guess she was thirty-eight years old. Nancy dug in her bra collecting money while telling Daren "I need four pounds for my cousin-"

"Get out ya doodies ma, you know yo money ain't no good wit me. I got-chu as soon as we break this shit down."

"Sure thing honey, and I'll make sure no one comes back here." Kasey watched Nancy go back in the house wishing Korita was like her.

Daren grabbed the AK from the driver seat and strapped it over his shoulder. "Help me break this shit down bro while you standin there lookin crazy. You always talkin bout you wanna ride." Daren popped the trunk then carried two duffle bags to the laundry table by the door that led into the house. Kasey joined Daren at the table with this head in the clouds.

"Bro what you tell Nancy about me?"

"Nun bro, now peep game."

Kasey watched Daren set up the scale and baggies on grind mode.

"Na for real big bro! You told her something to make look like a mark right?"

"What if I told her you be sneak jackin at night. Sqweak sqweak!" Daren joked making sounds like the bunk bed was moving. Kasey's face went sour until Daren said, "I'm just playin bro, now peep game."

Kasey watched Daren lean the AK on the wall with a brick ready. "Each of the four bags have thirty bricks. I paid $30,000 for 120 bricks which is $250 a brick. If I can sell each pound for at least $400 I'll profit $18,000 easy. I'm taxin but its dry in Riverside and I ain't takin Tentry chance to make people happy. What I usually do is break one pound down into ounces since this is a party. Then I'll do sixteen qp's, ten half a pounds and I'll most likely move the rest in pounds." Daren handed Kasey the rectangular brick with a quick glance at his phone. "You break one down so I can walk you through it." Kasey held the compressed brick in hand asking, "Dang big bro, are all the pounds big like this?" Daren took a deep breath to find his patience then explained, "It's two pounds bro bro, weigh it out so you can see."

Kasey turned the scale on and weighed the brick. "911 grams, its over big bro." Kasey looked up at Daren thinking something was wrong.

"It's coo bro, sometimes they come like that when you cop from cartels. Break all those into single pounds. I'll be right back."

Daren grabbed his phone and rushed to the trunk. His phone was ringing like crazy, but he ended the call to check if his main chick Trina had called. Once he saw that she hadn't he stuffed his phone in his pocket. He pulled the other two duffle bags of bricks out of the trunk then dropped them behind Kasey. "Speed it up bro bro! Time is money."

"Why don't you do it den?"

"Because you gotta learn bro, now turn up!"

Daren joined Kasey's side moving fast, breaking down bricks into half pounds. He watched Kasey find his grove with a mug of his face that soon turned to a face of concentration. An hour and some change passed by the time they had everything broken down. Daren knew if he was by himself he would have taken double the time to break all of this shit down. In the back of his mind he hoped Kasey would be wise enough to help him more often. Kasey helped Daren put the broken down bricks back in the trunk feeling like he was a part of the team. "It's like three pounds left over in loose buds and shake big bro."

"Keep it, sell it, smoke it. Do you bro," Daren said like he didn't care but he was really testing Kasey to see if he could stack some bread or not. Kasey held the stuffed gallon zip lock bag of shakey bud in a bear hug like it was a Christmas present. Daren stuffed Nancy's four pounds in a duffle bag with a box of gars and closed the trunk. On his way out Daren stuffed the AK in the bag as well along with the scale and box of baggies Nancy left out for him. Last but not least Daren locked the lac and put the keys in his pocket. All the while Kasey just stood by the door, pounds in hand with his mouth open.

"Now what big bro?"

"Now we trappin at the spot. Watch and learn."

Kasey followed Daren into the house, through the kitchen realizing how much he loved AC. Daren sat next to Nancy at the eight-man round table in the dining room. Kasey sat next to Daren with his stuffed bag of weed on display. From the dining room you could see straight into the living room, where Johnnyboy and his younger brother Arron lounged on the long couch playing Sega. Daren sat the duffle bag between him and Kasey, opened it then put the scale and four pounds on the table.

"For you ma, and I'm payin rent this month," Daren offered.

"No need child, this is more than enough. How much are they going for?"

"For you . . . umm. . .Gimmie $360." Nancy already had a few licks in mind being the fine wisdom that she was. Kasey and Daren watched her take her pounds down the hall to her room screaming, "Niesha! Daren's here would you hurry up!"

When Johnnyboy heard that Daren was here over the loud TV he stood shouting "Ay yo D! Wha's good family!" Johnnyboy dropped the controller, leaped over the couch and ran to Daren with open arms. Daren stood and welcomed Johnnyboy in a playful manner then they both sat down at the round table.

Johnnyboy asked, "What we lookin at fam?"

"It's all good, call everybody and tell 'em it's some good."

Johnnyboy pulled out his phone and began calling people with a mission to get it in. After a few calls Johnnyboy told Daren,

"Niesha in her room getting dressed D. But aye yo. I got some mad plays for days set up for you."

Johnnyboy glanced at Kasey in shock then looked again, "Oh snaps, wha's good lil bro!" Johnnyboy dapped Kasey up a few times in a playful manner that made Kasey laugh from all of the energy and excitement.

"But aye yo D. I need to make some money tonight. Phone bill due in a few days and I been trippen usin all my minutes like it's free n shit you feel me."

"Don't even sweat it. Ima hit you wit a startup kit." Daren shot back through the kitchen and into the garage. A moment later he returned to his seat with a QP and handed it to Johnnyboy. "Make ya money and give me $100 when you make it." Daren looked at Kasey like he was crazy as he said, "Bro, roll something up and loosen up. This is like my second fam. Stop actin like that."

Kasey grabbed a gar from Daren's bag, pulled a few buds from his bag of shake and began breaking it down. Johnnyboy pulled the scale in front of him to weigh out his normal five gram dimes, getting his roach on. It was cool too because Daren didn't sell small sacks so his and Niesha's friends had no choice but to buy from him if they wanted a quick smoke. "Just watch D, I'll make $230 in the next hour or so and get that bread fo you. Then cop a HP. Is that cool?"

"Cool as the frozen cool-aid cups Ms Wonda sell on Oak Dale street."

"AIIYYY!" Niesha screamed, running into the dining room. Even though she was dressed in a mini skirt, a polka dot sky blue tope with no shoes and half done make-up, Kasey agreed with Daren when he said she fine. Niesha hugged Daren from behind while whispering in his ear "Lia-Lynee and Crissa are on the way. Don't tell Lia-Lynee I told you, but she said she noticed you looking at her and she said if your done with Crissa pull her to the side."

Daren nodded, keeping it playa just as the doorbell rang along with his phone in his pocket. Already knowing what to do Arron paused the game, stood and ran to the door to answer. A preppy dressed white and black dude walked in. Arron locked the door and returned to his game while Daren's company made their way to the round table. Daren stood then made his way to the kitchen, motioning for Kel and his friend to follow. Daren noticed that Kel's friend held his bag tightly, ready for business. "Hold it down Kasey," Daren shouted.

Daren, Kel and Thomas stood in a circle in the middle of the kitchen with serious demeanors. "What y'all bring me?" Daren asked.

"Eight grand," Thomas replied, unzipping the bag showing Daren the money.

Daren stuck his hand in the bag pulling a knot of hundreds out. He put the money back in the bag dong some calculations. "390 a pop is the best I can do."

"As long as it's lime green, not that many seeds we coo with it Daren," Kel added.

Daren grabbed the bag to take the money from Thomas, but Daren and Thomas ended up in a tug-a-war match for the bag. Daren let go and almost spazzed out reaching for his Glock 9 behind his back. Daren calmed down remembering Kasey had his strap. -DING DONG- the doorbell rang along with Daren's phone ringing in his pocked. Daren looked to Kel trying to figure out what was wrong. "Kel, why famo trippen?" Daren pulled his phone from his pocket checking who was calling.

"Chill Thomas, I already told you Daren is good people and I deal with him all the time." Kels voice was soothing trying to calm the situation.

"You too friendly Kel! I aint' tryin to hear none of that. This is half of my bread and he already taxin. Just bring the bud and we trade, count, weigh the shit at the same time."

Daren nodded, ending Trina's call then ran into the garage. As fast as he could he stuffed twenty pounds into a bag knowing he needed to find time to call Trina back. He calmly went back into the kitchen, unzipped the duffle bag and placed the bricks on the counter. "Since we ain't got no trust somebody go get my scale form the dining room table."

"I got one right here," Thomas pulled a digital scale from his back pack's side pocket and put it on the counter. Thomas weighed the pounds one by one while eyeing Daren as he counted the money. Once they both finished Daren put the money in his duffle bag while Thomas forced what pounds he could into his bag. Kel had to hide a few bricks in his waistline and stuff a few in his pants.

"My bad D, I just been in some fucked up situations. One time I'm waiting just like this, and dude leaves out the garage with my bread. Then I'm black, dressed all preppy with my white boy here. Nigga's always see us as a lick." Thomas explained. "I told you Daren was good people man. You disappoint me. I can't believe you don't trust me."

"I do trust you, but this is business. And I'm not sayin you a bad dude D. But I ain't takin no more losses."

"I know I'm white and in the hood, but I feel disrespected Thomas."

Daren ran back into the garage after Kel and Thomas left the kitchen, still arguing. Daren put the money in the trunk telling himself to calm down in situations like that. His nerves was bad because he hadn't blew enough to ease his mind today. But he didn't blow much when he was on grind mode so that he could be sharp.

When Daren made his way back into the dining room he saw that Crissa and Lia-Lynee were on the small couch talking with a few of their home girls standing behind them. Crissa blew Daren a kiss, but Daren paid her no mind and returned to his seat at the round table. Daren noticed that a couple of blunts were in rotation. Shella and one of her big spending homeboys had just been let in by Arron. Before Arron could sit down the doorbell rang again. Arron huffed then quickly answered. Daren saw that it was Lavon, so he grabbed the bag by Kasey catching ghost to the garage. Again Daren popped the trunk, grabbed and stuffed ten pounds in the bag making sure to be careful with the AK.

Daren returned to the round table to find Lavon sitting across from him. "What up dough? I got $1200 for you." Lavon reached over the table, handing Daren the money. Daren slid Lavon three bricks after he counted the bread. Lavon put the bricks in his waistband with an adjust of his belt. After that he stood, took a long pull on a blunt that was passed to him then passed it along. "I guess I'm gone dough," he said in strained voice from the burn of the bud.

"You know you can chill right? This is a party."

Lavon looked around checking out the fine young ladies that had already gathered. "You know I'm on the run Dough, the wife gon be worried sick so I gotta get back."

"Alright G. Stay up."

Arron let Lavon out and three more people came in. Daren made a mental note to bless Arron's game for all of his troubles. Arron had been doing this for so long that he knew who Daren's and Johnnyboy's clientele was as well as Niesha's friends. This way people didn't get in who weren't wanted.

Daren laughed when he saw Kasey passed a blunt on auto pilot. Kasey was high as a kite with red and low eyes.

"Wuss-uhp Bro-ski," Kasey said in a long draw.

"Happy b-day bro," Daren laughed as he passed the blunt to Niesha.

Johnnyboy moved in blur, in the mix getting his skimpy sacks off. More people were let in and the party was definitely starting to jump. Lia-Lynee kept eyeing Daren but trying to play it off so Crissa wouldn't notice. Crissa moved through the small crowd and stood behind Daren. Once he finished serving someone she leaned forward speaking in his ear, "Since your not going to come talk to me can I please talk to you in the kitchen?"

"I need to grab some mo shit anyway. Bro you good?" Daren asked. Kasey's reaction was a slow nod, so Daren grabbed the bag with the AK watching more people join the party. He led Crissa into the garage, closed the door behind them then took a seat on the hood of the lac. Crissa stood between Daren's legs with a hundred lustful thought running through her mind.

"You see me working CC, I hope this is important." Daren tried to hide his annoyance but found his cool when Crissa looked deep in his eyes. She spoke with sincerity in her voice, not being affected by Daren's mood.

"I know your busy! You know I wouldn't have come if I didn't have something to tell you. otherwise I would have called and left a message."

"What is it CC?" Daren could hear his phone ringing away in his pocket. A moment of silence passed before Crissa blurted out, "I'm like, . . three weeks late and umm. . ."

"What! Is it mines?"

Crissa put her hands on her hips, looking up as she whined, "Oh my god your going to make me cry!" Crissa regained control of her emotions then looked Daren in his eyes again. "Of course it's yours, I'm not having sex with no one else. Your making it seem like ima hoe or something."

All Daren could think was: Damn, Trina gon kill me and ma never gon let me hear the end of this.

"So what?" Crissa asked, waiting for Daren to say something.

Daren's confession was heartless, "I need to see some test results. If it's' mines you know y'all good CC."

"If . . . What the fuck you mean IF? Why can't you just take my word and trust me?" Crissa's eyes watered as Daren tried to explain, "I wanna trust you CC but-" Crissa spoke, almost shouting over Daren, "You think ima hoe because we had sex on the first night."

"Naw CC I-" Before Daren could finish Crissa had already stormed off.

Ain't this a bitch Daren thought as he popped the trunk and put the bag in. "I can already see what type of night this gon be." Daren said to himself as he closed the trunk and chased after Crissa.

At the round table Niesha moved in Daren's seat sitting close to Kasey, eyeing him. "So your turning seventeen tonight?" she asked. Kasey nodded slowly, with a swig of his soda. "That's crazy. It just so happens that it's one of my home girl's eighteenth birthday today. She's on the way and you're going to like her too cause she's real real pretty."

"You gon put me in the doe or what?" Kasey asked, trying to fight his buzz. He denied another blunt in rotation with a shake of his head. When he held his stomach from a major munchie attack Niesha laughed, "You hungry boo? OMG I'm sorry I forgot to set up the snack table."

Niesha brought Kasey a turkey and cheese sandwich with a bag of cool ranch Doritos. Kasey attacked the food like a savage while Niesha set up the snack table right behind him. She continued asking him more questions, but he was so blowed and so much was going on around him he could barely pay attention.

Kasey denied another blunt attempting to shake back. Out of nowhere the round table was full and now the living room was crowded with over thirty people mingling and dancing to the music. It was something about this crowd that oozed money and the party lifestyle.

Johnnyboy ran to Kasey handing him Daren's $100. "Lil bro, I need a HP, QP or something. Where did Daren go?" Kasey shrugged his shoulders real slow mo like. "He followed Crissa outside," Niesha said.

"Lil bro, sell me a QP of what-chu got! I need to make some moves before it get too late."

"I ain't trippen, but most of its shake."

"Just look out fa me and Ima throw you some sells so we both eat."

Johnnyboy motioned for the dude in Daren's seat to move, then slid into the seat with the scale ready. "Fa-shooow," Kasey moved slow weighing the qp with ten extra grams. "Gimme the bread Johnjohn." Kasey joked, with his hand out.

"I got-chu right here lil bro," Johnnyboy had the money ready nodding, counting the $20 come up Kasey just blessed him with. Johnnyboy started weighing his skimpy sacks and people were already giving him money. In less than fifteen minutes his qp was gone. More people showed up, a few left and shit was moving so fast Kasey couldn't believe it. Johnnyboy sold three ounces for

Kasey and the rest of his nine qp's went for a hundred a pop like magic. After that Johnnyboy sat next to Kasey blowin big clouds, waiting. "They want pounds lil bro. This a party but a bid-ness at the same time. You gotta go get D asap."

Kasey stood with a long stretch, looking at the party. Thick smoke was in the air, the music was going, and bottles were being passed around. But most had eyes on Kasey, waiting for Daren.

Daren leaned in Crissa's driver seat door talking her down in his best Mack mode voice. Crissa held the steering wheel in a tight grip, facing forward, ready to pull off. She half listened to Daren plead his case, feeling heartbroken that Daren didn't believe her.

"For real CC, I wanna be in my child's life for the simple fact that my father missed most of mine and Kasey's. I wasn't callin you a hoe or none of that. I'll man up to mines wit out a problem. Just need you to be understanding from my point of view."

"Whatever Daren, just come to my doctor's appointment tomorrow so you can ask how soon you can have your DNA test. But I know it's yours."

Daren thought about Trina with a heavy pain over his heart.

"CC, I gotta tell you something. But uh. . " When Daren paused Crissa smacked her lips. "If it's about your girl I already know. So after you find out it's yours I hope you choose so we can be a family. . . Or let me know because I can't do this on my own."

"What you sayin CC? you thinkin about gettin a abortion?"

When Crissa stayed silent Daren started to say something fowl but Kasey approached the car.

"Big bro, they need pounds and I sold all my weed already."

Kasey gave Daren his $100 laughing and feeling good. "Dis from JohnJohn, he crazy den a mug big bro!" When Kasey saw that Daren and Crissa were in a heated moment he stopped laughing. Daren gave Crissa the $100 with a demanding plea. "Go guy you some food and please, I mean please don't do nothin dumb CC. Ima call you tomorrow."

Crissa laughed, "Ha! You always say that and don't call. When I call you you don't answer, and I be all sad. This is my life Daren! It hurst to be played and treated like shit."

"I said I got-chu CC, Damn!" It took all Daren had to fight his aggravation. Now he remembered why he didn't' answer her's or Trina's calls. The sex was great but the drama that came afterwards made it not worth it sometimes. Daren shut Crissa's car door then stepped back as she drove off.

"What happened big bro?"

"She havin a shorty, she say its mines. . . It's crazy because I don't know what to feel at the moment."

"Dang bro for real? You think she tryin to pull a trap move on you?"

"Naw bro, she not that type of girl. I'm the one who fucked up. I was feelin extra throwed and I don't be using protection when we be chilin. She thinkin about killin it if I'm not gon be with her. . ." Daren looked around then came back to reality, "Let's go inside Kasey, I just remembered where we are.

It was ten PM and the usual key hustlers waited to cop their bricks. Some had even dumped what they copped then returned to buy some more. Daren, Ms Nancy, Niesha, Johnnyboy, Arron, Shella, Lia-Lynee, Kasey and Daren's potna T sat around the round table in the dining room. Kasey took mental notes watching Daren sell pound after pound, HP's and a few qp's here and there till only the last pound of sack's remained. Not really feeling it, Daren gave Kasey the last pound and stood. "Handle this lil bro." Then Daren made his way to the garage.

Daren popped the trunk to gather all of his money, but his thoughts were scattered. "What am I going to tell Trina?" he asked his self. After he bagged the money he stuffed it under the spare tire. He flopped down in the lac's driver's seat and just thought. It's crazy when you truly love someone but make a big dumb mistake. He lit the remainder of his blunt from the ash tray thinking about how crazy life just flipped that quick.

At the round table Kasey sold two ounces for *80 with a fly decision to put four ounces together to sell a QP for $115. Kasey kept glancing in the direction of the front door searching for this pretty home girl that was close to his age Niesha spoke about. It was almost eleven and Kasey could hear Korita's nagging voice about being home by 2am. Kasey sold two more ounces to Niesha for $60, giving her a deal. A few minutes later the stripper Sharena Daren told him about came back through and bought the last HP then dipped when she found out that the bud was all gone. All Kasey could think was dang she fine. . .

Arron let Sharena out just as three women walked down the hall and stood in the living room. When they looked at the party everyone stopped for a few seconds, staring. Someone whispered, "is that Shay and her best friend Alexa? Why are they here? Who's that other girl?"

Niesha stood, moved through the crowd breaking her neck to hug Shay. "Happy 18th birthday!" Niesha shouted, slapping Shay on her plump ass. Niesha led Shay and her company to the round table.

Shay smiled as she said "Hi Ms. Nancy, everyone. This my friend Alexa and my cousin Courtney. My name is Shay for the lamo's who don't know."

Kasey was at a loss for words, stuck on Shay's beauty. He could have sworn Shay went to his school, and she wasn't eighteen. But she sure looked twenty-one wearing a black jean long sleeve jacket over a violet cleavage-showing blouse. Her denim jeans hugged her curvy hips, and her black heels made her look tall, sexy as well as classy. Kasey took notice of her short violet nails and matching contacts. Alexa and Courtney were dressed in a similar fashion, but Courtney had on coochie Cutter Jean shorts with an ass so fat, and Alexa had on a black jean mini skirt that almost exposed her bubble butt. Their skin tones were a few shades lighter than coco and they all had long black real well cared for hair.

"Let the ladies have a seat!" Nancy ordered.

Arron walked to the door to let a few people out, Johnnyboy raided the scraps of the snack table and Lia-Lynee stood to leave now that it was obvious Daren wasn't going to give her any play tonight.

Alexa and Courtney sat in the empty seats while Shay stood by Niesha fanning herself. Shay watched Kasey rolling the last of his shakey weed with a roll of her eyes. "What's that kill? Umm I was looking for some dro for my birthday." Shay blurted out. Kasey thought for a moment because he didn't want to sell his birthday dro sack. "I got some, but it's really my personal. Big bro chunked me a zone fa my b-day." Kasey pulled the ounce out of his pocket just to take a whiff. "How much you tryin to get?"

"What kind is it?" Courtney asked.

"Big bro said it's sour diesel." Kasey opened the bag so Shay sat in Daren's empty seat and put her nose in the bag. "Aw snaps you ain't tell me you had doe-doe lil bro," Johnnyboy exclaimed, leaning over Kasey to take a good look.

"We got a pound at the crib," Kasey bragged.

"Oh really, Daren never brings dro over. Just goes to show much he really loves us huh mama?" Niesha stressed. Kasey realized he shouldn't have said anything, so he explained, "Probably cause big bro don't smoke reggie so he don't sell dro."

"Well we tryin to get on his level! Where is um. . . Big bro?" Courtney asked.

"I want the whole ounce. How much?" Shay asked, taking the pen of money off of her jacket. "I got you cousin." Courtney said, digging in her designer purse. Kasey saw she was serious when she pulled out a wad of cash.

"Dangg, the whole thang! I haven't even smoked none yet." Kasey stressed.

Shay covered her mouth hiding a forced giggle, "sell us half at least."

Kasey thought for a moment not really wanting to. But Shay, her friend and Courtney were extra fine and they seemed like they was rich. All I gotta do is ask big bro to sell me some mo when I run out, Kasey thought.

"Gimme $140 for the half. I really ain't tryin to sell none but I guess since it's our b-day and all." Courtney counted the money and gave it to Kasey, not complaining about him taxing. Kasey split the ounce of dro and weighted it on the scale to make sure both sacks were fourteen grams. The smell of exotic loud made Nancy break down. "Shit, go ahead and sell me a gram of that honey."

Nancy slid Kasey $15 then Niesha and Johnnyboy did the same. Kasey weighed and gave everyone their dro feeling like the man. He leaned back in his seat real playa like as he lit his blunt of reggie. He took a few puffs then passed it to Shay. Shay passed the reggie along with her nose turned up then put a gram of dro in front of Kasey. "Can you roll it for me? My nerves is bad and it takes me forever to roll up." Kasey nodded then put a gram with Shays.

He broke the dro down eying Nancy, Niesha and Johnnyboy tuck theirs for later. Kasey rolled three rillos while listening to Niesha and Courtney make small talk. Kasey found out that Courtney was from the H and visiting Shay while she took a break from college. Johnnyboy counted his money behind Kasey wishing Daren had more weed. Alexa looked around searching for someone to talk to but none of these dudes caught her interest.

Kasey and Shay locked eyes a few times, smiled then looked away. Kasey would light a rillo, take a few puffs, cough then pass it to Shay. Shay would hit the dro hard, not wanting to pass it until Kasey passed her another one. "You blow like a G Shay. I'm so blowed I'm just here right now!"

"We come across some really good dro in my apartment complex from time to time. My mama know people."

Kasey wanted to ask Shay more questions, but the room started spinning. Again he started passing blunts along. After the second round of the blunts being passed in rotation Say shook her head in frustration.

"What's wrong mama?" Courtney asked.

"I'm not even high yet and the blunts are already too small," Shay whined.

"Wanna go hot box the bathroom?" Kasey asked. Without a word Shay stood, grabbed Kasey's hand and pulled him down the hall.

Di'lon and lil Chris pulled up in a '96 SS Impala. Chris parked his wip at the end of the long line of cars with his vision set on Niesha's house. "Let's go cus!" Lil Chris ordered while getting out. Di'lon followed behind lil Chris with a shake of his head.

"Daren not gon go for it cus. He ain't cutting no deals and he probly not gon fuck wit us in the first place."

"We'll see, he in my hood makin bread." Lil Chris flexed.

"I ain't tryin to be involved in no B.S cus, . . . For Real. I just got out and ain't tryin to go back fa no dumb shit."

"Well ain't that a shitty hand dealt. Yo fault for living in Money Lane."

Shay sat on the open counter space of the sink in the bathroom with her legs and heel's dangling. She watched Kasey concentrate on rolling a decent sized blunt of dro. Kasey felt her energy and looked up in a glance.

"You're not eighteen are you?" Shay asked.

"Nope, I'm seventeen." Kasey felt a little embarrassed knowing he was the youngest at the party.

"I'm seventeen too. Niesha lied to Nancy because she doesn't like minors coming to the parties your brother be throwing. You must be happy to have a brother like Daren."

"Fa-show, big bro been teaching me everything."

"Like what?"

"Like umm, . . . how live the game is but you gotta stack some bread for a lawyer n shit. From what I get from it all it's a lot of negative karma come from being in the game. So you gotta run it up while you on."

"You're going to be moving weight with him from now on?"

"Probly so, big bro already been putting me on." Kasey was feeling good, so he lit the blunt and passed it to Shay. She took a few puffs with a sigh.

"It's been a long week, so much stress has been coming my way from school and my grama. Me and my mama been bumpin heads a lot lately too."

"What they be doin to make you mad?" Kasey watched Shay smoke making sure her nails were out of harm's way.

"You know parent stuff. My grama's super strict with the stay in school and don't be havin sex talks I hate. My mama used to give me weed, now she switched up and I be like fuck that bitch. Honestly my apartment complex is full of dope fiends and drama. I wish had money to just pack up and leave."

"I know what you mean. Ma wont let me chill and do me, but all that's about to change."

Shay took another puff then explained, "My mother sells drugs too. She used to get her hands on a little bit of everything till her main plug got popped. They call him C-dre, do you know him?"

Kasey shook his head even though the name sounded familiar. "I used to move weed for my mama at school. I have a lot of friends that need bud. But now that I'm a senior she wants me to focus more on school. But I know she don't give a damn and its my grama in her ear. But maybe we can make some money together."

"How? I don't like a lot of them foo's at school."

"You don't have to. I'll bring you sales and you break me off."

Kasey thought about Shay's proposal and asked, "What took you so long to get here?"

"It's dry in the hood and I had Courtney drive me way to Adams Hill for some bars. I skipped school today for nothin cause they dry to. That's when Niesha called me all late about this party."

"How come you never talked to me at school? I coulda been got you some weed. And I'm pretty sure big bro could get you some bars."

"I didn't think you smoked and Daren don't be out there like that. I thought you was a good boy until I heard you got into a shootout with Tay Tay nem.'"

"It really was my potna stop six, I was just wit'em, so we clapped back."

Shay finally passed Kasey the blunt but he shook his head saying, "Smoke on beautiful." Shay smiled taking a few more prissy puffs of the blunt. She jumped down from the sink, put the blunt out in the ash tray. She moved close to Kasey, putting her chest close to his while tying her long hair in a violet scrunchie. "Ima be straight up Kasey, I'm tryin to make some money but I could find time for a homie lova friend." Kasey fumbled with his sack of dro not knowing what to do. Shay grabbed her phone out of her pocket, looking Kasey in his eyes. "Put your number in my phone so I can call you." Kasey did what she asked with his heart thumping loudly in his chest. Next thing you know Shay's lips touched his, . . . -DING DONG-- . . BOOM BOOM BOOM –

"Answer the door Arron!" Johnnyboy shouted, but Arron was too throwed from the drank and bud he'd been taking in all night. BOOM BOOM BOOM—

"Niesha! Get the damn door!" Nancy shouted from her room. At the same time Daren and Kasey ran into the living room asking, "Is it the cops?"

"I got-chu D, just chill," Johnnyboy whispered. He stumbled to the front door while Niesha turned the music down. Johnnyboy looked through the peep hole with a sigh of relief. "It's coo y'all, it's just Di'lon black ass with lil Chris." Johnnyboy answered the door with a "Wha's good fam?"

"I know Daren here, let me holla at'em," lil Chris demanded.

"Don't be comin ova here all hostile my G, the party ova-"
-MOW-, lil Chris slept Johnnyboy so clean then rushed into the
house, but Daren met him in the hallway in a stiff post up.

"We just tryin to talk business," Di'lon explained.

Kasey stood behind and next to Daren with the Glock nine
cocked and ready. Lil Chris bucked Kasey cappin "Lil cus gon kill
me in front of all these people? . . . Naw, he ain't built for no shit
like that. . . Neither one of you is or will ever be legendary K."
Lil Chris leaned in with a power punch, but Daren ducked under
his sloppy move letting off a mean upper cut. Lil Chris staggered
back to the door in a daze. Daren was on his ass with a stylish three-piece. Lil Chris put his arms up in a cage then pushed
Daren back for some space. They entered a blend that was blow
for blow for a minute until lil Chris backed up trying to regain
his wind. Lil Chris tripped over Johnnyboy's body just as Daren
threw a mean right hook that put lil Chris on his ass. "DIS-RE-
SPECT-FULL-ASS-NIG-!" Daren stood over lil Christ beating
his head in yelling like a mad man. "DON'T-TALK-BOUT-MY-
FA-THA-NO-MO! KILL YOU BI-BI-BI."

Di'lon looked at Kasey holding the gun then back at his bloody
lifeless homie. "Come'on Daren chill! Let us bounce." Di'lon
pleaded. When Daren didn't stop Niesha screamed, "DAREN
STOP BEFORE YOU KILL HIM!" She hugged Daren from
behind talking him down until he snapped out of his savage state
of mind. He backed up with the crowd standing in the living
room hallway trying to get a good look. Everyone was quiet wondering if lil Chris was dead. Di'lon dropped to his knees next
to Chris and sat him up. Lil Chris coughed blood but remained
lifeless.

"Get him to a hospital!" Nancy cried.

"Somebody help me get him to the car!" Di'lon yelled. When
no one moved Kasey put the nine behind his back then moved
to help.

Daren stood there in a spaced out daze until Ms. Nancy yelled,
"Pack it up people, party's over."

During the drive home Daren was deep in his thoughts while Kasey went on and on full of excitement. Daren blocked Kasey out trying to figure out what had happened. He just told his self to be cool, but he lost it . . . The thought dawned on him that he almost killed somebody today. If Niesha wouldn't have stopped him he wouldn't have stopped. .

"Oh God big bro! You was like Mike Tyson, Lenox Lewis and Muhamad Ali put together. DOWN GOES FRAZIER! Den you was on his ass like a shitty pamper . . I'm talkin homie couldn't rock wit you in the blend. Nothin from the shoulders. An den yo weave game so real. You gotta teach me ta scratch like dat! WHOO! This was the most turnt B-day ever. You was right too, the trap spot so live. You moved all that bud and I made like $1500 without even tryin. I hate history but now I love dead presidents. .

I see how you show love when you need to, but on da coo we could post up all day and really eat. I wanna be just like you big bro, smart, live from the shoulders and don't take no shit."

"Bro, I'm tryin to gather myself right now. Don't tell ma about the fight neither. And make sure you throw them bloody clothes away. If ma see that she gon have a heart attack."

"I got-chu big bro. And oh yea, I gave Shay your number and I'm probly gon need a phone."

"Understood bro." Daren turned the music up a little to let the music ease him mind.

Kasey pulled his money out to count it again thinking about the night and how live it is to have some freedom.

Shay so live, she like a classy hood chick who be up on game like a mug. Her cousin looked extra good, like grown woman fine. I think big bro should holla at her. She breaded up too. It's a drought in Money Lane for no reason. We could be makin stupid bread. I'm talking enough dough for every house in the hood to bake big stupid dumb cake. My only problem is I gotta figure out a way for ma to let me chill . .

CHAPTER 3

REAL FAMILY

Kasey woke, climbed down the bunk beds ladder still hyped about last night. When he didn't see Daren sleep in the bottom bunk his hopes of riding through the hood with big bro faded. . He checked the clock radio thinking: it's 8AM and Saturday. . Where could have big bro gone this early?

Kasey crept to his room door listening for Korita. He peeked into the empty living room glad that Korita was still sleeping. He quietly turned the doorknob to close the door so the loud click couldn't be heard. He danced to the end of the bunk bed doing too legit to quit. Just like he saw Daren do he moved the bed to the side quietly pulling the wooden floorboard up. He passed whispering, "Dang big bro! I neva seen so much money befo!" He grabbed his sack of dro, the weed tray, a rillo then rolled a blunt as fast as he could. After he rolled one up he gathered the trash and gar guts in piece of paper and threw it in the stash. Noticing his sack of dro was almost gone he opened Daren's pound for a bub. Big bro ain't gone notice, he thought. Sneak game on point he closed the stash, moved the bed back with another dance. "Uoo, wee" he whispered taking a pull on the blunt to taste exotic aroma.

If I go outside ma gon wake up like she always does. I probly should just climb out the window, . . Yea. . I gotta hurry too because she might wake up already. Kasey snatched a lighter from the nightstand, opened his rooms only window then carried a chair over. He climbed outside as fast and quietly as he could. He waited to see if he woke his mother, but no one came bursting in nagging. Cars passed up and down Money Lane as Kasey lit the diesel. He blew his wig back one deep trying to ignore the ass beating that would come his way if Korita caught him. His heart beat a thousand miles per second but after the sixth or seventh puff things began to slow down, looking fuzzy wherever he looked. He coughed into his shoulder a few times to muffle the sound. A minute passed before Kasey realized he was just standing there on stuck mode, enjoying the wind from the passing cars and the sun's warm morning glow. He relit the blunt, took a few hard pulls that made him hide his cough again. Swaying a little he put the blunt out in the windowsill then left it there. Kasey jumped in the window worming his way inside. He made hella noise but was to blowed to care. Making sure his half a blunt was outside the windowpane he closed the window. Moving ever so slow he turned the radio on. The room moved in a blur until he found himself in the bathroom. He brushed his teeth bobbing his head to cash money bling bling. Next he hopped in the shower just to stand there because the water felt extra good. .

I gotta figure out a way to cop some bricks wit big bro so I can stack some bread. I'm finna be the king of Money Lane. I'm talking big stupid dumb weight. All I gotta do is figure out a way to duck ma so I can turn up.

Kasey opened his eyes at the thought of a live idea. Me, Daren, Rich, Nancy nem could start a trap squad. . .Like a real family.

Kasey hopped out the shower, dried off finding his way into the closet. He threw on some creased polo jeans with a red mossimo shirt with some air max. Kasey felt his eyes get heavy, so he flew to Daren's' bed felling like he was on cloud nine. He flopped back on the bed thinking about how fine that stripped was, how fine Shay was. All he remembered next was seeing darkness.

The house phone rang and rang, waking Kasey up. He opened his eyes to Korita standing in his room's door with the house phone in hand.

"Kasey wake up and get this phone! It's some little girl, and don't be tying up my line acting grown, hell. . " Korita pulled the long cord in to hand Kasey the phone. "And be ready to go to grama's as soon as Daren gets back. She cooked for your birthday."

"Kay ma," Kasey said rubbing his eyes. Korita sniffed looking around as she left. "Smell like feet and weed up in here."

"Hey, it's Shay. What-chu doin?"

"I was blowed den a mug, fell asleep. I had to jump out the window n shit cause big bro was gone when I woke up."

Shay laughed, "How would you like it if I sneak in your window?"

"If I get caught ima get a well expected beat down. But it'll show be worth it."

Shay laughed again, "You are so silly. What are your plans for today?"

"Today really my b-day so my grama cooked. Everybody probly gon be over there and shit. I hate goin over there because it be borin."

"Sounds like you have a loving family that cares. I wish I had that."

"No you don't, they type of care isa nag nag nag. . ."

Early that morning Daren walked out of the cell phone store with Kasey's new phone in hand. He took the phone out of its box to check the phone's settings. It was a Motorola just like his, but it was a smaller version. Daren put Shay's, his and Korita's numbers in it to start lil bro off. Shay called Daren's phone a few times after Daren gave her the house number. Kasey and ma must still be sleep Daren thought.

Daren hopped in the lac feeling good that he copped it from Joe with the title. It turns out that it wasn't hot. Daren pushed the lac down Money Lane with a mission to get home for Kasey's birthday dinner with the family. He glanced down at his phone in his lap feeling a sudden hurt when he saw that Trina was calling. He answered mentally preparing for Trina's sassy attituded.

"Damn nigro! Am I your side chick or something? Why in the hell can't you answer my calls?" Daren took a deep breath then explained, "My bad Trina, I been busy. I've been meaning to come through, but you know how that go when I'm eatin."

"Don't give me that lame ass excuse. Make your way to my apartment. . . NOW!"

Daren thought about telling Trina the bad news over the phone, but he felt like he should tell her face to face. It was only right after all they been through. When Daren didn't reply Trina snapped, "Boy don't make me come to ya mama's and cause a scene. You know she gon be on my side cause you always doin me wrong."

Daren Huffed out of guilt and frustration, "I'm on the way T."

Fifteen minutes later Daren parked the lack in Trina's parking spot in the Living Square Apartments. It was the longest walk he ever had to take, like gravity was pushing against him. He stood at her door and just waited. He couldn't force himself to knock because he truly didn't want to face Trina. She was one of them down-ass hood chicks known from beatin hoe's up just because. Over the years she put Daren up on so much game with major licks in his phone, safe places to make transactions, sex and life in general.

Trina must have felt Daren because she opened the door with a sassy "Where's your key? And who's car is that?"

"Mine Trina, I just copped it."

"Where's your key Daren?" Trina asked more seriously, blocking the door.

Daren ducked and turned his body sideways squeezing past Trina to get inside. "I left my key at home."

Trina closed the door with a little attitude about how Daren was acting. She joined Daren on the Livingroom long couch eyeing him wondering why he wouldn't look at her, kiss her or give her the attention he usually did. Daren grabbed the remote from the coffee table searching for the right words. He changed the channels from Lifetime to B.E.T. still avoiding Trina's eyes. Trina's anger rose but soon turned to hurt as she thought; I know he didn't just walk by me without a kiss, hug or nothin. . . I must be the side chick for real.

Even though she was giving Daren the evil eye she was still beautiful to Daren. She had shoulder length black permed hair with smooth caramel skin. She wore a tight-fitting set of matching maroon booty shorts and shirt that showed off her curvy plump body. Her nails and toenails were painted red, and she smelled like she just got out of the shower.

Daren continued acting like he was watching TV until Trina forced her way, straddling him. She kissed him deeply asking, "I thought we agreed this was your home?" She caressed Daren's face kissing him again.

"You agreed and I don't be feeling like arguing all the time."

Trina smacked her lips as she moved to the side, facing Daren keeping a leg in his lap. "Are you serious? Twenty-one still living with your mama does not sound right. I thought we had plans to save money to get out the hood, get our G.E.D's and go to college to find true happiness."

"Things change T." Daren's avoiding Trina's eyes had her about five seconds from slapping five from Daren. "So what? A few days ago you were deep up in me, tellin me how much you love me. You gon take care of me. Now shit changed huh? I never tripped on none of your bull shit Daren! I lost two apartments because you sellin drugs. I sold my car to get you out of jail because I love you, believe in all your promises. Now things have changed . . WHY!"

"I pay for this apartment, an I'll get you another car T."

"That's not the point I'm trying to make Daren! Why have things changed?"

Daren remained silent causing Trina to cry, "You promised me a life of no worries, a real family. Now you stopped lovin me all of a sudden. Did you kill somebody? Huh, are you abot to go to prison? What is it?"

Daren cleared his throat to speak through his bitterness. "I'm finna tell you because I love you and I feel like you deserve the truth. But don't hit me T, I swear to god!"

"Boy ain't nobody gon hit you! Tell me what you did Daren, you makin me mad."

Daren took a deep breath finally looking Trina in her eyes. "I met this chick at a party, at my home girl Niesha's. . and um. . I been chillin wit her after I move shit. Sometimes I be too throwed and she um. . I got her preg-" SLAP! Trina reacted out of natural reflex slapping Daren so hard his nose started bleeding. Trina stood covering her mouth in a oop's gesture. Daren stood controlling his anger knowing they'd be fighting right about now but Daren knew deep down he'd done something forbidden.

"I told you not to hit me T, DAMNN!" Daren flexed. Trina's shocked turned to pain and blind hurt as she cried, "Oh my god Daren how could you?"

"I fucked up T. . . I"

"You said you loved me!" Trina screamed in a throat burning yell. She lost all control, hitting Daren out of anger and painful love. Daren blocked a few punches then wrapped Trina up trying to calm her down. She fought with so much pain that Daren had to slam her on the couch. He wrestled with her until she got tired. He lay close to her, his head on her listening to her cries. He whispered, "I'm sorry T" over and over as she wept with the deepest pain she'd ever felt.

"I'm sorry T, I messed up bad this time. I do want a life with you, but I knew you'd react this way-"

"GET OUT! GET-THE-FUCK-OUT!" Trina screamed releasing a newfound burst of energy. Daren weaved a few slaps running for the door. He shut the door quick fast in a hurry. He was surprised Trina didn't follow him outside. That let him know Trina was truly hurt.

Daren flopped down in the driver seat of the lac feeling lower than low. His sorrow turned to anger causing him to hit the steering wheel multiple times. "FUCK FUCK FUCK FUCK!" he yelled, wishing he could take it back. Daren's only thought was I just fucked off the best thing in my life for no reason at all. He lit his dro blunt from the ash tray and waited. Hoping Trina would come outside levelheaded so they could talk. Twenty minutes passed, ten more passed and once his blunt was gone he started the lac, reversed accepting reality. He drove down Money Lane feeling like the sour diesel soothed his painful soul. His phone rang in his lap, stopped then rang again two minutes later. His first thought was to throw it out the window.

"Hellow, what it is CC?"

"Did you forget about my doctor's appointment?"

"I had some shit goin on. Where you at?"

"I'm at the bus stop on Ocean Street in Riverside. My car broke down this morning so . ."

Daren huffed, "Don't get on the bus CC! I'm on the way right now."

"Sambo nem know me. I put on at school. I'm a real G in the makin. Ma just been trippin on me lately." Kasey confessed.

"I know you think I'm crazy but I'm a project baby and I'd love to have a mom like yours."

"No you don't Shay. She be makin me go to church n shit. Den if I talk she wanna beat on a nigga. Just let me do me is all I'm askin. If I wanna go to church it should be cause I wanna go."

Shay could tell that Kasey got worked up about the situation and his innocent anger made her laugh with a sweet warm feeling inside.

"Maybe you should ask her if I can go to church with y'all?"

"Kasey! Bring me that phone, HELL . . . Tying up my GOD DAMN LINE."

"OKAY MA, DANGG!" Kasey shouted back to Korita.

"Boy don't make me come in there. You might as well get ready so we can go. Hurry up so I can call Daren."

"I ain't tryin to go ma. Tell GG to send me a plate."

"I don't give a damn what you tryin to do. Bring ya ass cause you ain't grown. . "

"See what I'm talkin about Shay. Sometimes I be feeling like oohh I wanna run away."

Daren pulled up to the curb in front of the bus stop trying to change his mood. He was a firm believer in not letting bad energy control you, but he felt out of it right now. Crissa got in the passenger seat thankful to get out of the heat. Daren pulled off with a straight face letting Crissa know what was on his mind. "Look CC, if you carrying my child I don't want you walking through the hood like this."

"It's fine Daren. You act like I didn't grow up in Riverside or something."

"I don't care CC, it's not just your life in danger feel me!"

"Alright Daren damn! You don't gotta be so mean. And can you please roll a window down. That smoke is going to make me throw up."

Daren turned the AC off then rolled his window halfway down thinking: I can already see this baby mama drama is going to be some bull shit. Damn ma why didn't I listen to you.

To break the silence Crissa asked, "After my appointment can you stop by Sonic. I'm craving chili tater tots and pickles."

"I just told my T-jones I was bringing you to meet her. My grama's cooking for Kasey's b-day."

"you're going to tell them about us?"

"Nope, you are. I ain't wit all the emotional shit CC."

"So you believe me now or what?"

"I'm riden with you till we get a test. But I'm takin your word for it till then."

"You're the only person I had sex with since I lost my virginity back in high school, so it's yours. I feel like you think less of me for not believing me."

"Think less of you." Daren scoffed then continued, "I don't want you working at the stirp club no mo CC."

Crissa rolled her eyes, "I'm just a bar tender Daren."

"You act like bar tenders and serves don't get in where they fit in."

Daren took a deep breath to calm his nerves. "Listen CC, if this is going to work ima need you to listen to me. Certain shit ain't up for discussion."

Crissa snapped, "First off, I don't need no man controllin me! Baby daddy or whoeva. At the end of the day I have to take care of myself."

"CC, if I said I got-chu I got-chu. I don't want my B.M up in no strip club. That's messed up, don't you see that?"

"But it's fine for you to be in the stirp club, and it's fine when you was fuckin me on the side. But now that things are in the light it's a problem."

"All of a sudden you got a lot of sarcastic shit to say."

Daren started to blow up on Crissa but he pulled into the clinic on hush mode before he said something he'd regret. He parked searching for his sac of dro to roll up. He laughed to himself thinking about how Trina never tripped with him on small shit like this.

"So you not coming in?"

"Naw, just tell me what the doctor say." Crissa rolled her eyes seeing that Daren was serious. He had already split a gar down the middle with his thumb nail and dumped the gar guts outside.

"If I stop working at the strip club will you stop smoking. It makes you mean when you're not high."

"I don't be smokin bud to look coo CC I got a anger problem. Jane is the only thang that calms my nerves."

Crissa opened the passenger door to get out, but she sat there looking at Daren like she wanted to ask him how stupid he thanks she is. "Daren, I have bills' to pay, and I can't depend on you with your lifestyle. My mother's sick and I don't have much of a choice in life but to do what I gotta do." Crissa got out and shut the car door before Daren could reply.

Half an hour later Crissa got back in the car feeling cheerful from the loving embrace of the clinic's staff. She handed Daren her sonogram wishing she could prove to Daren that it was his.

I'm a month and I need to eat more and drink lots of water."

Daren took a quick look at the dark image, handed the sonogram back to Crissa, started the lack, reversed and mashed off.

"I'll take you to H.E.B. after we leave my GG crib."

"Aren't you going to show your mom and them the sonogram?"

"Nope, I already told you you are." Daren turned the music up and mashed the gas.

Kasey followed Korita into the living room of his grandmother's house without knocking because the front door was wide open.

"Kesha don't play with that plug baby!" Korita yelled as she picked her four-year-old niece up before she could stick a nail into the socket.

"Grampa Perry, do you see her, or do you need some new glasses?"

Korita asked not expecting an answer because all Perry did was watch jeopardy. She made her way into the kitchen yelling, "Brenda! Why aren't you watching my niece? And why is mama cooking by herself?"

"Umph, she must be waitin on you," Brenda mocked with a turn of her neck.

"It's okay Rea, they'd just be in my way. Now where is my grandbaby?" Gwen asked standing over the hot stove and frying pan. Kasey approached the stove with his hands in his pockets. "I'm right here GG."

"Well come give grama some love child!" Grama Gwen turned around giving Kasey and Korita each a quick hug. When she returned back to cooking Kasey reached for a piece of fried chicken piled upon the greasy napkin, but Korita slapped his hand. "Um umm, dirty hands Kasey. Wait till the food is done!"

"He's fine Rea, there's more than enough." GG explained.

"Thanks GG!" Kasey snatched a leg from the pile of chicken and bit into it like a starved animal.

"Thas crazy mama, you neva let us get samples before the meal. An I'm your oldest child," Domo complained.

GG took a golden leg and thigh out of the sizzling grease, smiling as she placed it on pile of chicken. "That's because none of my children tried to graduate from high school. Kasey's so smart I'm sure he'll be the first." GG spoke full of pride as she dropped more chicken in the pan.

"Thanks GG." Kasey shook the coming conversation and made his way into the living room. He stood behind the love seat checking what was on TV. "Boring, boring, boring. I hate Jeopardy. Papow Perry this is wack. Can we watch B.E.T?"

"We lost the remote. Sit down and learn something."

Kasey went back into the kitchen hating how lame GG's was. He stood in the middle of the kitchen trying to find something to do. Knowing Korita, they would be here four or five hours after they ate still doing nothing.

Korita held Kesha on a hip helping GG cook. A card game was going on at the diner table and no one was in the other rooms.

"Maaa," Kasey whined.

"What Kasey! Don't start bugging me," Korita snapped.

"It's boring ma, I'm tryin to play ball at the park."

"UM UM, wait till ya brother gets here." Korita checked the sweet cornbread in the oven thinking about making a mac-n-cheese casserole.

Domo pulled a card from the deck in the middle of the table and paused, "Mann that boy grown Rea, let'em go play ball."

"Ain't no body talkin to you Domo, please mind yours!" Korita snapped, facing Domo. "I bet you don't have the slightest clue as to where my nephew Tavious is."

"Free, being a young adult doin whatever it is they be doin. You can't be sherlterin that boy sis. If I was him I'da did you somethin a long time ago." Domo threw a card in the dead pile in the middle of the table making eye contact with Korita, hoping and ready for an argument.

"Would you leave me alone Domo, hell."

"It's crazy unk, whenever I tell her somethin all she wanna do is beat me for no reason."

"You hear that GG." Domo asked his mother.

Brenda grabbed a card from the deck, looked at it then shouted, "double tunk!" She placed three queens down on the table then grabbed the folded money next to the deck. She stuffed the money in her bra demanded for her double, meaning since she double tunked each person playing owed her money.

"Shit Rea, this all yo fault wit yo janky ass!" Domo shouted.

GG cleared her throat and politely asked, "Please watch you mouth child."

"Sorry mama." Domo gathered the cards to shuffle for the next game.

Kasey sat in the empty seat next to his cousin Kent watching money be passed around. With nothing else to do he asked, "Can I play?"

"You got some money?" Kent asked.

"You don't need to be gambling Kasey, hell . . . stop actin worsome!" Korita said, giving Kasey the eye.

"Well what on earth is my grandbaby supposed to do Rea?" GG asked.

"Yea mama!"

"I don't care Kasey, but I ain't givin you no money to be gambling!"

"I got some money from big bro for my b-day."

"Den you in kinfolk. Let me explain the rules real quick. This is Tunk. Each person playing puts up an Anny, we agreed for the Anny to be five dollars. The goal of the game is to fall or double Tunk to win the pot of money. . "

Domo passed out five cards to the five people at the table. Brenda acted like the law making sure the twenty-five dollars was counted and in the middle of the table. Kasey still hadn't annyed up and his confused face said it all. .

"A fall is to lay your cards down kinfolk, face cards and ten's are ten, aces are one. The lowest hand wins. But if you fall and someone is lower than you, they win the money, and you owe them the any fee. A spread is three of a kind, like three aces or queens. Or you can even spread by using three cards of the same suit in order."

"Like 5, 6, 7 of hearts?" Kasey asked with his five dollars in hand.

"Yep, and if you spread twice it's a double Tunk and the table each owes you the anny fee."

"So I should just fall after I spread and win da money huh ma?" Kasey asked, looking for Karita.

"I'm not helpin you gamble Kasey. Leave me alone boy!"

"Oh, I forgot about the automatick- - "

Domo cut Kent off saying "Anny up Kasey! Kent you shoulda taught' em befo you brought 'em!" Brenda took Kasey's five dollars, folded it over the rest of the money then placed the money next to the deck in the center of the table. "Person to the right of the dealer pulls first," Domo added.

Brenda's friend Brandy pulled a card, looked at it then threw it face up next to the deck. Kent explained, "That's the dead cards, you can only pull what's on top if you need it if it's your turn." Brenda pulled a card from the deck next. She kept the card down as she put it in her hand with her five cards so on one could see. She jumped back to look at all six cards then threw a card in the dead pile. "Ahh Haa, aint Brenda you crazy den a mug," Kasey laughed.

"Uh uh, cause see. . . Domo always cheatin and tryin to run game. Stick around, you'll see nephew."

"Yo fault fa holden ya hand out of course Ima look sis." Domo grabbed the five of hearts Brenda just threw in the dead pile. Kasey watched Domo place two fives out of his hand with the five of hearts on the table in front of him. Then Domo threw a dead card in the middle of the table.

"Dang, so I probably can't fall now huh kinfolk?" Kasey asked. . .

"Naw kinfolk, I wouldn't . . but if he high and you real low shoot ya shot . . . You know what they say, have nuts have glory. Domo play to double Tunk. Knowin him he probaly high." Kent pulled a card from the deck then threw it away.

"My turn, I fall with fourteen," Kasey said, throwing his cards down.

When Brenda saw Kasey's ace, five, two 2's and a four she said, "SHHITT!"

"Language Brenda! Or I'll wash your mouth out with soap damn it!"

GG covered her mouth with a quick prayer, "Oops, now y'all got me cussin."

Brenda grabbed the cards for the next game explaining, "That's a auto sweety. Forty-nine and fifty's are autos and fifteen and under are autos." Kent grabbed the twenty-five dollars and handed it to Kasey.

"Up the anny to ten dollars and a game and a side pot of five dollars each for first spread. We'll see how long his punk luck last." Domo boasted.

Kasey happily put his fifteen dollars in the middle of the table. "I'm in."

"These card do turn, don't go cryin to Korita when you loose all your birthday change nephew."

"It's ok aunt Brenda. I know when to quit."

Daren and Crissa walked in the living room smelling the home cooked meal.

"Perry you ain't dead yet? You need to burn off already!" Daren stated as they walked by. "You outa control, dope sellin, paints all off ya ass."

Perry's voice faded when Crissa and Daren walked into the kitchen. Daren tossed Kasey his phone with a "You lucky you my lil bro."

"Oh snaps my own phone. Now ma ain't gone be trippen on me. Thanks big bro."

Daren kissed GG on the cheek with a "my beautiful Grama, looking good and got it smellin good as usual."

"Nice to see you too grandbaby."

Daren kissed Korita on the cheek while easing baby Kesha out of her hands. "Look out unk, deal me in the next hand," Daren said, finding a seat at the table with Kesha in his lap.

GG glanced back at Crissa with a smile. "And just who might you be honey?"

"Hi, umm my name is Crissa Cromer and I . . "

Brenda cut Crissa off. "Crystal Cromer's your mother. We went to school with Crystal, remember Rea?"

"It's been so long I don't, but she sure is pretty Daren. You could use some meat on those bones girl." Korita glanced back keeping her question of where's Trina to herself. "Be nice to Daren's new girlfriend Rea."

"I ani't say nothin mean mama."

"I don't know about me being his girlfriend, but I have something to show you."

Korita faced Crissa as she dug in her purse. When Crissa handed her the sonogram Korita lost her breath.

"Oh my go-ahh. . .I'm about to be a grandmother."

"Well it's about time! The boy do everything else," Perry yelled from the living room. Daren shouted back, "You not even our real grampa! You here for no reason!"

"Daren please!" stressed GG.

"Sorry grama Gwen. Please tell you skin bag of a man to leave me be. My nerves bad."

Korita took hold of Crissa's hand and pulled her to the back. "I'm finally about to be a grandmother . . . Tell me everything."

Korita made Crissa sit at the edge of her mother's bed. She stood over Crissa asking question after question.

"Are you and Daren going to move in together?"

"Most likely not. My mother's on bed rest with umm . . . Brain cancer. So it's like her house is my house. It's been this way since my first year of college. She's the main reason I dropped out and got a job as a bartender at Paradise.

"Where's your father baby?"

"Dope fiend. Crack head, in and out of prison all my life. Besides that I don't know much about him."

"So you and Daren are just having sex or?"

"I mean I want a relationship with him, . . You know a real family, but I know he has other women in his life. I don't want to get an abortion but with my mother sick I can't do this on my own."

Korita sat next to Crissa and held her close. "If you ever need help you bring that baby to me do you hear me?"

"Yes ma'am."

"And if Daren puts his hands on you make sure to call me."

"Ok I will . . .-AHH" Crissa screamed, jumping on the bed when a rat passed from under them. Korita laughed then asked, "When's the next doctor's appointment, and how far are you?"

Grandpa Perry, Brenda's fourteen-year-old son Mike-Mike and the rest of the kids were in the living room eating on the floor and on trays in front of them. the rest of the grownups sat at the crowded dinner table with healthy plates. Korita made sure Crissa's plate piled high. The men ate with their heads down like savages while the women showed mannerism, keeping conversation going. Korita held Kisha in her lap taking turns feeding her and her niece. GG ate slowly feeling good that she could feed her family a good meal from her heart.

"Daren, my oldest grand baby . . . What are your plans now that you're going to have a family?"

"I don't know yet GG."

Brenda smacked her lips, "Kent 21 and just got out of prison for aggrobbery. Daren's most likely next."

Daren frowned at his aunt, bit his tongue then continued eating. Daren felt everyone's eyes on him, and it made him mad. "At least I know who's the father of mines while you talking Brenda," Korita snapped. Domo added, "Brenda stop actin all high and mighty like Mike-Mike don't be in the manor at age fifteen."

"My baby don't sell dope that's fa show! Humph."

"It's only a matter of time. Hangin with dough-boys you most likely gon be one over time."

"Would you shut up Domo, like you don't know what Tavious be doin." Brenda snapped.

GG shouted, "THAT'S ENOUGH, . . . Domo, why don't you get Kent, Tavious and Daren a job at the oil rig with you?"

"That's over with GG," Daren confessed.

"Yea, I'm good to GG. The oil rig is slave work and the death rate is high." Kent explained.

Perry yelled from the living room, "Well ya asses gon do something."

"GG will you please tell you half dead sugar daddy to mind his."

"Perry, please leave my grandbabies along!" GG yelled.

"We worry about y'all that's all."

Daren stood trying to keep his cool, "Why is y'all worried about me? Shit get on a nigga nerves. . .Mann I'm out!" Daren stormed out the house extra heated.

Crissa stood with her foiled extra plate, "Thanks for the meal. . ."

"You're more than welcome honey. Call if you need anything you hear." Korita and GG stood, giving Crissa a group hug. Crissa hurried outside feeling good from all of the love and support Daren had.

Kortia and GG sat back in their seats. GG had a stern gaze on Kasey, so he got up from the table to find a seat in the living room. Domo laughed trying to tell his mother and sisters the real, "Y'all can's shelter these kids. You gotta guide them with some sort of freedom. If not they gone bump they head even harder as soon as they get a lil freedom."

Daren drove Crissa to H.E.B in silence. When she went inside to shop he pulled extra hard on his swisher. After the bud kicked in Daren calmed down realizing his family cared about him but what else could he do in life. I ain't no nine to five nigga and school ain't my scene. . . Daren thought.

Crissa pushed the basket of groceries to the back seat and opened the door. She was surprised when Daren got out and helped her. Once they were back on the road Crissa smiled at Daren.

"What is it CC?"

"You have a really nice family. I wish I had a family. My mom's never really been there, and I don't know if she has brothers or sisters. I think she said she's a C.P.S baby. . . Thank you for that experience Daren."

"You're welcome I guess. They just make me so mad. Ma know what she be doin too."

"At least they mean well. I just want you to be here you know. I heard about what happened at the party with you and lil Chris. I know shit happens but you gotta learn to control the situation by controlling your actions."

"I know CC, and ima be here till the wheels fall off. . . With that baby I got-chu for life."

"What about your girlfriend?"

"I told her, and I think we done."

As soon as Daren said that his phone rang with a call from Trina. . . When Daren didn't answer Crissa crossed her arms with a sassy "whatever Daren."

CHAPTER 4

HOMELESS

O n the short ride home Kasey had his new phone glued to his ear with his playa swag on full attack. Korita drove laughing to herself at the sight of her youngest son with the seat back trying to be mack daddy. Kasey reminded Korita so much of her and Kay that she found herself having a flashback of one of the most special days of her life.

Thirteen years ago . . .

Kay blindfolded Korita and her patience was thin on the drive to wherever they were going. Korita sat up and alert in the passenger seat asking questions, but Kay remained silent. When she tried to peel the blindfold back for a peak Kay would say "Don't do that Rea, or you ain't gon get yo surprise."

"UOO boy you getting on my nerves. How much longer?"

"As long as it takes bae. Sit back and be the queen that you are."

A few minutes passed and Kay's old school began to slow down.

"What is this Kay?" Korita asked feeling the car stop.

"Bae, the sweetest joys in life come to those with love in their hearts and patience in every action." Kay turned his old school off and waited just because he knew Korita was always in a rush. On top of that she was frustrated due to their current living situation.

"Boy stop, you musta been reading them poetry books again." Kay stopped Korita from trying to untie the blindfold then hopped out of the car. He ran around to Korita's side to help her get out. Kay led Korita somewhere and all she could think was it's not my birthday so what could his crazy ass be up to. Kay led Korita into a yard, stopping at some steps. He stood behind her removing the blindfold while whispering, "it's in your name. My credit bad ass hell and I ain't neva had no job."

At the sight of her house Korita turned around and kissed Kay deeply. Kay searched his pockets until he found the house key explaining, "It's right next to the church and GG live right behind us on the next block."

Korita was too excited to listen once she pried the key from Kay's hand. She unlocked the door and ran inside.

I'm so happy to finally have a place to call my own. Thank God because I'm tired of living from hotel to hotel and holding and helping Kay sell his dope.

"We goin to church in the mornin Kasey."

"Ma can we pick up Shay?"

"I don't see why not. Now bring the food in and don't spill none." Korita parked in her driveway and got out. Kasey continued his conversation saying what he really wanted to say now that Korita was in the house.

"I know what to do wit it girl, you playin games. . Shh I'm a beast- -."

'KASEY!" Korita shouted form the porch.

"Shay, let me call you right back!" Kasey hurried up and put his phone in his pocket, got out and got the food out of the back seat. He closed the car doors with his feet. As he did so he had his eyes locked on Korita. "Comin ma" Kasey met Korita on the porch wondering what he could have did now.

"Don't lie to me Kasey! Are there drugs in my house?"

Kasey knew Korita was serious because of the way she stood, hand on her hip ready to slap five if she synced any type of hesitation. Knowing not to lie Kasey just stood there with his mouth open, heart beating fast with the heavy pan of food in his hands. Korita started to slap Kasey just because, but she knew he'd spill the tuna cheese casserole all over the porch.

"So you wanna play dumb huh? . . Okay, I got-cho ass." Korita stormed into the house and into Daren and Kasey's room. Kasey carried the food into the kitchen as fast as he could. As he set the food on the counter he could smell tobacco and loud ass dro all throughout the house. Kasey didn't now that with the AC off while they were gone it would expose Daren's hustle game.

Kasey stood in the door of his and Daren's room watching his mother hit the room like a storm. She searched every corner, the closet and Daren's and Kasey's drawers only to find nothing.

"I just had a lil weed fa my b-day ma. I left a piece of blunt in the window. Korita continued her search with fuss that made her angrier each passing second. "Bullshit Kasey! You think I'm dumb. I know Daren has drugs in here. You both always have new clothes, shoes. Where is he getting the type of money to buy cars and phones like it's nothing!"

Korita stopped searching and slowly approached Kasey with narrow eyes locked into his. "You know what, yo ass is going to tell me where you brother hidin all of his shit. Or I'm gonna make you finish school at grama's, then you ass is going to the army."

Kasey's eyes began to water as he cried, "I'll run away!" "You not old enough to be out on your own. . .I'll call the cops and have you ass in juvenile so quick. . .WHERE ARE THE DRUGS KASEY!"

Kasey looked at the floor under the bed.

"BOY AIN'T NOTHIN UNDER THE BED! I'M GONE ASK YOU ONE MO TIME. TRY ME KASEY!"

Korita's strained evil voice let Kasey know he was a second away from one of them ass whoopins so he hung his head as he made his way to the bed. He moved the bed to the side, pulled the floor board up and stepped back.

"Oh my god, like father like son" . . . Korita's voice was full of shock that changed to a fiery anger in the blink of an eye. "You wanna send me to the feds Kasey?"

"NO MA!" Kasey cried, -SMACK-

"I can't tell!" Korita shouted, as she slapped and beat Kasey down until he ran out of the house. She started to chase him, but she realized this wasn't his fault. At the sight of so much money, weed and guns she laughed. . . "Some things will never change."

After helping Crissa settle in Daren unconsciously drove down Money Lane in the direction of Trina's apartments. Daren called Trina back hoping that she wanted to talk because he really needed to vent to someone who semi understood him. Trina answered after a few rings, but all Daren could hear was heavy breathing.

"I'm on the way over there."

"How many times have I heard that. You mean tomorrow right?"

Daren could hear Trina's crackly voice and somehow he felt her pain.

"I'm for real T. I need to talk to you without you spazzin on me." -BEEP- Daren checked his phone with a glance and saw it was a call from the house. "Hold on right quick T, it's ma," Daren clicked over, "Please don't tell me your car broke down ma!"

"Your brother ran away! Find him before he gets killed."

"What happened ma?" Korita rudely hung up, so Daren clicked back over. Trina hung up as well which kinda made Daren mad. If it ain't one thang it's another, Daren thought as he turned off of Money Lane into Oak Ride. He called Kasey's phone while searching the streets. Even though it was late the blocks of his hood were still full of life.

"Bro, where you at? And why you run away?"

"Cause ma was beatin on me, she know about the stash cause I . . My bad big bro"

"DAMN IT KASEY! . . . How she. . ." Daren calmed his anger beating himself up mentally because he knew he shouldn't have shown Kasey the stash just yet. "Where you at bro, it's one in the morning."

"I'm at the park by Rich house," Kasey spoke with sorrow feeling like he'd let Daren down. Then he hung up.

A minute later Daren parked the lac in the empty parking lot of Oak Ride Park. Daren forced himself out of the car while searching for Kasey. He asked himself, "Why am I always in the middle of some shit?" He walked through the basketball court calling Kasey phone, but Kasey didn't answer. "Kasey!" Daren shouted but Kasey still didn't answer.

When Daren got to the sandy playground he could see Kasey at the highest part of the playground. Daren stopped at the sandy edge and yelled "Com'on bro, before you get us killed in a drive by."

Kasey climbed down and met Daren on explain mode.

"It's my fault big bro. I was blowin and it smelled like dro and cigar in the whole house."

"It's alright Kasey. I'll take all the blame. Nothin is going to change."

"Ma gon kick you out cause I messed up." Kasey cried.

"Don't even trip. I'm neva home anyway besides to sleep." Daren put his arm around Kasey's shoulder and walked with him back to the lac.

"But I don't want you to be homeless big bro."

"Don't worry lil bro, everything happens for a reason. I learned that about life a long time ago."

❖ ❖ ❖

Daren parked the lac behind Korita's car and waited. "Don't talk and stop crying bro. everything is going to be alright." Kasey nodded as he and Daren got out of the lac. They stood before Kortia sitting on her porch chair smoking a cigarette like a burned fuse. She had Daren's' duffle bag on her side showing no emotion.

"Look ma, you know it's my stuff. So why you beatin on Kasey fo?"

"Because he lied to me, and I know his ass is sellin drugs with you. That god damn K is a murder weapon. What the hell is wrong with you Daren?"

"Well he wasn't sellin drugs wit no-body. I barely showed him the stash last night because I gave him some weed for his b-day."

Korita pointed at Daren and spoke with a painful anger, "Y'all thank I'm stupid. Got drugs, guns in my house like I didn't tell you not to a hundred times. How did you get ya father's gun anyway?"

Daren and Kasey remained silent watching Korita take a hard puff of her cigarette. She spoke through the smoke like it didn't bother her. "Musta been Richard. A damn shame. Forty years old and still gang bangin. I want a better life for you and Kasey, Daren. Do you remember the night your father died?" Again Daren and Kasey remained silent so Korita shouted, "DO YOU?"

"I do ma," Daren answered.

Korita's tears fell as she stressed, "I won't sit here and let that night replay itself. An I damn sho ain't gon let you get this house shot up."

"It's understood ma. But don't punish Kasey for my wrong doings."

"Go to your room Kasey." Korita smashed the butt of her cigarette in the ashtray with extra force. Once Kasey was inside Daren told Korita the truth of their reality. "Living in the hood we don't have high goals and dreams ma. Ain't no I wanna be a doctor or lawyer when I finished school because those opportunities ain't given to us. You of all people know that life ain't simple. I do what I do so we can be alright."

"You have to find another way Daren. That's all I'm asking."

"Whatever that way is I'll be on the lookout for it. Till then I'll still do what I do for you and Kasey." Daren picked up his bag then stopped, looking Korita in her eyes. "I'm sorry ma and I'll love you no matter what."

"I don't want your drug money Daren!" Korita cried.

"You really don't have a choice ma."

Korita dried her eyes and took a shaky breath. "I'm going to get a job at the nursing home with Brenda's friend. She said she's friends with the manager."

"Coo ma, let me know if you need help with anything."

Daren took a few steps towards his lac, but Korita weekly cried, "Wait Daren." Daren stopped with his back to Korita watching the dark streets. "Think of your child. You have more than enough money to stop what you're doing and get in school. Why is the street life your only option?"

"Because ma. That's all we was given when we freed as slaves. . . .the streets. I gotta stack up as fast as I can before the baby born. I really been chillin outa respect for you. but I gotta get in the wind now ma. I can't have you, my queen slavin in no nursing home for long. I'll be back to get some of my clothes tomorrow."

Just like that Korita watched her first born jump knee deep in the streets of Money Lane.

Daren parked in Trina's parking spot and turned off the engine. He pulled extra hard on his blunt of dro thinking about how real this was. I got guns, drugs and way too much bread on me to be homeless. Trina's too emotional so I probly shouldn't stay here to too long. If I do I'll most likely end up in the county. So what am I doing here? Because I love her more than anything and love is blind.

Daren grabbed his phone from his lap and called Rich. Rich picked up on the first ring, "The wisdom of a O.G is only gained by the way he plays the game. What it B like young dough?"

"I got in some shit wit ma. She kicked me out and now I'm homeless."

"Neva that, my door is always open young dough. Or we can get you a spot in a cluck name. Just come through."

Daren looked up to see Trina standing in her apartment door, dressed in a sexy black nightgown. Her beautiful face was full of buried anger. But how she stared at him pulled him in. It was strange how he liked Trina's attitude. She had that sexy I know what I want outa my man, and she wasn't afraid to let him know. At the same time they could talk about anything and find a solution.

"Ima see if Trina trippin, I might slide through tomorrow. Oh yea before I forget. I'm on the clock full time now."

"If that's the case then you definitely need to come through. Be easy young dough."

By the time Daren hung up Trina was at his driver's side window looking in. Daren opened the car door and waited for the bull shit. Trina stood with her hands on her waist asking, "Talking to your baby mama?"

"No I wasn't Trina."

"So now I'm Trina! How come you didn't come in Daren?"

"I was tellin Rich how I'm stuck out." Trina could see Daren's worry and wanted to know what had happened. Just then they locked eyes when they heard gun shots close by.

"Daren please come in, its dangerous out here this late!" Trina demanded.

"I got too much heat on me if you start trippin Trina."

Trina smacked her lips with a sassy, "Boy ain't nobody finna trip wit-chu, you did what you did already, and you can't take it back. Now come in so we can talk."

Daren shook his head. "Nah, you get in and we can talk."

Trina rolled her eyes then noticed the bag in the back seat. "Who's bag is that and why do you have that big ass gun with you. At least hide it."

"Kasey was blowin and ma made him give up the stash."

"So she kicked you out! Ha, I would have done the same thing. Yo ass is goin to the feds fuckin wit Rich and them cartels." Trina laughed at Daren in an open long laughter. She controlled her reaction when she saw how down Daren was about the situation.

Trina walked around the lac thinking about how much she wanted this. But she didn't want it to happen like this, with him getting another female pregnant. Oh my god why do things happen to us like this. I guess I have to ask myself if I can still love him, be with him with another in his life.

Trina got in the lac and shut the door just as Daren shut his car door. Daren lit his half of blunt and held it in as long as he could. On the exhale he asked, "You wanna smoke?"

"You know I don't usually but yo ass been stressin me out lately."

Daren opened the glove box and gave Trina a gar then pulled his personal sack of dro out of his pocket. Daren smoked his half a blunt down to a doobie while watching Trina roll up. It was something about the woman that made everything she does sexy. Trina split the gar down the middle with her nails, emptied the gar guts outside. She sat with her legs crossed skillfully breaking sticky buds down and lining the dro in the gar.

"Why do you think I lie to you?" Daren asked.

"Because you don't want to hurt me. But with the shit you do you hurt me anyway so."

"The crazy part is you think I lie to you when I keep it one hundred. It's crazy how you know more about me than ma or Kasey. Know why?"

"WHY?" Trina asked, rolling the blunt like a pro from the many nights of practice from rolling Daren's weed.

"Because you're my only friend. But you be putting too much pressure on me. Tryin to change me. Force me to do things I don't know if I'm ready for."

"So you distance yourself from me and get some random bitch pregnant."

"She not random T, I told you I met somebody at a party at my home girl Niesha's, I also told you I wanted you to meet her. I can't make you understand how hard it is to control my want for a woman. I wanna try things and experience life to the fullest. You said you'd be the one who'd be open to try things with me but your emotions get in the way and you always start trippin."

"Yo nasty ass just wanna have threesomes all of the time Daren!"

Daren took a deep breath. "These is the arguments I don't be tryin to have. Light the blunt please." Trina lit the blunt to try and ease her pain and stress. "All I can be is real Trina. What man doesn't want threesomes? What you fail to see is that I want you involved in whatever I got goin on. What happened to the Trina I knew back in high school? The one who was down for whatever?"

"I grew up Daren. America paints this picture of a happy family with a house, a white picket fence where we grow old in marriage. But all that seems like its fairy tale because all I see is single mothers, a high death rate and you headed straight to prison."

"My hustle game to hard and I'll never going to prison."

"Umm hum, you said that about getting caught by your mother and getting another bitch pregnant." Daren hit the blunt real hard thinking about how Trina must feel. Lord knows she's supposed to be my one and only.

"I know I messed up T, and ain't no way to fix it. But I still want you in my life. In my heart I feel like we were in more than just a relationship. Tell me what I gotta do for us to be together. If we can't be together then at least continue to be my best friend."

Trina took the blunt from Daren and took small puffs until she coughed. Once she caught her breath she told Daren her terms with a straight face. "We're going to enroll in GED class as a start. I know your still going to hustle but we know that the good of the game don't last forever. Try to make it work with your baby mama for your child's sake. My last hope is that you get us out of the hood like you promised."

"I don't know about the school thing T, Ima try but-"

"But what-" Trina cut Daren off bringing her crazy side back in a flash.

"Nothin, . . Does that mean we can't have sex?"

Trina took small puffs feeling hella good. She felt so good she let the following thoughts run through her mind without judgment.

I'm horny as hell, high and I ain't got no panties on. It's been ten days since I had some dick and umm. . he is still technically my man with his dirty dick ass. . . God why didn't he wear a condom?

"Do you have condoms Daren?"

Before Daren could tell Trina he hates condoms Trina passed him the blunt with a "I'm good on that." The way she spoke and moved slowly made Daren laugh because Trina never smokes, and he hadn't seen her this way since high school. "Of course I got protection. I just hate. . ."

Daren stopped talking because Trina stretched her left leg over Daren's lap. "We can have sex only tonight till you figure something out. For fucking me over you gotta tongue my clit till I cum three times before you get any."

Daren knew that could take a while, but he didn't care. He just wanted to make Trina feel good. Daren's eyes found Trina's fingers rubbing and caressing her womanhood. Her mouth was open, tongue out and Daren like the way she hummed and moaned. "UHOO I'm so horny boy, . . Shit I need it bad right now!"

Daren dropped the blunt in the ash tray and was already on his way down for a late night snack. But Trina caught Daren's head with her palm and a teasing taste of her fingers. "Come in for the buffet!" Daren watched Trina open her car door and make her way inside.

I love buffets Daren thought as he reached in the back seat for the AK and his bag. He stuffed the Ak in the bag and gathered his blunt from the ash tray. He almost broke his neck trying to get out, lock the car doors and run inside after Trina. He hurried into the apartment thinking about how he was going to give her all of the tongue and dick she could ever want to make her stay.

Once he was inside he locked the front door and stashed his bag in the back of the living room closet behind all of Trina's junk. He had a bag of clothes and few pairs of shoes in the back from when he sometimes stayed over. Now more than ever he wanted nothing more but to live with Trina, but he knew that thigs would never be the same between them.

Daren stripped down to his boxers with his blunt still behind his ear. He rushed to Trina's room and stopped in the door at the beautiful sight of Trina laying in the center of her bed, propped up on her fluffy dark silk pillows. Her night gown was above her waist, her legs were spread wide. She was in her own world rubbing her womanhood in circles. When Daren approached the bed Trina dug her caramel painted toes in the bed to hold off her orgasm. "Hurry daddy. SS-ah, I'm about to come!" Daren dove in headfirst ready to be her sex slave. As soon as Daren's tongue ran up and down her womanhood Trina's orgasm ripped through her body. Her back arched as she uncontrollably grabbed the back of Daren's head and mashed his face deep into her sex.

Trina calmed down and Daren tongued her to another trip to cloud nine. Trina felt satisfied but she still wanted some good strong D. She knew what she told him, but she pushed Daren down on his back and rolled a condom on his manhood. She skillfully straddled him and slid down with a low hum while looking Daren in his eyes.

She rode him in a slow up and down rhythm until his manhood was good and wet just like she liked it. Trina leaned close to Daren's face and kissed his lips, all the while she never stopped her pleasure and pain.

"Why does love hurt and feel so good at the same time?" she asked.

Daren didn't answer but he thought about how painful life could be. Trina's love was so good and tight that Daren came before she could come again. Trina was so emotional she didn't care about the task she had given Daren. She was so hurt that she lie on his chest and cried.

"You're not homeless. You can stay with me if you don't stay with her."

Not wanting to argue Daren hugged Trina close. "Ok T, just don't please don't leave."

Around two in the morning Trina fell into a deep sleep. Daren tossed and turned thinking about how everything was on him now. Everyone depends on me and I'm homeless. Ain't that a bitch. Daren hopped in the shower then put his clothes back on. With no other option he hopped back in the lac on a mission to see what Rich had to say. On the way back to Oak Ride all Daren could think about was how Trina wanted so much from him. I know she wants the best for me, and I owe her everything for being there for me through all of this. I'll take the school thing into consideration but right now I gotta stack some bread real quick. I need my own spot like asap.

"We really could get our own spot with all the bread we be makin with Rich. Sometimes I be feelin like we some bums because we always here or there." K-9 vented to the homies.

"D-woo was the first one to challenge. I'm straight. I love chillin right here. On O.G porch, wit the homies. . . watchin the block waitin for whatever. Look at the bright side. We ain't gotta pay no rent every month. Rich always feed us. And if you stay in the wind the fed's will have a hard time catchin you or clockin your moves. The couples hoes I be putting dick to in Oak Ride always need extra money for rent, this or that because a 9-5 just ain't whas up. Plus we ain't neva had no job to get a crib."

"Rich said he'll get any of us a spot in a smoka name." Daren added.

The homies surrounded Daren, D-woo and K-9 knowing the debate was about to turn up now that Daren brought a new perspective to the block.

D-woo passed the blunt to Daren pointing out one important fact.

"Rich always be tellin me that it's always a possibility that the smoka could get into some shit and fold on you. you can't depend on no dope fiend doin what we do. I'm good dawg. You askin fa mo problems and responsibility. You can't get comfortable in this lifestyle."

The homies nodded in agreement putting their two cents in. Daren started to say something, but Rich poked his head out the front door and saw the homies huddled up. He huffed with a shake of his head then took a step outside. He closed the door behind him and before he could say anything K-9 apologized. "Our bad O.G. We know we suppose to be watchin-". .

"Naw, hold on my young G's. . It's obvious we need to have this discussion again from a different point of view so it will stick this time. Let's use chess, it's a game of war symbolic to the battle field of life. The two women in that house are queens. I thank y'all all can agree with that. They do a lot for us even though at times they get fed up. D-woo and K-9 I like to thank of y'all as my bishops or horse's. Daren I wanna say he holds the power of two rooks. I would say he could do more if only he would embrace his position in this army. The rest of y'all represent pawns and everyone knows pawns might grow to be the next king or any piece of the chess board. But before that can happen certain work must be put in buy these pawns. Now what should happen if the kingdom should fall?" Rich paused looking everyone in their eyes.

"We got-chu O.G, keep our straps ready and watch the streets." D-woo shot out."

"That's all I ask . . Young dough, would you be so kind to come inside?" Rich asked. Daren's phone rang in his pocket again and he knew it was Crissa calling this late because she'd been calling ever since he left Trina's an hour ago. "Let me go check on something real quick Rich and I'll be right back." Rich nodded then went back in the house when the homies gave their full attention to the dark block.

CHAPTER 5

TWO SIDE OF THE HOOD

Bright and early Sunday morning the pastor of Living Faith Church led the choir in singing melodies from heaven. Everyone wore their best suits, dresses and church attire. Many had their hands up in need of a blessing. Kasey wasn't one of them. he hated the small hot church that would quickly get packed. He dreaded being forced to come and he was still mad at Korita for what happened last night. But most of all Kasey worried about Daren because his situation was his fault.

Kasey shook his head at his mother and grandmother in the row in front of him. They both had their hands up singing louder than the choir. For this reason Kasey learned long ago to go deep into his own world.

Sometimes Tavious helped Kasey pass time with low conversations and jokes. But right now Kasey thought about his position in the hood and what he should do to stack some bread without Korita finding out.

Tavious leaned in close to Kasey and whispered, "Cuzzo wha's good? Sorry I missed your dinner last night. Me and some of the homies had a long meeting N shit."

"It's coo kinfolk," Kasey said in a gloomy whisper.

Tavious nudged Kasey with love and concern in his voice. "You ain't gotta act like cuzzo! Just cause we from two different sides of the hood. We still fam no matter what."

"It ain't you kinfolk. I just got a lot on my mind."

"I was hopin Daren came to church with y'all. I really needed to holla at'em."

"About what kinfolk?" Next to Tavious, Domo leaned forward and gave his only son and Kasey the keep it down gesture. Domo pointed to GG and Korita like they was the law.

"Coo pop's," mouthed Tavious then Tavious leaned in closer to Kasey's ear to speak more quietly. "The homies of Riverside messed up about how Daren put lil Chris in the hospital. On top of that ain't no crips in Riverside really eatin. I was hopin Daren would mess with me off the strength that we fam. To stop all of the beef between Oak Ride bloods and Riverside crips."

"Sorry to tell you but I got big bro kicked out last night. But I been thinkin about runnin away so I can get on the grind."

"Daren gon put you on?" Tavious asked with wide eyes because of how green Kasey was. "Sorta, well I could really go talk to Rich myself but ma. . . She be trippin on me fa no reason."

"I already know cuzzo. Where Daren stain at?"

"Wish I knew. I been worried about'em. Den he got some chick named Crissa all emotional. I think she bout to have his baby."

"NO shit! Crissa Cromer from Riverside. The strip club bartender from Paradise. Everybody been tryin to hit dat. Her mother's a brain dead dope fiend."

"Kasey's mouth dropped with a "Dang I ain't know none of that."

"Yea cuzzo . .But drop that. When you hear from Dough tell'em I need ta holla at'em."

"Ima call'em after church." Tavious nodded but he could tell Kasey was unsure. The soul soothing music came to a stop letting everyone know to take their seats. Domo leaned over making eye contact with Tavious and Kasey.

"Y'all please keep it down so GG don't get on my ass."

Kasey leaned over and whispered, "Got-chu unk, but umm ask ma to let me go chill at you crib after church. I need to get out the house before I go crazy."

Domo gave Kasey the thumbs up then sat back.

BOOM BOOM BOOM – Daren jumped out of his sleep to find Rich standing at the passenger door of the lac, looking in the window. Daren rubbed his eyes to wake up then leaned over to unlock the door. Rich opened the car door with a frown on his face. "Why sleep outside when my home is your home young dough?"

"I was arguin with BM and it was late when I got back. It didn't feel right to disturb you at four or five in the morning."

Rich nodded understanding Daren's' logic but confessed. "I'd rather be disturbed then have you sleep out here in your wip. It's not safe young dough. Now come in and have some breakfast. I see we need to talk history, so you understand where I'm coming from."

"History about what?" Daren asked grabbing his phone and sack of dro from the seat.

"The history of two sided of the hood young dough."

Daren followed Rich into the house thinking about how he always wanted to know why Riverside and Oak Ride beef on some murder game type shit. It had to be more than some blood and crip beef when you look at how much life had been lost over the years. Daren checked his phone and saw that it was 8am before he stuffed it in his pocket. He adjusted his Glock 9 behind his back with a quick nod to the two homies who sat on the porch.

From the look of the house Daren instantly knew why he didn't want to live with Rich. D-woo, K-9 and several other homies slept on the couch, floor or leaned up against the wall. A few homies were seated at the dinner table with their heads down snoring. Daren stepped over a few sleeping bodies to make his way into the kitchen. He joined Rich at the glass kitchen table and saw that the kitchen was small and worn down, but all of the appliances were band new. Janice was at the stove cooking bacon and cheesy eggs while Vicky stood next to her at the counter making plates and drinks. Daren's mouth watered at the sight of fluffy biscuits in the pan.

"Vicky give young dough a few slices of my bacon," Rich ordered.

"Some huh? Rich must love you Daren. We soppose to be his queens and we don't even get bacon." Vicky joked.

"I know right," Janice agreed causing both women to burst out laughing.

"Aye! Will y'all keep it down? I need to tell young dough something real important." Rich spoke in a calm soothing voice, but his demeanor was serious. "It's time for everybody to wake up anyway. Their plates are ready," Vicky said as she grabbed two healthy plates and took them into the living room. The whole house could hear Vicky yelling, "K-9, Woo breakfast. Y'all get y'all stanky asses up!"

Rich took a phone call which caused Daren's eyes to wonder. He watched Vicky take plate after plate into the living room. Vicky and Janice were fine, and Daren liked how they kept things in order and this gloomy house full of life. He wondered if Trina and Crissa could ever live under the same roof. But that seemed like a distant fantasy because Trina was crazy, and he was finding out that so was Crissa.

Rich hung up the phone watching Daren's wondering eyes all along. Rich chuckled before he began, "yeah young dough, it's all a part of the game. But you and I know it's not a fa-show thang. So I just live in the moment. I care for you and them young bloods like the O.G's and homies cared fa me when I was tryin to grow hair on my chest chin and nuts. Kay was one of those rare people that gave his last to make sure others were straight. That's why I think he was so fortunate."

"How can he be so lucky if he dead?"

"It would seem that way for those who don't know the history of the hood young dough. See, Money Lane leads to I-10 which is one of the main highways that go up north. Of course you know down south is where the border is and where most of America's drugs come in. Think of this city as a pit stop for drug traffickers. Now be it luck or ya father's drive and compassion to make it out of poverty he met one of the plugs main potna's at the strip club a week before you was born. Back then I was a petty crack hustler nickel and dime'n to eat. I met your father at several spots where the homies trap and parlay. The city of Money Lane been a gold mine it's just hard to find a reliable plug. I witnessed first-hand how a hustler come up and try to control the game. But somehow they always fall off. I jumped off the porch at age fourteen and since then I been at spots that jump like the Manor and over on Harrison Street. The ambitions of a young hustler had me well connected in the hood. So when Kay came to me with a partnership opportunity I didn't hesitate to jump on my blessing and curse. Together your father and I flooded the streets with whatever the truck brought, and we kept our prices low to move mass quantities. When you move a lot, and you move it fast with no error that's what makes the cartels happy."

"You never told me why my father got killed."

Rich took a deep breath before he explained, "Prior to your father locking in with the plug a Riverside crip named C-dre ran some big numbers for the plug. When your father and I jumped on the scene things changed. Our prices got better and C-dre became less dependable to the plug. Eventually C-dre robbed the plug of a fronted shipment then caught ghost. Now the plug only does business with me as far as Money Lanes goes because I fill the needed void with your help as well as other playa's in the game. But back then I didn't understand equality as your father did. It was his idea to do business with Riverside O.G's to keep peace. Money wasn't right and jealousy built over time. A deal went sour causing Kay and a few other brothers to get into a shootout with some of Riverside's homies. Kay ended up doing some time for aggravated assault. I held it down with the plug till Kay came home. We thought the beef with Riverside was said and done because Riverside found a new plug. But that plug turned out to be the feds in disguise. When Kay came home I embraced him like he did me. Together we ran the operation with such finesse that we were looking into expanding. We had sight's set on San Antonio being that the tone is forty-five minutes away but things don't always work out the way you plan them."

When Rich didn't continue Daren demanded, "What happened Rich?"

"Be easy young dough! This is why I never told you. I know you remember that night because you asked me for the AK. When I tell you this don't act on my words. The past is the past." Daren nodded with a straight face. He was trying his best not to cry and go shoot up Riverside.

"C-dre popped back up on the scene meeting Kay at the strip club to try and cop multiple times. I vaguely remember Kay saying C-dre and some of his goons shot your father's apartment up when they stayed in the living square. Your mother and father were homeless for a few months, living from hotel to hotel. They couldn't get a spot with bad credit and a low work income, so it was hard for them. Especially with your father moving weight. Your father lucked on Ria's house, paying a pretty penny under the table if you catch my drift. He was saving to start something righteous before he was killed that night. We don't know if it was C-dre that killed him but I'm certain it was Riverside. I begged your father to get a place closer to mines so we could watch each other's backs. . but your father's answer was always, "Rea gone trip if I live like you". . with all that being said I worry about you being ducked off in Riverside. Before you would hit and burn off, then chill for a while. But now you plan to be on the grind full time just brought complication you dough."

Daren shrugged his shoulders with a sudden attitude, "I'm good on Riverside. I got family over there and I stay strapped."

"That's RIIGGHHTT, ol unkle Domo," Rich said with a long draw of his words. "Domo and I used to do business back in the day. But now he play it safe. A hard working man."

"More like a slave. GG want me to work with him, but I need some right now money. I'm about to be a father."

"Is that RIIGGHHTT, Congratulations . . When should we celebrate."

"As of right now I need 100 bricks asap. I can't afford to celebrate right now Rich."

"Yeah young dough but ah. ." Rich paused and pushed his gold Armani frames close to his face. "Tha's why I'm so worried. You one deep in enemy territory with all that weight. No matter how much you don't wanna be a part of this organization you're still royalty. A royal blood by birth because of your father's legacy. The O.G's of Riverside know who you are young dough. . . What happened to lil Kasey? I thought he was going to be ridin with you from now on."

"Nah. . .He got into it wit ma last night. Now here I am."

Daren thought about the fight he had with lil Chris the other night then asked, "I'm short on options. What do you think I should do?"

"Take two of my most trusted soldiers with you and stay out of Riverside as much as you can. D-woo is a certified killer and I trust'em with my life. K-9 is a born hustler with wisdom and fiery street smarts equal to yours. They've been working for me for a minute. With them I pray you'll be protected."

"If I try it your way you gotta tell'em to let me do me."

Rich chuckled then explained, "you don't realize the power you could have if you'd just embrace your position in this army. But I'll make it understood young dough."

Vicky brought Rich and Daren plates fit for kings and left the kitchen with Janice. Daren and Rich ate in silence, deep in their thoughts. Once they finished eating on cue Vick brought Rich his silver tray of grape swisha's, a lighter and sack of purple looking buds. When Vicky sat the tray on the table Rich slapped her ass. Daren watched Vicky walk off looking back with a lustful smile.

"I love those women. I don't know what I would do without them." Rich slid the tray to Daren with a wink. "Roll up and burn one wit ya O.G."

Daren's plate was still half full because he didn't have much of an appetite with no green in his system. Daren pulled out a purple exotic looking bud from the sack. When he saw the crystals he had to ask, "What kinda dro is this?"

"It's called granddaddy purp. It's a special strand grown in Austin." Daren began rolling up while Rich took another call.

"Um. . . Tha's riigghht, . . Not a problem at all . . No rush, me and my lil brother here waitin on you." Rich listened for a moment then said "Understood . . I'll ask him but most likely we'll need to get together. Just let me know when you in route." Rich ended the call with a straight face.

"What he talking bout Rich?"

"They wanna know if you'd be interested in moving other thangs?"

Daren's facial expression forced Rich to explain. "The Mexican cartel we deal with has much more to offer than just bud. The higher ups have eyes on us and they sometimes want more product moved for their services. ."

"I only wanna move bud Rich."

"That's fine for now. Another question. Do you want me to plug you in so you can do your own transactions? I don't charge you nothin over the original price tag but if I'm going to be making these major transactions in my spot on a day to day basis I think I require some compensation."

"I already seen the plug. The big es'e that was here the last time I came with Kasey."

"That wasn't the plug. To meet the plug you and I are going to have to take a trip down south, cross the border and stay for a day. I only ask because the plug is rightfully yours. Plus with the numbers you putting up there shouldn't be a middle, forth and fifth man. FYI, it's rare that the plug wants to meet new faces. But when I told him you're Kay's son he insisted."

Daren thought; I ain't tryin to be way in Mexico, this shit is getting real. I feel like I'm movin too fast. Trina wants me to focus on school and look for a way out the game. But if I meet the plug I'm jumpin in waist deep. The game crazy ain't it?

"I'd rather just keep goin through you Rich. I ain't trippin if you charge me." Daren lit the purp hoping Rich wouldn't charge him too much.

Rich sighed while running a few numbers through his head. "I thought you would say that. Umm an extra ten dollars a pound is love to you on my end. Regardless I don't want you to get used to doing your transactions here. Which means we need to get you a spot. Your package will be here shortly. Now pass the purp young dough." Daren did what Rich said then grabbed his plate for some more of Janice and Vicky's good food.

Riverside. .

Domo parked his raggedy Buick Skylark in driveway and killed the engine. "Y'all don't be hot boxin in my house, and if you get the munchies eat a sandwich." Domo looked Kasey and Tavious in the eye to make sure they heard what he said. Domo got out of the car first and walked to the front door like his back was hurting. Tavious and Kasey got out and found seats on the top step of the porch. They watched a few cars pass by in silence until Kasey mumbled, "I ain't got no weed cause ma took mine last night."

"I got a sack from Johnnyboy but it's hella skimpy cuzzo!"

Kasey could tell that Tavious wasn't tryin to smoke what he had so he formed a plan. "Look kinfolk. Just burn one wit me and I'll call big bro to drop me somethin. Once I get on I gotchu. Den you can call ya homies and tell'em it's good. But make sure everything straight wit'em."

"A-ight cuzzo," Tavious stood with a stretch then disappeared into the house. Kasey pulled out his phone and called Daren. The phone rang then went to voicemail. Kasey hung up and tried again but still no answer.

Tavious returned ten minutes later with a loosely rolled skimpy blunt. "What big bro say cuzzo?"

"He ain't answer," Kasey replied sadly.

"Let's just chill and put one in the air. I really need to go to the Manor, but I know Daren ain't gon come there from how he move."

Tavious lit the blunt smokin it like it was a cigarette.

"Ma would probably flip out if she heard I was in the Manor."

"Ain't no body gon tell her unless you do cuzzo."

Tavious passed Kasey the weed already thinking about that sandwich. "Di'lon and nem on the way. So just C coo cuzzo."

Daren moved in and out of his closet packing shoes and clothes. When he came out of the closet for the last time Korita was standing in the door. She had her arms crossed feeling hurt but still remaining strong in her wisdom.

"Daren please stop this and come back home."

"Don't worry ma, you look beautiful by the way. Did you like the pastor's word?"

Daren sat his bag down by the door then checked his dresser for his key to Trina's apartment.

"It was good baby, and I prayed for you the whole time."

"Thanks ma. I be needin your love and prayer . . .Where Kasey?"

"I let him go to Domo's till later tonight to give him some space. I can tell he's still mad at me for what happened last night. I don't think it was the beating so much that got him mad. It must be because your gone. We both want you here because it's been only us for so long, but I can't have you doin what your doin here. Even if we have to struggle."

Daren's eyes were open wide, and he couldn't believe what Korita just said.

"YOU LET KASEY DO WHAT?"

"I let Kasey go to Domo's with Tavious. Kasey's getting older now and with you being gone I have to give Kasey a little bit of freedom Daren."

"Come'on ma you trippin. You got Kasey on Riverside with no strap."

Daren began moving as fast as he could, grabbing bags and the last of his belongings. Daren ran out the door with Korita right on his heels shouting, "I trust my brother Daren." Korita stopped on the porch telling herself. "I trust Domo more than I trust yo drug sellin ass . . . Oh, excuse me Lord." Korita turned her nose up at the two people in Daren's lac dressed in red. All she could do was shake her head and go back inside.

The blunt was almost gone because it burnt like it was nothing but paper. Tavious and Kasey looked down the street and saw three people dressed in blue hoodies, blue jeans that were creased down the middle with some fresh air max on their feet. "It's coo cuzzo. I.G and Di'lon my homies." Tavious tried to pass the weed to Kasey, but Kasey was already blowed. "I met Di'lon already. I wonder why I never see them at school?"

"Cause most of us from Riverside go to Hastings High School. You can chill cuzzo, the homies already talked about this."

Tavious stood when his homies walked in the yard and locked C's with them. Tavious locked C's extra hard with I.G and gave him a brotherly hug. Kasey stood nervously dusting himself off. Di'lon looked Kasey in the eyes and told him, "Thanks for help-ing me the other night."

"It's all good. I know y'all was tryin to eat." Kasey replied.

"Kasey this is I.G, . . .I. G this my kinfolk Kasey. . oh and that's Camron."

Camron remained silent standing behind Di'lon.

I.G nodded letting Kasey know, "Lil Chris my cousin. He almost died, lost a lot of blood and shit."

"My bad for big bro. I don't know why he be trippin. But ima mess wit y'all you know." I.G put his hands in his pockets frowning at Kasey.

"Do you have to wear all of them dead colors? No offense."

"I'm just sayin I.G, it's a Jordan set."

"You sho right." I.G said sarcastically. I.G spotted the lil piece of blunt Tavious was babysitting and took it. I.G smoked the rest of the blunt in one long pull until it was a doobie.

"So what you gone be workin wit?" I.G asked, flicking the doobie in the street.

"I don't know yet. I'm tryin to get in touch with big bro but he ain't - - "

Domo opened the door and eyed everyone with a mean mug. "Tavious I thought I told you not to be smokin in the front yard!" Before Tavious could say anything Domo shouted, "An now y'all havin gang meetings."

"Pops chill, we discussin the act of peace I was tellin you about."

Domo looked at Kasey, Di'lon, I.G and the hooded homie and shook his head.

"Hi you doin Domo sir." I.G said.

"Acts of peace my ass. Y'all go to the park or something. This ain't the chill spot. And come back when the street lights come on."

"Coo pops." . . Tavious led the way with his arms around Kasey's shoulder.

CHAPTER 6

TRUST ME CUZZO

Daren mashed the gas to Riverside thinking to himself; ma trippen, she know Oakride got historical beef with Riverside. I hope nobody try to get all lil bro because of the B.S with lil Chris the other night. I understand she tryin to give Kasey some space but things ain't gravy around that way right now. Kasey know it too.

Daren was shook out of his thoughts by D-woo smacking him on the arm saying, "tell'em young dough, K was the livest thing coming out of Oakride. . On blood, he is Oakride."

K-9's phone started ringing causing him to pick it up as he said, "I already know about legendary K. My unk used to ride with Rich and K back in the day." K-9 answered his phone and listened, then demanded, "how much is left? Just cook that up and I'll be through there in a sec. . ." K-9 hung up the phone and continued glorifying K, "hell yeah, unk told me K was a true G. One of the honest loving people you always want to be around but will turnup zero to a hun real quick to protect his."

D-woo rubbed his hands together excitedly explaining, "On topa dat the work K put in around the hood is the reason I got a itchy trigger finger now. Nobody's murder game was as official as K's."

"Say D, Ima need you to swing me by a few spots to drop some work off when we get done," said K-9.

"I got you, jus let me find lil bro real quick."

ZZZT! ZZZT! ZZZT! Daren looked down at his phone in his lap and saw it was Kasey. "Speaking of the! Hello! Bro you good? I'm headed your way now. I can't believe you just shot over to Riverside naked. No backup, strap or nothin."

Kasey replied, "Big bro chill, I'm alright. I was posted up with Tavious at uncle Domo's but now we at the park."

"In Riverside? Who's we exactly bro?" asked Daren.

"Um Tavious, and . . ah. . everybody."

Kasey's lack of explanation aggravated Daren. "I'm on the way lil bro," stated Daren then hung up.

Daren was mad at Kasey because it seemed like he listened to nothing he been teaching him over the past few months. The main thing on Daren's mind was how could Kasey put himself in a situation like that. Kasey didn't know anybody on Riverside and we only see Tavious at church and family get-togethers. I could be walking into a trap right now. D-woo and K-9 ready to earn stripes. . . Tavious . . It don't matter if he's family he not a Riverside OG. .

When Daren turned the lac into Riverside neighborhood both D-woo's and K-9's eyes opened wide. When they grabbed their straps Daren explained, "I see y'all already on alert. Kasey done got himself in the mix with our kinfolk and some kats from Riverside. He say everything is all good, but you never know. Let's just play it coo, get bro and dip."

K-9 mentioned, "We got a bunch of weight and guns on us D."

"I'm D-woo, ready to body something whenever wherever."

"It ain't gotta be all that. Ima scoop lil bro and dats it," said Daren.

Riverside park was located in the heart of Riverside. A green river ran down the park's center giving it it's name. when Daren crossed the bridge and pulled into the park it was jumping and people were everywhere. The parking lot was half full of cars and people in groups smoking, shooting dice, females choosin and a ice cream truck sat on glossy twenty-inch rims. At the basketball court a four on four full court game was going on that accumulated its own crowd. On the other side of the park were kids playing on jungle gyms, wrestling with each other and just being kids.

Tavious, Kasey, IG, Di'lon and a few other Riverside common folk stood close to the basketball court in a circle, smoking a black and mild. Everyone was on edge because they knew how hot headed Daren was. Everyone who was anybody in Riverside had been laced up, but you never know which way things could turn when a red lac pulls up in a crip neighborhood.

Kasey hit the black once and passed it not liking the taste. He spit the nasty taste out and said, "When a red lac pulls up y'all just be coo. . . It's my bro. Ima go holla at him and make sure everything is good."

"Who he gon have with wit'em?" asked I.G.

"Kinfolk, just tell'em everything good with us as far the historical beef," said Tavious.

Most of the park stopped doing what they were doing when they saw Daren's red lac pull into the parking lot and do a loop around. Daren could have parked in one of the many empty parking spaces instead he looped around once more checking out the scene. When Daren spotted Kasey he reversed into one of the spots by the basketball court.

Daren kept the engine running with the K in reach on the floor of the driver seat. Kasey ran up as Daren rolled down the window. The moment Kasey was in ear's reach Daren shouted, "Kasey! What the hell is wrong with you? You over here posted when these dudes won't hesitate to kill you! Did you forget whose son you are or what hood you from? Or maybe you forgot I dam near killed lil Chris when he tried to jack us the other night. ."

Kasey leaned in the car window saying, "bro chill, don't worry . . everybody's coo. They more worried about you and who you coming with . . Look, I got the 1900 you blessed me with and need eight pounds."

Daren only shook his head then scanned the park looking for his no good kinfolk. I know it could only have been Tavious Daren thought. Daren huffed then said, "bro, go get Tavious. I'm taking y'all back to uncle Domos."

When Kasey rejoined the circle everyone was staring at him trying to gauge the situation. Kasey shook his head with a sigh and said, "Y'all can relax. Bro not trippen, well on y'all at least. . He actin real paranoid though. He wanna take me and Tavious back to uncle Domo's."

Tavious locked C's with all the crips then he and Kasey made their way to the lac. They both got in the back seat and Daren pulled off with the quickness. The whole ride to Domo's Tavious kept glancing at the bulge under K-9's shirt. Tavious couldn't help but wonder what was on the minds of his lo-key enemies and how long the peace would last. Kasey sat between K-9 and Tavious with is head down, money in hand . . . thinking; why bro trippen when Tavious is fam. .

Daren pulled up and parked in front of Domo's and just sat there not hiding his anger. Daren stared out his window and Tavious could feel the obvious tension. "Daren, trust me cuzzo. Lil bro in good hands. I promise."

Daren snapped looking back saying, "So what, I'm jus supposed to let lil bro post up over here. . In Riverside. . Hustlin when you know our hoods beefin."

Tavious spoke calmly, "I already hollered at the O.G's and Kasey good. We jus tryna eat kinfolk."

Daren turned back around and said, "Eat! . . Uncle Domo know y'all doin this?"

"Naw, but I know how to do my shit on the low. . . We gon bust down in the back yard. My pop's be tired from workin at the rigs all day anyway." Daren shook his head whispering to himself, "this is crazy kinfolk." Kasey handed the money up front and waited for Daren to take it.

"Let me holla at you Kasey," said Daren, getting out of the lac and heading to the trunk with the keys in hand. Kasey and Tavious got out, happy to be out of the car's negative energy. Tavious took seat on the porch and Kasey met Daren at the back of the lac as he popped the trunk.

"Kasey, you sure about this. I really don't trust no one over here. At the end of the day you still from Oakride. And that alone ain't gon sit well with some of these Riverside KAT'S." Kasey shrugged his shoulders saying, "Tavious talked to the O.G's big bro, and he's fam. . . This is the way to stop the beef . . don't you see?"

Daren thought about what Rich said about his father standing on equality and keeping both sides of the hood fed, but still. .

"Why are you so trusting of everybody? I already told you there ain't no such thing as friends in this game. Family won't think twice about crossing you when it comes down to money."

"I gotta take my chance and live life bro," said Kasey. . Daren sighed as he gave Kasey his Glock 9 from his back saying, "Jus be safe bro." Kasey took the gun with a look of honor feeling like he'd just been given his brother's blessings. Daren got Kasey's pounds together thinking, . . if ma find out Kasey gon be ina world of trouble.

Daren left without saying a word to Tavious which kinda made Tavious feel some type a way. But his whole mood changed when he saw Kasey walk up the porch with pounds stuffed in his pants. "Let's go to the back cuzzo," said Tavious leading the way.

To the side of the houses back door was a faded plastic table with four chairs set up where Tavious would usually post up. He dubbed it the chill spot till Domo would run everyone off from them smoking and being too loud when he's trying to sleep.

Kasey started emptying his pants then paused with a sudden "DAM!"

"What's wrong cuzzo?" asked Tavious.

"I got these bricks from big bro and forgot to ask him for a scale, baggies."

"I got you cuzzo, I gotta digital in my room. It's been a minute since I used it because I haven had no use . . . Pockets ain't been right, no what I mean." Kasey nodded half listening. Tavious got the drift and crept in the house.

Kasey looked at his four green bricks of two pounds each and thought about the best course of action for breaking down his bud. Since he would most likely be on the move he decided to break all down in qp's except for one. One qp he break down in dime sacks. If he need to break down more sacks he'll just break down another qp on the spot.

Tavious came out of the back door with a box cutter, scale and some baggies. Kasey went to work, and Tavious just stood there watching. Kasey glanced up at his kinfolk every so often replaying Daren's words in his head over and over. . .

Family's usually the first to turn on you when it comes down to money.

"You prolyl gon need a backpack too cuzzo."

"Hell yeah," said Kasey in realization.

"I'll let you borrow one of mine. . . But do me a favor cuzzo. . ."

"What's up kinfolk?" asked Kasey, making eye contact with Tavious. . .

"Front me a half pound till I get on my feet."

Kasey was unsure and Tavious could tell from the look of Kasey's troubled thought. Tavious begged, "C'mon, trust me cuzzo. . .If you can't trust yo own family who can you trust. I'm putting my neck on the line with the homies to make show you good ova here."

Kasey felt wrong not putting his own kinfolk on, and besides . . Tavious did get him a pass in Riverside.

"Alright kinfolk, but I'm only gon front you a qp. Jus give me a hundred next time you re-up wit me."

Tavious replied, "No doubt cuzzo, I'll have that to you tomorrow after you get back from school."

"Bet," said Kasey.

Tavious broke his qp down in skimpy five gram dime sacks like Johnnyboy did. Kasey realized Tavious was trying to come up but roachin the game didn't seem playa at all. Kasey rolled up and burned one with Tavious like he promised, however Kasey didn't hit the weed too much knowing he still needed to sell some weed. I don't wanna take none of this home even though big bro left me a live stash spot. . , Kasey thought.

"What's IG number?" asked Kasey.

Tavious gave Kasey the number off the dome then said, "I really need to make some moves cuzzo . . You can ride orr . ."

"Naw I'm good, let me call for a ride."

Tavious gathered his skimpy sacks in his shirt and went inside thinking Kasey was calling Korita.

"Shay, what you up to ?" asked Kasey.

"Nothing, riding around with my cousin. . Why? What's up?" she asked.

"I need a ride, ask her to come scoop me and tell her I got gas money."

Kasey didn't bother to tell Tavious he was leaving he just left. With a backpack full of weed and a nine behind his back Kasey walked down Riverside Street until he spotted Courtney's white Pathfinder cross over one of Riverside's bridges. Kasey hopped in the back seat and sang, "smells like dro and pretty ladies." Courtney and Shay looked back at Kasey and smiled. Shay tarried to pass Kasey the blunt, but he said, "Naw I'm good, I'm high than a mug." Courtney and Shay laughed at Kasey's smooth cloudy mood as Courtney pulled off.

"Shay you better keep him girl. He is too cute."

"Would you be quiet Courtney." Shay turned in the passenger seat to where she made eye contact with Kasey.

"Can you take me to Riverside Park real quick?"

"Are you sure?" asked Shay with deep concern. .

"Yea I'm sure. . I'm good, . . we good. . Trust me."

Kasey called IG just to be on the safe side.

"You and your brother must have a nice setup for you to have a cell phone." Said Courtney, prying for information. "Yea, me and bro good," replied Kasey, not giving up any info. . . Shay smiled at Kasey and blew him a kiss. Kasey gave Shay the come sit back here with me gesture and she mouthed "hold on."

As soon as the Pathfinder parked in Riverside Park Kasey hopped out to calm the worrying eyes. When IG saw it was Kasey they met with a small crowd of people who were dressed in blue. Shay and Courtney watched nervously while Kasey had a conversation with the group. Kasey sold IG and a few others a qp, then the crowd got bigger. After all of the commotion died down Kasey hopped back in the Pathfinder. When Courtney drove off IG tried to see who pushed the whip but couldn't see clearly through the tent.

Shay eyed Kasey as he counted money wondering how he was able to do that. "Fastest 900 dollars I made in my life," joked Kasey like he did this often.

"Where to now balla, and you don't have to give any gas," said Courtney.

"Shay, can we go post up at yo spot."

"Umm, NOO! Let's just keep riding around," said Shay with dreamy eyes.

"I got weed on me and a strap. Just so you know."

"Courtney straightened up and said, "It's ok, I'll drive extra careful boo."

Shay turned around saying, "Plus, I can help you move some bud and to do that we need to stay in the wind . . .But can we stop by the corner store while I make some calls?" Shay put the blunt in the ashtray while Courtney drove like a pro explaining, "Sometimes I drive from here to Houston with fifty pounds, with this dude I was messing with."

"He pay you for that or what?" asked Kasey . .

"He better," said Courtney, letting Kasey's mind wonder.

Courtney parked at a gas pump and handed Shay twenty dollars for gas. "Anybody want anything?" asked Shay.

"A honeybun, a big red and some cool ranch Doritos," said Kasey handing Shay five dollars. "I'm good mama," said Courtney.

When Shay got out of the car Kasey watched her ass wondering how it fit perfectly in those tights. He liked how hood and at the same time how classy Shay and Courtney dressed. These were the type of chicks he could see himself with. When Kasey looked forward Courtney was turned facing him, lookin him up and down. "What up ma," said Kasey trying to be cool.

"You, Pa," Courtney shot back sarcastically. .

Kasey laughed then asked, "Why Shay don't wanna go to her spot? Her parents be trippen or somethin?"

Courtney rolled her eyes as she said, "Not at all. . .Shay's a little girl boo. Looks like you need a grown woman who can do for you if you catch my drift."

Courtney motioned for Kasey's phone and he gave it to her like a moth drawn to flame. She put her number in his phone saying, "How are you going to get around when I go back to the H tomorrow? I can come back every weekend if it's beneficial. And I know I can make a whole lot more money than Shay can. . . Just let me know."

Shay walked out of the store with a bag of junk food and Courtney quickly changed the subject. Shay pumped the gas and Courtney turned around to touch up her makeup in the mirror. All the while she was eyeing Kasey. Kasey looked down not knowing what to do or think. Shay got back in the car, but in the back seat with Kasey. When Courtney pulled off Shay stressed,

"I can't believe you were in Riverside dressed like that! Where were you coming from anyway?"

"I was with my kinfolk Tavious."

"Tavious is your cousin? Oh my god Tavious is hell," laughed Shay.

"Why you say that?" asked Kasey.

Shay explained, "His homegirl Tiffany is one of my bar connects. They throw wild parties every weekend with a lot of hard drugs. I tried powder once and um umm, . . . Never again."

"Tavious be doing powder?" asked Kasey in shock. .

"Not sure, I don't go over there unless they got bars," said Shay.

Kasey saw Korita was calling and ignored the call. Shay saw Kasey's worry and sudden anger, so she asked, "Is everything ok?"

"Yea, what's the plan?" asked Kasey.

"Umm, we're going to stop by my apartment to pick up Alexa, and I got you a few sales here and there. . . but it's mostly sacks."

Kasey nodded, sat back then said, "fire the weed up."

The sun was long gone, and Tavious was two doors down at Tiffany's house. Tiffany and her sexy chocolate girlfriend Janette held what Tavious called THE BOX. His box was a storage place of powder, exo's handlebars. The items of the box were supposed to be for sale, but they were often passed around like candy during the wild parties that were frequently thrown.

Tavious sat in the middle of the long couch, between Tiffany and Janette, with his face in a pile of cocaine. When Tavious sat back up he said, "Gotta love salt and peppa." Tiffany and Janette started giggling then took turns doing normal lines. "Did y'all call Mike and T yet?" asked Tavious.

Tiffany cooed, "NOO!" from the head rush then started laughing.

"We'll call them later. Right now we're trying to play hide and seek with the black mamba."

Tavious said, "Shit, I'll hide him whereever you want. . .Grab your bong Tiff." Tiffany handed Tavious the bong and he stuffed almost ten grams of bud in the huge bowl and fired it up. Tiffany and Janette began chanting, "smoke, smoke, smoke." In the spur of the moment Janett pulled off her shirt, exposing her C-cup chocolate breasts. Tiffany did the same and screamed, "snort one between the girls."

Before Tavious could answer the bong was taken from him and Tiff lay in his lap. Tavious buried his face in Tiff's B-cup breast taking a strong snort and kissing everywhere. When Tavious sat back up he spoke in his best rich white man's voice with his pointer finger up, "I do concur, that this is going to be hellofa night. ."

Chapter 7

Rebellious Teenager

Kasey sat in the back of math class nodding in and out. He hated math, the only thing he was interested in counting was dead presidents. Kasey shook his head attempting to fight this sleep, remembering; I'm trippen, I got ten dimes stuffed in my socks. I gotta stay on point. I really need to talk to Shay to let her know I'm holdin. . It was live chillin with them last night. But I still don't know what to think about Courtney. I've been thinking about Shay all night. I'm really feelin Shay but I don't know how to tell her I want to be with her. . Is it too early for that? . . I shoulda asked big bro. .

"Gotta use the restroom.."

Kasey stood and left to the student bathroom without permission. . He called Shay and she didn't answer. Kasey put his phone back in his pocket to wash his face trying to wake his self up. Once he finished Shay was calling him back. .

"Ay ahh. . I got a proposal for you. I got some bud on me and I need your help moving it."

"I got you, meet me at the vending machines at first lunch."

Kasey forced his self to go back to class and flopped down in his seat. His teacher noticed Kasey's lack of paying attention, as well as his grades were slipping but she didn't feel the need to press the issue.

When the bell finally rung Kasey stood and smoothed the wrinkles from his red and white Nike outfit. His clothes and red Nikes made him think about Daren. How he got Daren kicked out and still Daren left him a lot of shoes and clothes he couldn't fit and didn't like. How can I repay big bro for everything he done for me when he got everything. .

Kasey snatched his book bag from the back of his seat and made a bee line out the door. When Kasey met Shay at the court-yard vending machine she was looking extra good. She had her long black hair down to her shoulders, looking like she had a perm. She had a light sheen of makeup done. She wore a purple DKNY shirt that showed a little cleavage and some matching baby fat violet jeans. She wore a pair of three-inch wedge heels that showed off her small, well pedicured feet and purple painted toenails.

Shay gave Kasey a hug and asked, "How much you got on you?"

"I got like ten nice dime sacks, you got any custos on dack?"

"Sure do! I know six people that want one right now."

"Where they at?" said Kasey, looking around.

"Slow down track star," said Shay with a quick giggle. Kasey watched her make a few calls and smile at him. "Follow me," she said, and Kasey joined her side saying "I'd rather we walk together. . "

"Like a couple?" asked Shay, making eye contact with Kasey. . . Kasey shrugged his shoulders letting Shay think about it. Shay led Kasey to the second floor of the school to where the bathrooms were. This is the science, home-ec, honors society part of this building. No one comes here during lunch. I used to meet people here when I used to sell for my moma." Kasey began to reach into his socks, but Shay stopped him and said, "go in the restroom just to be on the safe side."

Kasey stopped and said, "You used to meet dudes in the bathroom."

Shay smirked and shot back, "You wish you were one of those guys don't you?"

Kasey's mouth dropped in awe. "Boy I'm just playin, what I look like."

"So what we got goin on right now?" asked Kasey.

"I got one person I can trust gather all the money and meet us here so we don't attract so much attention. They said if your sacks look right they want eight dimes altogether."

Before Kasey could brag about his sacks a skinny black kid wearing a daffy duck shirt, polo jeans and some Chuck Taylor's approached. He and Kasey silently went into the bathroom. A moment later Kasey and dude came out the bathroom both feeling like they both had won. "Let me know if they need more, Chewy," said Shay. . .Chewy remained silent and burned off.

Kasey and Shay made their way back to lunch and Kasey tried to give Shay ten dollars for her help. "I'm good, just look out later on if I ever need you. . ."

"Coo, ay you really live Shay."

"Well thank you, I try to be. I'll most likely get those other two sold before lunch is over." Kasey nodded then said, "at least let me buy you lunch from the snack bar."

"No sweat, but tomorrow it's on me." Said Shay with a wink.

❖   ❖   ❖

A month later. . .

Daren was fed up with the zoo of everyday life that went on at Rich's spot. It was like a non-stop party spot with people in and out at all times of the night. That had Daren on agg because he hardly got any good sleep. Not to mention all of the guns and durgs that were kept in Rich's room. Daren imagined Rich had enough of everything which was enough to get everybody a fed case.

The final straw was when Daren was woken out of his sleep to take one of D-woo's home girls to the hospital. Kesha got fuck in by the homies at another spot, then everyone came to Rich's for a celebration. Kesha was beyond loose, and tonight was the night she decided to snort a quarter ounce of cocaine.

It was three in the morning when the party finally died down. Daren and K-9 were at opposite ends of the long couch, laying on the armrest's knocked out. Daren woke to being smacked in the head when Kesha fell on top of him foaming at the mouth, having a seizure. Everybody else was too trowed to drive which meant Daren had to rush her to the emergency room.

The sun crept in the sky by the time Daren got back. Daren told Rich he couldn't live like this, and he'd take his offer up on finding him a spot. "I'm tired of going back and forth to Carissa's, Trina's and here," Daren told Rich.

"Understood young dough," was all Rich said. Daren could tell Rich was hurt that Daren didn't enjoy his lifestyle, but it was what it was.

Rich got one of the smokers from the Manor to put to a two bedroom apartment in their name for Daren. For a spot in the hood it wasn't your typical closet-sized apartment. Daren actually like living in the Fairway Apartments. It was up-scale compared to the cracked out Manor or Charles 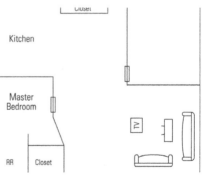 Andrew Section-8 Apartments. Daren made sure to get a spot in the back of the Fairways and on the second floor to keep jackers out his mix. Plus Daren liked to cheef in his down time. What Daren liked most about the Fairways was there was hardly any major traffic or drug activity. He was low key, and he could move as such.

Daren was sitting on his couch blowin and looking at all of his Jordan posters and bulls hats he hung on the wall. This felt so good he wondered why he hadn't got his own spot a long time ago. He enjoyed the freedom of being able to do whatever he felt like doing and no one could tell him any different.

Daren was also able to kick it with Kasey more often because Kasey's school was right down the street. Lately Kasey and Shay had been popping up and chilling. Daren was cool with it because it allowed him to keep an eye on Kasey. Korita would call Daren and tell him how bad Kasey was getting. In the end Korita and Daren agreed to let Kasey chill at Daren's' giving him a little more freedom.

Daren sat there enjoying his new-found freedom and peace of mind when Crissa popped in his head. He had been meaning to swing by and check on her because the last few times he stopped by on the fly he could have sworn her smelled a hint of smoke on her clothes. Daren thought to himself, I ain't dumb, but Crissa's an emotional rollercoaster. She's just as bad as Trina in her own way. . . Ahh, let me go check on this girl.

Daren rolled another blunt then hopped in the lac, heading to Crissa's. He pulled up and parked then snuck up to Crissa's door. He knocked once and no one answered. Daren could hear the TV on loud, so he knocked again. It was hot out causing Daren to sweat as well as get angry. Daren checked the door, and it was unlocked. This girl outta there, thought Daren as he let himself in. Daren walked in to see everything was alright as far as the house was concerned. But the first thing he smelled was cigarette smoke as soon as he stepped in. When he made his way down the hall and into the living room he saw an older woman in a hospital bed with a bunch of medical equipment around her. He continued further in the house until he reached the den. He couldn't believe his eyes when he caught Crissa red handed with a cigarette to her lips. Daren didn't hesitate to walk up on Crissa and snatch the cigarette. Daren could tell she was terrified from both being caught and not realizing someone had snuck up on her.

Daren spoke while trying to control his anger, "First off why is the door unlocked for anybody to walk in like I did?" Crissa rolled her eyes and looked away. "And second, why you smokin squares carrying my child?"

Crissa rubbed her temples and replied, "Daren. . you don't know the stress I'm under, . . You really don't. . "

"Like what CC, like what?" Daren demanded. . .

"MY mom is brain dead from meth and dropping acid. On top of being pregnant I have to pay bills, change bed pans and give her sponge baths. You don't know how much I worry when I have to leave for work. I have no time for myself Daren. . .And you wanna walk in here all high and mighty like you're the world's best support system. You don't even come inside the clinic with me for my checkups. I didn't' fuck me and get myself pregnant, YOU DID! . . I'm doing my best with all of this. If you don't like it I'll just get an abortion Daren. . I swear I will."

Daren saw a flash of slapping the shit out of Crissa but he remembered she was pregnant and he didn't beat females. . but Crissa knew how to push his buttons. Daren took a deep breath and sat next to Crissa.

"Look CC, you should have kept it real with your situation from the jump. I didn't know you had all this goin on. How can I help if I don't know. And make no mistake this is a two way street. I didn't force open your legs, you gave it up. We too old to be arguing like teenagers. We need to think and act for the future of this child. . Give the baby a chance CC, that's all I'm askin."

"What kind of man sits in his car smoking weed instead of checking on the development of his child?"

"You right CC, you got that. Ima step up. . But please don't go an do something we both gon regret." Crissa crossed her arms and stressed, "Then don't make me regret being pregnant by you. I need help Daren and I'm not just talking about grocery money and rides to the doctor. I need you to really be there for me." Tears started slowly rolling down Crissa's face. Daren pulled her close seeing all of the pain his baby mama was actually in.

Kasey and Shay were still doing business on the low at school. Everyone at school could see that their relationship was beyond friendship and a lot of dudes that tried desperately to holla at Shay didn't like that. After school Kasey would take Shay to Sonic then head straight to Daren's' apartment, which he had a key to. Shay still didn't want Kasey to come to her apartment so whenever she got a chance she would sneak into Kasey's room window at night. They would lay close on Kasey's top bunk kissing and talking in low voices. They would occasionally sneak back through the window and smoke a blunt or two.

Tonight was no different than any other. He and Shay lie close in his bed, under the covers talking low and listening for Korita. Shay whispered in Kasey's ear, "why don't we ever use the bottom bunk. It's squeaky up here."

"Naw that's big bros bed."

Even though Daren had his own apartment Kasey secretly whished Daren still lived here and things were like they used to be. Kasey had a sudden munchie attack and asked Shay, "You want a sandwich or something?"

Shay shook her head, looking in Kasey's eyes giving him a sexy smile.

"What's on your mind?" asked Kasey.

"You," whispered Shay while rubbing his manhood through his Jordan shorts. Kasey instantly got hard and nervous at the same time. Shay leaned over and started kissing Kasey deeply already having what she wanted on her mind. She started undressing and Kasey just sat there thinking, this is so real. . . Before Kasey knew it Shay was straddling him, kissing him asking, "are you going to take your shorts off or do I have to do it for you?"

Kasey helped Shay pull his shorts and boxers down as they switched positions. When Shay felt Kasey's nervousness Shay asked, "What's wrong?"

"I never done this before."

Shay covered her mouth to conceal her burst of laughter then said, "That's ok, I got you." Kasey couldn't put this feeling into words. He had to slow down or he would come as soon as he got in. Kasey stopped and asked, "Should we use a condom?"

"Just go slow babe, and pull out when you fell yourself about to come." Kasey found his rhythm and a few moments later there was a loud cracking sound of wood splitting. Boom – Kasey and Shay fell down to the bottom bunk as the old bunk bed collapsed with a loud crash.

Korita burst in Kasey's room like the FBI. "Bad ass kids. . . I knew I was hearing something." Sahy and Kasey slowly stood feeling embarrassed. Shay wrapped herself in Kasey's cover while Kasey covered his manhood with hands, looking for his boxers and shorts. . . Korita shook her head with her hands on her hips. "I knew you was up to something Kasey. It ain't that much tossin and turnin in the world."

"Alright ma, let us get dressed," pleaded Kasey. .

Korita shouted, "Y'all ain't got noghitn I ain't seen before. Put some goddamn clothes on. . standing there like adam and eve. . .you must be Shay, with you fast ass."

"Yes ma'am," said Shay while finding her clothes. .

"You Kasey's girlfriend or are y'all just having sex?" questioned Korita. . .

"Why, danng maaa. . .Let us get dressed," whined Kasey in embarrassment. .

"Don't get yo ass beat in front of your company . . Kasey. . .Y'all get dressed, playtime is over. . .And it's a school night. . .C'mon Shay so I can take you home." Korita left Kasey's room wondering how long they've been having sex and if they've been using protection. . .

As soon as Kasey went to school that morning Korita decided to go snooping in Kasey's room hoping to find condoms. If he was going to be having sex he should at least do it safely.

Korita searched Kasey's room thinking; I'm not mad Kasey's becoming a man, but the last thing we need is a baby on the way and he hasn't graduated high school yet. I know he won't talk to me so I guess I'll have to get Daren to tell him about using protection.

Korita searched Kasey's closet from top to bottom on the cool looking for weed. His shoe boxes that were empty didn't have any weed or condoms. She checked Daren's spot under the broken bed, and it was empty as well. Next she checked Kasey's drawers and saw a wad of money big as day in a rubber band. All thoughts of condom went out the window when Korita's intuition confirmed Kasey must be selling drugs.

When Kasey got home from Daren's around nine like he usually did Korita met him in the kitchen as he raided the pantry. . .

"Ma where the brownies at?" shouted Kasey. . .

"Yo high ass ate'em all," said Korita, standing behind Kasey.

Kasey turned around to see Korita with that 'I ought to slap the hell out of you' look. .

Kasey had his hands up in explanation mode, "Look ma, sorry bout Shay, we was just . .-"

Korita spoke over Kasey with a shake of her head, "I'm not worried about you getting ya dick wet, you're seventeen. . . But what's this?" Korita pulled out Kasey's money and set it on the kitchen counter.

"Money ma."

"No shit smart ass, where'd you get it?"

"Big bro gave it to me."

"I know damn well Daren ain't gave you no seven grand. Don't insult my intelligence Kasey."

"I'm not ma, for real for real."

"Umm hum, don't get yourself into no shit Kasey," Korita threatened.

Kasey snatched the money off the counter and left the kitchen in a hurry. Kasey closed his room door and flopped down on Daren's mattress and box spring. He called Shay thinking how close that was, he had just got rid of the last of his weed at school today and it's a good thing he left his strap at Daren's. Ma really on my ass. . . it's like she got a knowing superpower. . .

The next morning Kasey set foot on Park Village High School looking fresh and clean, in his normal wear of jeans, jays and a polo shirt. He was on a mission looking for Shay when campus security approached him. He spotted them through the crowd of kids and panicked because he had seven grams of OG cush for him and Shay as their smoke sack. He had the dro in his sock hiding it from Korita and he completely forgot about it. Not wanting to take a chance Kasey ran off campus and headed straight to Daren's. Kasey let himself in and immediately called Shay and told her what happened. Daren wasn't home so he called Daren and told him what happened as well. Kasey rolled up a blunt and smoked it stressfully, worrying about what could have happened. . . Why would the school laws be lookin for me Kasey thought.

Daren came home around two and sat his bags down on the coffee table. "Ma called, the school called her and said you ran. . They just wanted to ask you some questions."

"I had some dro on me bro, I had to dip." Explained Kasey. .

Daren sat down with Kasey and grabbed the half blunt from the ash tray. Daren lit the blunt and held it in for as long as he could. .

"You might as well go home and face the music. You didn't get caught with nothin so what's the worst bro."

"Ma be gettin on my nerves bro."

"I know how she get but you gotta live with her at least till your eighteen."

Kasey remained silent deciding to roll another blunt of cush. .

"Ma told me she caught you and Shay. . Was you. . I'm mean, did you strap your jimmy?"

"Nag, nag, nag, nag. . . Dat's all ma do. . She making me crazy bro."

"I'll take that as a no. . .Just trust me bro, you don't want what comes with a kid right now. . .The baby ain't even here yet and I'm goin through it with Crisssa."

"Hello," said Kasey answering his phone.

"Chewy got popped with a few sacks and blamed it on you. . .Which is crazy because I sold all your weed yesterday," whispered Shay. . .

"That's crazy, . . ." said Kasey. .

"I know babe, they called me to the principal's office and asked me about you but I kept it G. . Security searched me and didn't find anything, so I went back to class . . "

"Punk ass Chewy. . .why they call him that anyway?" asked Kasey.

"He sells acid on gummy bears, so they call him Chewy. . .But I think we need to chill for a while. . "

"I'm really gettin tired of school. ."

Daren listened to Kasey's conversation and thought; lil bro must be in trouble. . . I told him not to be sellin bud at school . . .

CHAPTER 8

SHAY'S STORY

S hay skipped her last class and walked to Daren's so she could be with Kasey. She wanted to talk to him because she could feel his frustration. She also wanted to talk to Kasey and ask him why he never popped bar's or x with her. Shay didn't pop x a lot, but when she did pop a few bars she would feel Kasey's mood change. Shay felt like this was one of those unspoken things that needed to be discussed.

Daren let Shay in and told her that Kasey was in the spare room. Shay made her way to the guest room and found Kasey in the corner, seated on the floor rambling in a box of his things. Daren's' guest room was made into a mini gym, but Kasey slowly began collecting things like a desk and a roller chair. Daren even gave Kasey a small safe, but Kasey didn't use it because he liked to hold his money and be flashy with it.

Shay pulled the roller chair next to Kasey and kissed him. She could tell she slightly raised Kasey's spirits, but he was still down about the situation. "I never thought it was that serious, I hate snitches Shay. I wish I woulda known Chewy was a whole dope fiend."

"Why you say that?"

"Dope fiends aint' gon keep it G. you know. If you in the game, why can't you just take yours." Shay let the silence linger for a minute then asked, "What's the farthest you'll go with drugs?"

"I'll never do hard drugs. Bro said they dope fiend drugs that get you hooked. Ima whole G so that's over with. . ."

"Kasey, all drugs get you addicted, so that doesn't make sense."

"Yea, but those drugs will have you doin any and everything to get'em."

"Soo . . Do you think less of me because I do bars?"

Kasey didn't want to answer so Shay exclaimed, "Be real with me Kasey."

"Shay, . . I umm. . . I feel something for you I never felt before and it's crazy. . l wanna be around you all the time and to not bring bad energy I try look at what I like about you. I think the worst things a person can be in life is a dope fiend, thief and a liar. From what I seen so far those drugs bring out that type of stuff in a person."

"I know what you mean, trust me. I deal with it on a daily basis. Drugs are just a realty cope and my reality sucks."

Kasey shook his head while saying, "I don't like seeing you on bars Shay."

"I can tell, I only do'em when I'm with Alexa. . .She's the reason I started."

"Can I ask you a favor?"

"What is it?"

"Can you stop doing bars?"

"I'll try Kasey. . .If you do me a favor."

"Whatever," replied Kasey. , while putting most of his money in his safe.

"Just keep my mind away from this place."

Kasey nodded wondering how bad Shay's life at home could really be.

Around ten Daren dropped Shay off at her apartment complex because Korita kept calling, wanting Kasey home. Kasey watched Shay step inside her apartment door, drop her book bag off then shoot out the door before Daren drove off. Kasey wished Korita let him do what he wanted like Shay's parents. If ma would just chill sometimes we'd be alright, Kasey thought.

The feeling of Daren parking outside of Korita's house was dreadful. Kasey just sat in the passenger seat with his head down, knowing he was about to get a beating. "Go ahead bro, if ma hist you or tips out too bad just call me."

"So you not comin in?" asked Kasey sadly.

"This on you bro, I told you not to be sellin bud at school, when you make decent bread on Riverside." Kasey gave Daren the four grand in his pockets knowing Daren was right. "Hold this fa me, you know ma gon be trippen even though I didn't do nothin."

"I got you bro," said Daren wondering why Kasey carried so much money on him.

When Kasey walked in the living room Korita was sitting on the couch smoking a cigarette. She never smoked in the house which let Kasey know he was in real trouble. To his surprise Korita was calm as she said "have a seat." Kasey sat on the edge of the small couch, as far away from his mother as he could. "The school called me today-."

Before Korita could finish Kasey explained, "I didn't do nothin ma!"

"Then why you run Kasey?" exclaimed Korita. .

Kasey started to lie but Korita said, "I knew yo bad ass was sellin drugs at school. You been skippen class and ya grades slippen. I can't believe you Kasey." Kasey could only drop his head and wait for his beating. "Do you wanna stay here?" asked Korita.

"Where else ima go ma?" asked Kasey, on the brink of tears.

"Well then some things gotta change. You are to focus on your schoolwork and nothing else. You not going to Domo's, Daren's and your girlfriend ain't comin over for a month. You might as well give me that cell phone too."

Kasey stood suddenly feeling bold. "Ma why you gotta act like this?"

"You ass shouldna been sellin drugs at school. Now do what I say or get your GED and take your drug sellin ass somewhere else. I'm not going to jail behind you Kasey."

"How you gon take my phone when big bro bought it fa me?"

"I don't give a damn who bought it Kasey. Now give me the phone!"

Kasey felt a beating coming so he tossed the phone on the small couch behind him and ran to his room. Slam- "Don't slam my goddamn door Kasey!" shouted Korita. .

Did that already Kasey thought, wanting to spaz out. He paced back and forth not knowing what to do. Kasey was so heated that he hit Daren's punching bag till he ran out of breath. He sat at the edge of Daren's bed with a mean mug thinking: How she gon take my phone. . Ma trippen for real. Then she gon try and ground me on the slick. . Tombout I can go where I always go. . She don't know me. . I might as well got caught by the laws and faded juvie.

In a sudden burst of anger Kasey got up and punched his window. The widow shattered cutting Kasey's hand in the process. The damage was already done so Kasey opened his window and jumped out. He took off running down Money Lane ignoring his mother yelling from the porch, 'KASEYYY!!"

Kasey stopped on Shay's porch and wiped his tears away while catching his breath. Once he straightened himself up he knocked once and stepped back. He hid his bloody hand behind his back trying to slow his jumping chest. Shay's mother answered the door looking crazy as ever.

"Baby, who is you?"

Kasey lost his words when he saw Shay's mother. She had tangled curly weave, and two open faced gold teeth that she kept sucking on. She wore a pair of blue jeans as some cut off shorts, some sunflower flip flops and thin black sleeveless shirt with no bra. She held a Heineken in one hand and a Doral cigarette with a long ash in the other.

"I'm Kasey ma'am. Is Shay home?"

"That grown heffa around here somewhere. Why ain't you calla?"

Kasey tried not to look at Shay's mother's enormous breasts that swung freely in her loose shirt.

"I . . I . . Lost my phone," stuttered Kasey. .

"Well child, I'm Arlene. . All I can tell you is come in and wait for her." Arlene noticed the small pile of blood that gathered behind Kasey on the porch. Her worry kicked in causing her to grab Kasey's arm and pull him inside. She and Kasey stood in the kitchen while Arlene searched for paper towels but found none. She settled for a dirty kitchen rag to wrap Kasey's open wound with. Arlene sat Kasey on the small couch in the living room kindly explaining, "Shay's hardly ever here baby. She sleeps here then takes off to school. After that she's gone most of the night sooo. ."

Kasey must have lost a lot of blood because his hearing was fading in an out and he was seeing things. He thought he was trippen because he couldn't believe the place he was sitting in.

"Are you Shay's boyfriend?"

When Kasey didn't answer Arlene began rambling on and on about Shay doing this and Shay doing that. Kasey tuned her out as the reality set in about his surroundings. The TV was old and had a pair of pliers where the TV knob was supposed to be. The antenna was made of foil and everywhere he looked he saw black bald spots in the carpet. Roaches of every size you could imagine came to Kasey's attention that made Kasey's' chest pound again. In the kitchen there was about a weeks' worth of dishes in the sink full of dark dirty water. The tan couch Kasey sat on had bald spots and it was black in certain places from being worn down.

This place is nasty thought Kasey. How can Shay live like this. Even though ma make me mad I'm glad she forced us to keep the house up.

After a roach ran across Kasey's shoe he sook it off even though it was gone, then stood up. "Can I borrow your phone please?"

"It's off right now baby, but you're more than welcome to wait till Shay comes home." Kasey was already heading to the door saying, "I'm coo, I'll wait outside for her." Kasey sat on the porch and could feel his skin crawling. Arlene stood behind him asking him, "what happened to your hand? Why you out here so late? Don't you have school in the morning? What's yo mama's name?"

Kasey didn't answer the first time, but Arlene asked again so he broke down and explained his situation. Kasey looked at the dirty kitchen rag with disgust then flung it off on the slick. Arlene wasn't paying attention, talking about whatever she was talking about at a hundred miles per hour.

Kasey looked down the curved street of Charles Andrews Apartments with interest, seeing opportunity. He could see multiple people standing around smoking and selling. Music could be heard like this was the place to be. Then he saw dope fiends ten times worse than smoker joe walk up on doughboy after doughboy beggin. One of the young hustlers slapped a fiend in the face with his pistol, making the smokers scatter. Then everything went back to normal. Kasey watched Shay's reality and knew why Shay was the way she was.

It was about twelve at night when Shay came walking around the corner. Her mouth dropped at the sight of her mother standing behind Kasey, with her hands on her hips with no shame.

"UUOO mama! Why you outside looking like that?"

Arlene dug in her nappy weave to scratch her head "Lookin like what SHIIIT!"

Shay met Kasey as he stood, noticing the bloody dirty rag.

"Kasey what are you doing here?" Shay asked trying to hide her embarrassment.

"Ma tried to punish me for what happened at school."

"Why didn't you call me?"

"She took my phone, so I broke the window on accident."

"Oh god," sighed Shay, grabbing Kasey's hand and pulling him inside and upstairs. Arlene followed them inside closing the door behind her saying to herself. "SHHIITT, I looks good honey. . ."

Kasey sat at the foot of Shay's bed taking in the details of Shay's clean kept room. His thoughts were; How is Shay always so classy, and in high spirits all the time living like this? Where she get the money for all this stuff and why does downstairs look so bad?

Shay sat Indian style close behind Kasey, rubbing his back and comforting him. Kasey looked to his left at Shay's closet noticing the double doors were missing. Her closet had no hangers, and all of her designer clothes were folded in neat stacks on the shelf at the top of her closet. Her classy heels, pumps and flats were all lined up at the bottom of the closet and well taken care of. She had a Sony radio on her nightstand beside her bed that made Kasey wonder why she didn't have a TV. But he guessed why would she need a TV if she's never home to watch it. To Kasey's right was a mahogany wood dresser with a big mirror attached. Her room's walls were bare except for a framed picture of Whitney Houston.

"You really broke your window and ran away?"

Kasey changed the subject asking, "How you live like this Shay?"

Shay smacked her lips, "I don't have much of a choice Kasey. That's why I stay gone all of the time." Kasey stood, walked to Shay's dresser mirror. His bloody clothes caught his attention at first then he flicked one of Shay's heart charmed necklaces. He turned around and leaned on Shay's dresser, looking into her eyes. It was like he could see her pain and he knew the real her now. The Shay under her mask of fake happiness.

"Tell me what's goin on Shay?"

"UUOO boy that's why I didn't want you to come here!"

"Well, I did. . An I need to know the real. You my homie lover friend, why you hidden this from me?"

"Because Kasey, you don't understand."

"Help me find understandin den Shay."

Shay took a deep breath then explained, "For as long as I can remember my mama and her boyfriend Money sold crack. My mama met Money after my father got killed in a armed robbery. Money's actually the one who got my mother hooked on whatever drugs they be doin. Now my mama and Money sell crack to support their habits instead of making money. This whole apartment complex is section eight and Money's not supposed to be here. But he gets an S.S.I check and pays the rent, so my mama's basically using him to keep a roof over our heads. My grama Bernice is the real stability in my life. She makes sure my mama buys me the things I need. But most times my mama can't even do that, so I call my grama and tell. My grama pay's my phone bill, buys me clothes and hygiene and bitches my mama out when she don't do right. My grama sometimes threatens to call C.P.S and housing on her but I don't think she'll do it. But my mama be scared so she bribes me with $80 every time Money gets his check, so I keep my mouth shut. I use that to get my way and do what I want."

Kasey thought; dang, here I am complainin bout ma when I'm really good. But I still wish I had Shay's freedom to do what I want. I guess you can't have the best of both worlds. Or the good without the bad.

Shay fought her tears as she continued, "It's bad here Kasey. My mama sells crack in and out of the house all night. Some nights I can't sleep because dope fiends be fighten over who knows what. My mama and her friend Dee Dee go boosting and stealing from wherever. That's how I get some of my clothes. . But my mama doesn't do it for me. Most of the good stuff goes to the dope man. I be scared that my mama might not come home one morning.

There's a lot of people that sell drugs around here, mostly crack, meth bars and rarely heroin. All that makes this apartment complex dope fiend central. It's almost as worse as the Manor except mostly everyone does good business here so there's not too many shootings going on. I make my money by selling bars but most times its hard to find them if it's not the first of the moth. You don't realize how much you help me with the little you do for me. That's why I'm so glad you came into my life. I didn't want you to see my reality, bit that's it. . . that's my story."

"I don't like it Shay, I can't stand to see you like this."

"If I had a choice I'd live another way Kasey, but I don't."

Kasey shook his head wit a frown as he said, "Ima try to talk to big bro to see if I can stay with him so I can do more for us. I'm not feeling ma's B.S right now anyway."

"What are you going to do about school?"

"I'm really done with school. I ain't learnin nothing and I'm really tryin to get on the grind full time."

"So you're just going to drop out?" asked Shay.

Kasey replied, "Naw, ma said something bout a G.E.D, so I guess I gotta get out and get it on my own. Plus you my best friend and I gotta make show we straight."

"We're going to make sure we straight. I'm the one who keeps putting you in position..." Joked Shay. Then she handed her phone to Kasey and said, "Now call your brother."

"Yea, you show right. . he proly worried like a mug."

As soon as Kasey called Daren pulled up like he'd been close by. Daren's ballen ass was probaly at the strip club next to my apartment Shay thought. As soon as Shay lay down for the night Alexa called, turnt like it was the weekend. "Come back over girl, why'd you leave?" asked Alexa. .

"Kasey was at my house girl, he's so crazy. He got into it with his mama for what happened at school."

"Every sence you met him you always leave me dry. Come back to G-baby's. . Cory, Camron, and Duce Duce are all here chillen."

"Terra went home?" asked Shay.

"Yea why?" "Because you're the only girl there with all those guys and we both know G-baby and Kam don't understand NO."

Shay heard someone talking in the background then the phone hung up. . "UUOO this girl makes me sick," said Shay, pulling herself out of bed and getting dressed.

When Shay knocked on G-baby's door he answered saying, "Shay, come in girl." He tried to kiss Shay but she big faced him back saying, "Move punk." She squeezed passed him and joined Alexa in the living room. She was seated between Kamron and Cory smoking and drinking, watching BET's uncut. G-baby flopped back in his recliner chair and started bobbin his head to the strip club video and music.

"Alexa, come here," demanded Shay. .

"No wait, Cory went to the back room to get this new drug," explained Alexa.

"It's the best drug in the world," added G-baby.

"Sit down Shay, let's get fucked up," said Alexa. .

"Ah, No, we have school tomorrow Alexa."

Cory returned from the back with a tray that had a bust open balloon that was full of a thick brown sugar substance. Cory set the tray down on the coffee table and waited for Alexa to try it. Cory already had lines chopped and separated. "What does it do?" asked Alexa. . Shay snatched Alexa off the couch and pulled her to the side. "Bitch, what do you think your doin?" asked Shay. Alexa was swaying and slurring her words as she explained, "bitch, they gon pay us five hundred dollars each to get fucked up and have some fun."

"Ah, uh, you're already messed up, and I'm not about to let them run a train on you dummy," Shay whispered.

"I know what I'm doing, I just thought you wanted to get paid. ."

"Not like that, Alexa lets go!" Shay whispered, trying to pull Alexa out the door. Alexa wrestled Shay causing G-baby and his potnas to stand up.

"Ay leave her alone Shay."

"Shay stepped back and said, "You know what. All you niggas are wrong. . .She's seventeen with y'all old asses." Shay stormed out of the apartment thinking how could Alexa stoop that low and be that dumb.

CHAPTER 9

IT'S I.G NOT Y.G

Kasey ran through his G.E.D test making educated guesses. He turned it in feeling confident that he'd at least pass. The instructor followed Kasey into the hall where they met Korita, sitting on a bench against the wall. Kasey couldn't help but check out elegant ladies of St. Philips College. Kasey wondered why he never seen any of these people when the college was just outside Money Lane's city limits.

Korita stood and shook the instructor's hand with a fake smile. "Thank you so much. How long till we get his test results?"

"It usually takes about two weeks. If they come in before that I'll give you a call."

"It can't be faster than that? Asked Kasey.

"It's graded by a separate institution young man."

Korita grabbed Kasey's shoulder with a strong grip speaking through grinding teeth, "STOP BEING RUDE, . . Let's go." Korita's monstrous face changed back to its smile as she pulled Kasey out.

Korita drove home with the radio off while Kasey browsed through his phone settings. Kasey knew his mother was beyond mad at him, but he didn't' care. He had his mind on his and Shay's future and making money. Kasey reached to turn the radio on, but Korita slapped his hand.

"I know what's going through your mind Kasey. You think you don't need school and you think you gone be the next drug lord with your brother but mark my words son this is going to come back to bite you in the ass."

"I'm not tryin to be no drug lord ma. I'm jus ready to do my own thing."

"Umm humm, hard head make a soft ass. I'm not finna argue with you."

"Why you actin mad ma, you gave me options, so I picked one."

"I'm not mad, I'm just disappointed. I wanted you to be successful in life legitly. Your father died doing what he did just for that house and a little bit of money. He was this close to gettin out the game and didn't make it. He would always say that he wanted you and Daren to be the ones to break the chain of drug sellin, prison time and our family dying for no reason."

Kasey huffed then explained, "look ma, Ima young G jus tryina see what the world has to offer. I don't know why you think Ima be sellin with big bro just cause I wanna move out."

"Run game on somebody else Kasey, I'm ya mama. I tried to lead you away from this life and here you are running headfirst into it." "I respect your rules ma, and I can't have you beatin on me and takin my phone. So Ima jus leave. Ima always love you but I gotta go."

"I know you're going to stay with Daren. My question is are you going to get a job?

"Probably not ma."

Korita just shook her head fighting her tears. They rode the rest of the way home in silence. All Kasey could think about was how he could elevate the money making process with I.G and them. I figure if I give them better prices they'll bring me more money. Everybody wana eat. . .I jus gotta put'em in position.

***

Kasey packed his clothes, shoes, CD's and hygiene as fast as he could. He called Daren to let him know he was ready and waiting on the porch. Korita didn't come outside and lecture him or see him off. He was glad she didn't come to nag but at least wanted to tell his mother bye. She must really be messed up Kasey thought.

Tavious kept calling Kasey but he didn't answer. He already knew I.G and some of Riverside homies needed to re-up.

This gon be too live. Now I can really stack some bread. . Just think about how much money I made in the past month. I started with eight bricks and made nine hundos the first day. By the end of the first week I made another nineteen hundos, plus Shay helped me pull in four pushin sacks at school and her apartment. . . the nine, nineteen and four hun put me at thirty-two. The second week I coped twelve bricks from big bro for 3,120. . .Rich raised the price ten dollas a pound big bro said, so I just pocketed the extra $80. . Den I pulled in two grand off five bricks, plus Shay moved a whole brick fa me in sacks. A quick twenty-eight hun. .

Week three was crazy. My last six bricks jus disappeared between postin with big bro at Nancy's and chilin wit I.G nem at the park. That Thursday and Friday I made twenty-eight hun, which put me at six grand. I back doe coped a lil ten bricks that night just to keep feeding I.G nem. I moved all ten my Monday with Shay's help. That's when Chewy told on me. . .That put me at seven grand and four hun. . . That's some fast money and I couldn't move like I wanted. . Now it's goin down.

Daren pulled up and helped Kasey load his stuff in the back. . "Where's ma?" asked Daren in a rush hopping in the car.

Kasey was right behind him. "She trippen bro, she mad. Like she was cryin." Daren pulled off asking, "You good bro?"

"Yea, kinda don't like leavin ma by herself like dat. But I gotta be able to do me."

"She gone be straight. I stop by all the time to check on her. She just too emotional, that's all. She really need a man in her life."

Kasey never thought about that. He couldn't see another man being in the house with them.

"I don't know bout all that bro but look . . I got seven grand and four hundo's . . It's 7540 for twenty-nine bricks. . ." Kasey paused to let Daren think about what he was asking. "I got you bro. Now let's talk some rules. You gone have to go half on the rent, and we gone try and keep the in and out traffic down. You can have the guest room but I'm leaving my weights where they at. Just like ma's we gone keep our spot clean."

"Fa show," said Kasey feeling good about stayin with big bro again.

Once they got to Daren's they brought Kasey's belongings upstairs and got right to work. Kasey broke ten pounds down in qp's, two pounds down in sacks and he split the rest of his two-pound bricks into single pounds just like Daren taught him. Since Kasey was using the living room Daren broke some heavy weight down in the kitchen. Daren made some phone calls while breaking down his double bricks. He didn't move anything but whole bricks now and his one-man operation was constant and steady. But now Kasey had joined the team full time.

Daren finished calling everyone back then shouted to Kasey from the kitchen. "ay I'm glad you here bro. Remember, stay sharp, move smart and let's get this bread. Now that you on the grind full time I want you to try to only carry what you know you gone move. Unless you can stash some bricks at Shay's or something. I know you cool with them Riverside katts but don't get too comfortable.

"I got-chu bro."

"and one more thing. Wrap your jimmy and try to keep it in the guest room when Shay come over."

"I got-chu bro."

Daren dropped Kasey off at Domo's then pulled into the HEB parking lot as a cover to deliver. Monza was a friend of Daren's who he went to school with. She had been buying three pounds from Daren every week since he got on the grind full time. She said she wanted nine pounds this time because she'd been stacking. Daren didn't think nothing of it because she'd been off and on since high school. Daren frequently used the HEB as a cover to make his drop offs go smooth. Daren called Monza as he parked in the middle of the parking lot next to a grey Silverado. He sat there smoking a blunt of his favorite sour diesel. Monza finally walked over and hopped in the front seat of the lack. Daren loved him some Monza in a homegirl type of way. She was cool, down to earth and had an ass so fat with emerald eyes. She said her family was from the islands, but she loved the city life.

Daren put his blunt in the ash tray. "What's good, gorgeous?"

"Shit, you know. . Tryin to get paid."

"That's a bet. . "

"Say, you know I.G." Daren shook his head so Monza continued, "Some crips from Riverside talkin like they got weight. So I tracked them down and found out it was I.G black ass. and he ain't got nobody's weight. It turns out he cops from your little brother and they speak highly of him. . What's his name?"

"Kasey, . . you think lil bro ok over there?"

"Hell yeah, he's Riverside's meal ticket. Word on the street is if you touch your brother the OG crips gon put a price on your head. ."

Daren got lost in his thoughts till Monza changed the subject. "Anyway, . . I know I usually grab three but my cousin threw in with me but he didn't' wanna just come up off his money like that. I was wondering if I could let him hop in with us."

Daren shook his head saying, "you know I don't like meeting new faces. But ima fuck wit-chu this one time." Monza called her cousin and he slid into Daren's back seat real smooth like.

"What's good D, I heard some good thangs about you."

"It's all good, I got you right here," said Daren as he touched the bag under him. "We agreed on 2960 right," said dude handing Daren the money.

Daren started counting the bread and quickly realized it was only 100 dollars in ones wrapped in a few twenties. Daren looked back and Monza's so called cousin had a 44 pointed at him.

"YOU WANNA BE A G, HERE GO DAT GANGSTA SHIT RIGHT HERE. . PASS THE BAG BACK. ."

"And run them pockets to balla," added Monza. .

Daren slowly did as he was told while looking Monza in the eyes. "It's like that Monza. .?" asked Daren.

"Nothing personal. . I told you I was tryina get paid. . Lil bro woulda got it too if he wasn't protected by I.G. ."

Daren could only sit there in shock, watching his bread blend in with the many cars and HEB shoppers. .

Tavious, Kasey, I.G and Di'lon sat at the chill spot in Domo's back yard. Di'lon and I.G bought two pounds a piece from Kasey for 360 each. Tavious finally paid Kasey the hundred dollars he'd been owing him and tried to cop another qp for a hundred. Kasey felt so good to be free he tossed Tavious a half a pound and said, "keep ya money kinfolk and stack some bread this time. . Ima be back tomorrow if y'all move fast enough but I ain't tryin to chill."

I.G smacked his lips and said, "This shit already gone. You need to go wherever you go and bring some more on some right now type shit."

Kasey leaned back in his chair real player like, capin "I got-chu Y.G, . . Where we going?"

I.G stood in a playful manner, flexing like a pit bull. "It's I.G NOT Y.G, BIG DOG. RAWF RAWF." I.G's vicious imitation made everyone laugh hard enough to lose their breath and eyes water. The weed had them feeling good and there was so much money to be made.

Once everyone calmed down Kasey said, "I thought it was Y.G, why they call you I.G?" "cause Ima G, a Trey 7 Gangsta crip."

"MY bad Y.G," Kasey said not realizing it.

"IT'S I.G" screamed everyone at once. The stomach felt laughter broke out again lasting for a while. Tavious rolled in the grass holding his stomach laughing and saying "cuzzo a foo, ahhh."

"I know it's I.G I jus wanted to make y'all laugh," said Kasey as he called Daren. Daren didn't answer so Kasey called again still getting voice mail. "Big bro ain't answering, I guess we dead till tomorrow."

Kasey stood and took the blunt that was passed to him. He hit it real hard then passed it to I.G. "I'm gone y'all, kinfolk. . . stack some bread for real."

"A-ight cuzzo, Fa sho fashow. . But ay. You know Daren gon be trippen about you walking across the hood by yourself. Why don't you wait for a ride."

Kasey straightened the nine in his waist band saying, "I'm riding wit nina and extend. . .I ain't even trippen." I.G stood and locked C's with Kasey's B saying, "On the set aint' nobody gon fuck wit you. you good big dog, rawf."

Kasey dapped everyone else up, checked his pockets to make sure his money was there, then left Domo's back yard on a mission.

Kasey climbed the steps of Shay's porch and knocked on her door. A tall, dark, skinny dude with two long braids and a mouth full of gold teeth answered. Kasey looked dude up and down trying not to laugh at his high black shorts, holey muscle shirt and beat up reeboks.

"Is Shay home?"

"Naw, you know goddamn well she ain't." Dude slammed the door in Kasey's face and turned the metal locks.

"Hoe ass ol nigga, lookin like cracked out flavor flave," said Kasey as he sat down the porch's first step, thinking I shoulda called in the first place.

Shay answered on the first ring. "It's so different not seeing you at school. Where are you?"

"I'm at your house." Kasey could hear other females laughing in the background and music playing.

"I'm on the way right now. Did my mama let you in?"

"Nu hu, some dude answered the door then slammed it in my face."

"Who money don't worry bout him, he's like that all the time. . I'm on the way though!"

Daren sped home like a speed demon and parked the lac in front of his apartment with a loud SKIRRT! "FUCK, FUCK, FUCK!" shouted Daren while beating the steering wheel.

No strap, they got me for like five bands too. I don't know where Monza stay no mo. . . She done moved so many times. . I can't believe I got caught slippen like that, . . I know better. ."

Daren grabbed his phone and saw a couple of missed calls but he was too mad to focus. His only thoughts were, I need to buy another gun. I should have listened to Rich and kept D-woo and K-9 with me but that ain't my style, riding with a bunch of kats. . .Just think if we get pulled over with all the shit they be having we goin under the federal prison. . . For life. .

Daren forced his self out of the lac and stormed inside talking to himself. "I need a blunt to the dome, then I'm going to the pawn shop. . . Mama always said never trust a big butt and a smile."

Kasey sat on Shay's porch rolling a blunt. By the time he finished Courtneys' white Pathfinder pulled into the apartment and parked next to Arlene's beat up green Volvo. Shay, Courtney and another pretty yellow bone Kasey didn't know got out of the car looking equally beautiful. They all wore matching outfits of yellow shirts with white jean booty shorts. Shay and her friend wore white flats and Courtney had a pair of white heels on her feet.

"Where's Alexa?" asked Kasey. .

Shay shrugged her shoulder as they sat down on both sides of Kasey. . Kasey noticed how Courtney broke her neck to sit next to him. "This is Terra," said Shay, reaching for the blunt. . Kasey gave her the weed thinking about what Courtney said about a grown woman doing more for him. Kasey felt something for Shay, but he'd never been in a serious relationship before, nor has he been with a grown woman like Courtney. She oozed confidence, sex appeal, and a sense of direction.

"Where you been all day?" asked Shay as she lit the blunt.

"I took my GED test. Then I moved my stuff ova to big bro's. After dat I was at my kinfolks with I.G and nem."

Terra's face frowned up as she said, "Why to hangin around I.G, . . EWWL."

"He coo, we be getting money together. . What's wrong wit em?"

Terra looked Shay in the eye giving her the tell him gesture.

"Kasey, I'm going to tell you but you have to promise not to get mad."

Kasey looked Shay in the eye trying to figure out what could make him mad. . ."Tell me Shay."

Shay passed the weed to Terra knowing Kasey would get mad. But Terra was right. She should have told Kasey long time ago.

"Me, Alexa and Terra used to chill at Di'lon's apartment in the Manor every day after school. Di'lon's parents would let everyone chill in the room upstairs where we would have shake that ass competitions with Di'lons sister Ebony." Kasey asked with a frown, "Why y'all booty poppin in Di'lon's room?"

Terra laughed at Kasey as she said "Di'lon and Eboni share a room."

"Hell naw, y'all bullshittin." Kasey looked back and forth to Shay and Terra not finding their joke funny at all.

"I'm being for real Kasey. Their room is the maset bedroom upstairs. All they have up there is two queen size mattresses on the floor. Two chairs by the open window with a fan in it because it's so hot. For some reason the AC is broke upstairs."

Courtney stopped Shay's story saying, "Damn, you two bitch's know I smoke too right?" Terra giggled "my bad" then passed the weed.

Shay continued, "You think I live bad, there's never anything to eat over there. The only thing they own is a pile of shoes and clothes thrown in the closet. Their room has a bathroom, but the toilet don't flush, so they fill up a bucket of water in the tub to make the toilet flush. But with all the bad we used to have fun."

"Why would I get mad though Shay?"

Shay and Terra leaned forward, locked eyes and busted out laughing. . . Courtney passed the blunt to Kasey. He took a puff then passed it to Shay.

"We used to spend the night over there, well everyone did. At any given time there would be like fourteen of us in that hot ass room. We smoke talk and listen to the radio. But when the lights go off it was a different story. The closet was the sex room and if you went in there you knew what was up.

One night Alexa, Terra and I were sleep with Eboni on her mattress. I was at the edge of the mattress in and out of sleep when I spotted I.G crawling over in the dark like he was a black ninja. He lie next to me all night tryin to holla and get me to go in the closet with him. He was persistent, trying to feed me ex'os and grabbing on my titties and trying to put his hands down my shorts. I had to keep making him stop but he thought it was a game."

"Stop lying Shay, you was letting him touch on you," laughed Terra. .

"Oh my god girl I was not."

"So did you go in the closet with him or not?" asked Kasey.

"No I didn't, I put that on everything."

"Since Shay's going to babysit the blunt, can I buy some weed or wha" asked Courtney. "All I got is my smoke sack on me, but here." Kasey split his personal sack of dro down, tore the bag in half and gave it to Courtney.

"The reason why I brought it up is because I.G is nineteen and he knows Shay just turned seventeen." Said Terra. When Kasey didn't say anything Shay said, "Say something Kasey."

"I ain't got nothing to say. It ain't like we together."

"Do you want to stay here with me tonight, so we can sleep in a bed?"

"I'm not really tryin to stay here Shay, too much goin on."

"Plus don't forget I'm here," said Courtney. .

"Somebody's in a bad mood all of a sudden," whispered Terra.

Shay stood in front of Kasey trying to look in his eyes. Kasey looked down and began rolling another blunt. Shay smacked her lips with a scolding look at Terra. "I knew he was going to get mad about the I.G situation. That's why I never brought it up. I just didn't want you to hear it from someone else. Do you hear me Kasey?"

"I'm not mad about the Y.G situation, so just chill Shay."

Courtney laughed as she told Kasey, "You do know it's I.G right?"

"Yeah, yeah, what eva. . Let me call big bro and see what's up for tonight."

Daren told Kasey he didn't feel like doing nothing else today. Kasey didn't ask why because he felt the same way. Kasey told Daren that Courtney was going to give him a ride home so Daren could chill. Daren dipped to Trina's without word to Kasey. Daren needed to vent, as well as some TLC that only Trina could give. At the end of the night Daren sat on the floor, leaned up against Trina's couch, between her legs. She massaged his shoulders while Daren pulled hard on his blunt. "I can't believe I let myself get got like that. . "

"I told you, you were getting way to comfortable with people. Regulars or not. You still gotta be on point babe. . . If I see Monza ima beat her ass."

"Don't get involved in my business. Ima handle it. I'm just fucked up right now."

"I know you're probably thinking you wish you had your gun, but what if they would have killed you, or you killed them in the middle of HEB parking lot?"

"I ain't tryina talk about it no more T. ."

"Fine, lets go in the room so I can make you feel better."

Kasey, Shay and Courtney sat together on Daren's living room couch smoking in silence. Courtney wasn't feeling Kasey's vibe, so she left thinking she was a third wheel. After the second blunt Kasey said, "This I.G play makes me think about your past. . .and I know you not a virgin."

"I had sex with one person before you."

"Tell me about it Shay."

"Are you sure? You're already mad Kasey. I had a boyfriend before you named Treyvon. He was from Riverside but transferred to Park Village sophomore year. I won't lie when he asked me out I just wanted to have sex with him. Alexa, Terra and all of the girls I hung around with had already lost their virginity and I was horny than a bitch. Trevon and I would hide in my room every night, don't give me that face like Ima hoe Kasey, . . .Let me tell you the whole story."

"Alright, Shay, . . Go."

"I was afraid to do it my first time, so Treyvon asked to tongue my clit. It felt so good, and it became the normal thing for us to do. He was patient and understanding with me and the next thing I knew we had been together for months and he still hadn't had sex with me. . I loved him for that and finally I decided to let him have some."

"Where's he at now Shay?"

"He umm has two murder cases from a robbery gone wrong. He and some of his potna tried to rob some outa town dro plug they had. He was sixteen and stupid now with a thirty-year sentence."

"If we get together and I get some sometime are you gone leave me lonely?"

"I'm gona be real with you and say I don't know. Right now we just living in the moment. But who knows what lies ahead."

"It's just that I.G my potna and now I don't know if I can have him around you. . ."

"Kasey if I.G was really your potna and he knew that we're ina relationship, and he tries to holla at me then he's not your potna. Just like if I try to holla at him I'm not really your girl."

CHAPTER 10

TRAP LIFE

Shay woke up at seven to get ready for school. She eased off of the couch to not wake Kasey, wishing he was going to school with her. She felt glad that she was able to open up to Kasey because now they had a deeper understanding and trust. They had just went to sleep three hours ago but Shay felt so energized from being around Kasey. He's so bright, driven and crazy with his silly self she thought.

Shay got dressed in some dark tight denim jeans with jade colored matching flats and a blouse. After brushing her teeth and washing her face she tiptoed into the kitchen and began making fried egg grilled cheese sandwiches.

Kasey woke up to the smell of butter toasted bread and smiled. He sat up, checked the time on his phone then made his way to the source of the smell. He found Shay in the kitchen cooking and was drawn to her side.

"I didn't know you could cook."

"I really can't, but when you have a mama like mine you learn to fend for yourself."

Kasey stood there admiring her beauty thinking; it's official, I wana be with this girl forever.

Shay glanced and saw Kasey smiling and asked, "why are you so happy?"

"I was thinking, and I was jus wonderin if we together or not."

"Do you want us to be together?"

"Hell yea!"

"Well so do I but from what I just told you last night this fast life scares me. I was born in a gutter Kasey. I can't understand why you want this trap life. The money's good, but the bad is even worse."

"I know Shay, Ima be extra careful."

"That's what they all say. Lucky for you I'm your down ass chick who's a vet in the game." Kasey changed the subject and asked, "Where you goin?"

"School of course, DUH." Kasey laughed and said, "oh yea," not really wanting Shay to leave. "If we're really going to be in a relationship that's going to last, we need to figure out a better way for us to make money with the money we have."

"Like what Shay? Now that I'm free I been feeling like I am the trap life."

"I don't know Kasey. But do you see how my mama and money live. I don't want us to be like them in the long run."

Shay kissed Kasey, grabbed two sandwiches and ran out the door. Kasey locked the door behind Shay then went back into the kitchen on cloud nine. He put the two sandwiches Shay left for him on a plate and found a big bag of hot Cheetos from the kitchen closet and a cold sprite from the fridge.

He sat back on the couch with his food thinking how live this was. Kasey took a few hard puffs of his half smoked blunt in the ash tray then started eating like a savage wild animal. He laughed because he could hear his mother naggin. But now he was free to do what he pleased. Kasey lie back down, and Courtney's sophisticated sexiness flashed through his mind. If I wanna be with Shay that means I can't be with any other woman but her. I should ask her what she thinks about that. Plus I feel like Courtney came to Money Lane with a motive. She said she moved big shit before, maybe I should put her in position.

❖   ❖   ❖

Kasey rudely woke to Daren slamming the front door.

"My bad bro," Daren said as he joined Kasey on the long couch.

Kasey sat up asking, "What's wrong bro?"

"I got, got last night bro. They caught me without my strap."

Kasey grabbed his 9 from under the couch and said, "What we waitin on? Let's go light em up!" Daren pulled two 45 Ruger handguns from his back and set them on the coffee table. "The only problem is I don't know where he/she stay at."

Kasey sat back and huffed, "Damn big bro. . "

"I know lil bro, now I'm hella paranoid. I'm not trippen on Shay but we not finna have the whole crew in the spot. This where we keep all our weed, guns, bread. I just had a reality check on how real the trap life can get if you caught slippen. ."

"I got-chu bro, if anything I'll just chill at Shay's or uncle Domo's more."

Daren nodded remembering what Monza said about Kasey being protected. Kasey watched Daren take his guns to his room in a depressed like mood. Kasey lit the rest of his blunt and thougth; damn, if they got big bro I know ima easy target.

Kasey got in the shower, brushed his teeth and got dressed in a grey polo shirt, black creased jeans, grey timberland boots and a Raiders fitted hat. After that Kasey gathered the rest of his weed from his corner of the guest room and broke it all down in Qp's at the lving room coffee table.. While at work his phone rang and he didn't want to answer but did anyway.

"What's up ma."

"Baby are you ok?" asked Korita.

"I'm good ma, why you askin?"

"I don't know baby; I just got a bad feeling and I'm worried about you."

"I'm here at Daren's chillin ma, I'm good."

"Why don't you come by the house and let me cook you something."

"I was just about to go chill with Shay ma, but I'll come over in a couple of days though. . I promise."

"OK baby, I love you."

"Love you too ma, and when I come ova I want fried chicken and mac n cheese." Kasey ended the call feeling his mother's sadness in her voice. As soon as he sat the phone down I.G called.

"Turn up with us big dog, rawf rawf raawwff!"

Kasey laughed as he said, "stop playing, what's up wit it?"

"Same shit different day. At Di'lon's waitin on you. Domo's grouchy ass started trippen se we had to burn off."

"Hell yea, well big bro sleep right now and I ain't tryina hop on the bus wit the rest of the issue on me."

"Don't' trip, I'll cop a dope fiend rental and come scoop you."

Kasey thought about what Daren said about being paranoid then told I.G "I'll be at the Block Buster on Money Lane."

"Fa shit show, we on the way."

Kasey ended the call and stuffed all the weed in his backpack, tucked his nine behind his back and hit the door thinking, I am the trap. . .

❖   ❖   ❖

The Manor gave Kasey a bad feeling off the rip, but he played it cool and followed I.G and Di'lon up the steps to Di'lon's apartment. Kasey looked down the dark halls of the apartments seeing dope fiends and prostitutes

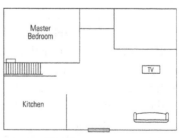

Dillon's House

that had no shame in their game. "Hey sweety," said a woman in fishnets, heels and a tight top.

"How you doin," said Kasey trying not to be disrespectful. "That come wit crabs Kasey, let's go," warned I.G.

Kasey followed I.G and Di'lon into Di'lon's apartment and closed the door behind him. "Lock the door or what?" asked Kasey. .

"Naw, you good," said Di'lon. Kasey watched Di'lon disappear into the kitchen while I.G flopped on the couch in front of the small tv. Kasey looked around and it was actually clean but there wasn't much furniture. The living room only had a long couch, a tv on a nightstand and roll of wire that was hooked to the house phone was on the floor in front of I.G.

"Pull up big dog, so we can eat," said I.G.

Kasey nervously asked, "Where's Tavious?"

"Domo got'em doin yard work, working like a Hebrew slave. He'll come through later." Di'lon came out of the kitchen with three barrel juices and passed the red one to Kasey as a joke. Kasey watched him sit on the floor in front of I.G and watch tv like this was the norm.

Kasey still stood with his back to the door looking crazy. I.G glanced back and laughed, "Ain't nobody gon put the feets on you, come chill!"

Kasey shook of his nervousness and joined I.G on the couch. I.G pulled a folded paper full of numbers from his pocket while grabbing the house phone from the floor. "I got a bunch of licks set up, but we both need three pounds," explained I.G. Di'lon continued watching TV while passing Kasey $1,080 and I.G did the same.

"Y'all move hella fast," said Kasey counting the money.

"The Manor jump's ten times faster than Riverside Park. You gone see." I.G began making calls just as Di'lon's mom came out of her room in a pink bathrobe and some matching house slippers. Kasey's mouth dropped when he saw the skinny woman stop in front of Di'lon and block the TV with her hand on her hip. "Hey Ms Fay," said I.G, hanging up the phone.

"Hi I.G, and why yo nappy head ass on my phone. And why y'all not upstairs with the rest of the hoodlums."

Dil'lon said, "mama it's too hot up there."

"Ms Fay why you trippen, you need some weed or something."

"You betta know it. Y'all must gotta buncha weed in my damn house." Ms Fay paused looking Kasey closely in the face. "You must be Kay's boy, look just like em."

"Ye-Ye-yes ma'am," stuttered Kasey, looking at I.G.

"Stop actin like that before we really put the feets on you. Get the weed out, Ms Fay ain't trippen." Ms Fay snapped her finger in a wave saying, "why would I trip when ima hustler honey. I sell tabs and work all day long. As long as I get broke off, humph." Kasey nervously put his back pack in his lap then began giving I.G and Di'lon their weed. Ms Fey eyed Kasey and asked, "What the half pounds goin fa?"

"I told you ima give you some weed Ms Fay, damn," stressed I.G.

"I ain't talking to you Isaac. Now shut up."

"Two maybe 210, it really depends on who it is," said Kasey.

"Boy what's yo name?"

"Kasey ma'am."

"That's right, how's your motha?"

"She's fine I guess. We been getting into it a lot so I had to move out."

"Well, you welcome here any time baby. And call me Ms. Fay. . Ma'am makes me feel old." Kasey tried to hand Ms. Fay a qp, feeling guilty for having so much weed on him. "I don't need no weed baby. . I.G gon break me off later."

Kasey watched Ms. Fey waltz into the kitchen, easing up a little thinking; it's some crazy moms in the world.

I.G made a couple more phone calls while Di'lon broke a qp down in zones. Five minutes later someone knocked on the door. "Come in!" shouted I.G, knowing who it was.

A tall rough lookin black dude came in, handed Di'lon some money. Di'lon counted it then handed dude three ounces. Dude looked at the sacks then left without a word. "Unless it's something big, then next one on me," I.G told Di'lon.

"It's understood cus."

A woman walked in a minute later. She was a little chunky with short curly weave, dressed in a blue jean shirt and short set with sandals. "I.G, Di'lon what y'all got going?" she asked.

"Trappen, I know you need something," said I.G.

Tameeka smacked her lips as she said, "y'all nigga's always tryin to sack a bitch down. Let me get a hp or something."

I.G looked at Kasey, so Kasey said, "220." Tameeka began counting money from her bra as she said, "And tell Ms. Fey I need a fifty pack."

"I'm in the kitchen Meeka," Ms. Fey shouted.

Tameeka gave Kasey the money and he handed her two qp's. . As she headed to the kitchen I.G said, "don't be expectin this all the time neither."

Once Tameeka got her work and left Kasey asked, "it's gon be like this all day?"

"Fucken right, everything you got in that bag gon be gone before six, maybe befo that."

"Straight up," Kasey said with a bob of his head.

I.G dialed another number as he said, "Straight up, you keep giving us good prices and we gon look out for you. Now roll something up big dog."

Daren woke up and just stared into the darkness of his room. He was having a hard time shaking his depression, but he knew he needed to get on the ball because the streets never sleep. Daren pulled himself out of bed and went into the living room to find Kasey gone. He then returned to his room, turned the light on and began counting the money between his box spring and mattress. Daren had each thousand dollars folded and wrapped in a rubber band. As he counted he thought to himself; I took a loss but I'm still $143,000 to the good. I been moving 100 bricks a week for the past five weeks at 370 a pound. Things really been slowing down since I been on the grind full time. . . I guess I would move 120 in one night because I would only stang twice a month.

DING DONG! The doorbell rang and Daren thought, "what the fuck, no body know I live here but . . . Daren grabbed the K from under the bed and crept through the apartment. When he looked out the peep hole he saw the heavy but muscular built Hispanic that always be at Rich's when he needs to re-up. Daren put the kay behind his back and answered the door, slightly cracking it open. "An ajar door means I am not welcome. It breeds bad blood."

Daren opened the door a little more, "Rich ain't here."

"I do not wish to speak with Rich, I've come to speak with you. Can I come in?"

Daren saw that he didn't really have a choice and let the man in. The Hispanic watched Daren lay his K behind the couch then they both took a seat. The Hispanic took a seat on the small couch...Daren sat on the long couch smelling the man's strong cologne and taking in the man's stylish silk suit, dress shoes, thick rope chain and dragon medallion.

"I am Verdugo. I work for some very powerful people and I have been sent with a proposition for you."

"Like what?" Daren asked.

"Let me tell you a story first. When these powerful people purchase the product you crave so dearly, they pay a very good price as a result in them buying in bulk, some even go so far as growing their own mota, coca...whatever...Either way it is costly and such investors require insurance on their money. Let us say a truck of 3 tons of this and that crosses over the border. It will stop at the first major cities such as San Antone, Dallas, Houston and Money Lane. Now the reason Rich is given such good prices is because these cities are the insurance. Meaning a fourth of the product is sold in bulk to rich at 250 a pound, which normally gives us a small amount of our investment back. The big ticket is up north, where one pound might go for $1200 to $1400 a pound. But it is a great risk getting a truck up north which makes it a gamble on my bosses end." Verdugo paused to let this information sink in.

"So you want me to buy more pounds."

"Preferably… Yes… We need you and Rich to buy at least 200 pound or more each, every time an eighteen wheeler passes through this city."

Daren sat there in shock thinking; the trap life just keeps pulling me deeper and deeper. Rich said trucks come twice a week, sometimes three times… Verdugo cleared his throat while straightening his collar even though his collar didn't need fixing.

"I see that you are undecided, but I am well are that you have the means to deliver the currency required… So I will give you two weeks' time to think. But be aware, these powerful people insist on this matter or you as well as Rich may lose this business connection. Also, if you choose to further our relationship prices will drop to 200 a pound."

Verdugo pulled out a card from his pocket and placed it on the coffee table. "I will be in touch, or perhaps you should call me as soon as you make up your mind." Daren watched the connects middle man stand, shocked at how fast things were moving. "Did Rich tell you I was here?"

"Oh no, it is my job to watch our investments. And if you didn't know you are very much that… Good evening Mr. Daren… Also, your usual 100 pounds is already with Rich."

Later that night Daren and Kasey sat together at the coffee table doing their usual. Daren just got back from Rich's with his hundred bricks. He broke pounds down while listening to Kasey brag about how fast I.G nem move. Kasey counted $10,920 and gave it to Daren for forty-two pounds. Daren began giving Kasey two-pound bricks on at a time. Kasey was so turnt he couldn't stop talking. "For real big bro, I luv this trap life. I sold six pounds for 360 each to I.G and nem, sold a couple of half pounds for 220 then sold the rest for $400 a pound. So really I spend $7,500 for twenty-nine bricks and made $11,150 in one night. Ima pocket the extra $230 left over and buy a cable box and probably somethin nice for Shay and ma. . .Tomorrow when I go over there I bet Ima move all I cop from you right now."

"Don't get too comfortable over there bro, keep in mind that's still Riverside."

"Big bro, I'm not even on Riverside no more. I'm at the Manor."

Daren paused and said, "bro, the Manor's hotter than fish grease."

"But it's ten times liver than Riverside. I jus gotta be like you big bro, get mines and get out. It's always gon be hot where it jump at."

Daren finished giving Kasey his weed then began counting the money Kasey gave him. The money was on point which made Daren think; with the numbers lil bro putting up I might have to call Verdugo tomorrow. Lil bro takin half my 100 bricks off the rip. . . Life is crazy ain't it??

Kasey broke ten of this pounds down into forty pq's then took all his weed to his corner in the guest room. Kasey put thirteen pounds and seventeen qp's in his bag thinkin this gone be so live. My only problem is, how am I going to come back to get more when I run out. I probably need to get a bigger bag. . or. . I could stash some shit at Shay's like big bro said. . . Naw. . .

Shay woke Kasey up for their morning phone call while she got ready for school. She told Kasey how much she missed him and how mad she was that he didn't stop by yesterday. But it was Friday and they would spend the whole weekend together he told her. .And he kept their first real date a secret.

After his phone call Kasey peeked in Daren's room to see that Daren was already gone. Kasey thought; big bro be on the move for real. . I need to get like him. I really need a whip. Kasey hopped in the shower, then brushed his teeth thinking how Shay was right. They really needed a bed for the guest room. Plus it didn't feel right having sex in the living room. What if big bro walks in like ma did. Kasey browsed through the guest room closet and picked out some all-white jays #7's, some black jeans and a white and green button up Tommy Hilfiger shirt.

Kasey moved fast with his phone and back pack in hand and hit the door. As he locked the door he called I. G. hoping it wasn't too early.

"Big Dog what's popping, I got the rental on stand by."

"Bet, I'm already at the Block Buster. Where you at?"

"We at Di'lon's waiting on you. I was just about to call but we figured you was asleep."

"Don't nothing come to a sleepa but a dream," said Kasey.

The trap setup was just like the night before. Kasey and I.G were on the couch and Di'lon was on the floor watching BET. This time I.G and Di'lon bought five pounds a peace from Kasey. An hour passed and I.G sold 7 of Kasey's qp's to different people for $115 a pop, while constant traffic came in and out for sacks and work. The house phone rang and I.G answered...

"Yeah, he right here." I.G tossed the phone to Di'lon telling him "We ain't cutting no deals cus." Di'lon listened then said "Fam's letting the q's go for 115, even if you wanna pound.. Ain't no body got it on deck in the manor so take it or leave it." Di'lon listened for a minute then asked Kasey, "You tryin to sell three pounds for 13 hundred..." I.G shook his head no but Kasey said "Hell yeah, I'm trying to dump this shit as fast as I can."

"But we gotta take it ova there," explained Di'lon, hanging up the phone...

"Hell naw, tell 'em come get it. You know we don't move across the apartment on foot," said I.G... Kasey stood as he said "Let's just do it I.G, we already taxin..." I.G took a long exhale

then said "That's all you got left is them 3?" Kasey nodded…
"Well leave our straps here just in case. This ain't Riverside."

I.G, Kasey and Di'lon speed walked down the street that ran
down the middle of the complex. Before they could get to the
building they were headed to a white van pulled up and 5 jump
out boys rushed them. "Run Kasey," shouted I.G, while making
a beeline to the gate and hopping the fence. Di'lon ran towards
the jump out boys creating a distraction. "What we do wrong of-
fica's. Me and my mama just moved here from outta town and –"
One of the jump out boys grabbed Di'lon's arm while the other
chased Kasey down. Kasey was a little too late to react and two
of the jump out boys caught Kasey in mid jump of the fence and
wrestled him down. The back pack was the only thing on their
mind and when one of the jump out boys opened it he smiled…

"Dispatch 21, we have one in custody… Possession with in-
tent to deliver."

Di'lon was searched and let go, then he ran, hopped the fence
joining I.G. They watched Kasey get hand cuffed and thought
damn.

CHAPTER 11

WELCOME HOME BRO

"You have a collect call from – Kasey Gibson."

Daren listened to the automated voice message and shouted "FUCK!" while going through the necessary motions to accept Kasey's call. When the call went through Daren asked, "What happened bro?"

"I got caught up in the Manor. I was moving too fast, den I didn't run when I shoulda." Daren just sat there shaking his head, listening to the details. .

"What they offerin?"

"Six months state jail, they not tryin to give me probation because I tried to run. . " Daren tried not to show his anger as he asked, "Why you ain't been called Kasey. You've been gone for a week?"

"I just been thinkin a lot that's all."

Daren took a deep, deep hurtful breath not liking the pain he could hear in Kasey's voice. To be truthful Daren felt like this was his fault.

"Put me, ma and Shay on your visitation list. . Ima send you some bread and some books. Stay focused, workout and before you know it you'll be home again."

❖　　　　❖　　　　❖

Dear son,

First I want to say that I love you. I know that this is not my fault when you make your own choices in life. But as your mother it's my job to guide you. especially sence you don't have a father. No parent wants to see their child locked up in a place like that. My mama used to say a hard head make a soft ass. Now that you got some time to think maybe you'll find the true meaning of what that means.

In other news Crissa's about to pop. I can't wait to see my grandbaby. It's a girl and they named her Imani. I got a job at the nursing home and I'm going to send you $60 when I get my first check on Friday. .Why haven't you put us on your list? Write me back ok, I love you son. .

Kasey closed Korita's letter and thought; ma still on that b.s but she right though. . I wasn't thinkin straight. I shouldn't have been in the Manor, and I should been on my p's and Q's. .

Kasey put his mother's letter down and picked up Shay's. . He looked around the dayroom thinking I never wana come here again. There were fifty-six numbered bunks all around the dayroom's walls. White painted brick walls separated every two bunk beds. Kasey thought it was crazy how every corner had a blind spot where the picket or camera's couldn't see. That's where it went down at. In every corner inmates were either smoking, shootin dice, tattooin or getting their scratch on. Kasey could only shake his head and hope no one got caught. Because he hated being on lock down. .

Kasey opened Shay's letter…

Dear Kasey,

Hey babe, How are you holding up?? I can only imagine how much it sucks in there but I'd rather you be there then out here right now. Everyone's dying and I feel like it's a blessing you're away from all of this...

Daren's really crazy babe... some shit happened and umm.. I'm sure he'll tell you... Any way I dropped out of school. I've been real stressed out lately for a lot of reasons.. The money you helped me save is gone and my mama been getting on my nerves so much to the point that I want to move out. There's only one problem with that. I'm almost five months pregnant..

WE'RE HAVING A BABY!!!!! I hope you're not mad at me for not telling you sooner, but I didn't want to worry you while you're in there.. Now that you're on your way home I wanted you to know what's going on with me.

Write me back and tell me what you think, and why haven't you put us on your list?...

P.S, my friend Alexa died from a heroin overdose.. I was so sad, and I cried so hard..

Kasey closed Shay's letter and asked himself "Am I ready to be a father? Damn this shit crazy.. Looks like I ain't got no choice though... If I add it up it had been about five months since I been gone.. Now I really gotta stack some bread... Get my own spot..."

"What you sitting up there looking all sad fo youngsta? You finna be home ina couple a wake ups..." An old school inmate sat at the dayroom table close to Kasey's bunk watching him the whole time.

"I just got some crazy news schoo, my girl having my kid and she ain't tell me till now.."

"So what you gone do youngsta?? What's the game plan?"

"I know my big bro finna put me back on... I'ma stack up and take care of mines. I just need to get outta here.."

"I ain't gon sit here and preach, cause you got ya mind made up-"

"I'm open to wisdom, this time made me sit back and open my eyes… lace me up."

The old timer explained, "I was in your shoes not too long ago.. I was young hustling, got caught with a lil or nothing then sat in prison with a child on the way. Right befo I got out a older kat told me what I'm bout to tell you. Get out the game befo it's too late. But I couldn't see no other way and now this is my life… the penitentiary… After I do this two years state jail I'm going to the feds to finish my sentence on a dope case… what I did, it's a long story and I been in and out of prison for 25 years. My family fell off and I'm ashamed to see my children because Ima dope fiend and they don't know me. The sad truth is when I come home ina few years I'm jumpin right back in the game because this all I know. ."

Kasey couldn't sleep thinking about everything that happened so far. . Even with Old Schoo's story he still felt like he could play the game well enough to stack some bread and get out the way. . .Kasey sat up, grabbed his pen and pad from under his bed and began writing a letter. .

Dear Shay,

What's good Bm, my bad for not writing or settin up my visitation list but I needed to fall back from everyone to get my head on straight. . Plus I feel like if my absence doesn't make you sad then me being there had no meaning to you. . I was wonderin what was keeping you writing me when I never wrote back. . I'm glad we gon be a family Shay and I found out that blood makes you related, but loyalty makes you family. So to me we've always been fam and I've always loved your character. A Old School told me this; a woman will always love a man for three things. His power, wealth and character. Most fellas will only love a woman for their beauty. I've come to find that I love your character because even if I lacked power or bread my character can always attract a beautiful woman. And a beautiful woman can always bring money and power to me. . .This time made me see you've always been that loyal love by my side. Through you I learned that listen and silent are spelled with the same letters. I know you think I do but I never looked down on you for having a past before me. What matters is what we build from now on. .

I've grown Shay. I been reading the Prosperity Bible, Message to the Black Man, Marcus Garvey and Malcom X books big bro sent me. Now I see life through new eyes. I gotta know what makes you happy, . . Sad. . because I never want to see you cry. I never want to forget how you look, feel and taste. . For some reason you never told me your dreams, so how can I make them reality. What thoughts keep you up at night? I think about how you're my best friend and I'm putting together a plan to give you and my child the world. . You're my first and only love and even if I do wrong, acting out of human nature you will forever have my heart, soul . . Even if you decide to throw it away. .

I love you Shay, . .

Kasey.

Daren waited in the parking lot of Dominguez State Jail in his 'Lac, trunk knocking listenin to I ain't mad at cha, by 2 Pac. Kasey walked out the front doors wearing a white commissary tshirt, shorts and some white sneakers. Daren got out the Lac and embraced Kasey with a strong brotherly hug.

"Welcome home bro…"

Daren held Kasey's shoulders while looking him up and down. Kasey gained some weight and was cut up with that fresh out glow. Kasey posted up with Daren and Daren was quick on his toes, posting up with him. "Now that's what I'm talking bout," laughed Daren as he and Kasey circled each other trading a few licks. Daren caught Kasey with a strong fast lick to the chest. Kasey backed up out of breath but Daren embraced him again saying "I see them old schoo tantry nigga's had you them pads…"

"Hell yea, and I did good too. I wasn't smoking none of the money you was sending me. And it's crazy cause this place is flooded with every drug you can think of.."

"Bro, If you woulda came home a dope fiend I woulda beat you up for real."

"I'll never fall victim like that!"

"Man it's so good to have you home lil bro."

"I's good to be home, but I gotta ask you something serious big bro."

"What ever it is ask me in the whip, penitentiary makin me break out in hives…"

Daren and Kasey hopped the Lac and hit the road. Daren had the music down the 45 minute drive back to Money Lane, listening to Kasey prison stories. Daren couldn't believe Kasey had been through so much in 6 months… But you know what they say about state jail… It's rockin and rollin with out a second thought because everyone's going to do their time no matter what.

After Kasey finished his stories Kasey asked "Did you hear about Shay?"

Daren shook his head… "Shay's five months and I want her to come stay with us. And it won't be for long bro, I'ma stack and get us a spot…"

Daren excitement made Kasey's worry fade. "That's live bro! Crissa's about to have Imani any day now. You know you good. We'll move the weights to a storage till you ready… Now all is left is to celebrate…"

"Strip club," said Kasey with wide eyes… "How you gon get me in?"

"Just let me handle that… Not about this Riverside situation. I told you not to be messin wit them kats. Now you a felon and on the radar."

"It wasn't I.G nem fault bro, I froze up and laws was everywhere. On da coo I-G a good dude and his hustle game hard. I was thinking about fromin a trap squad, but in a safer location.

Major money can be made and we can lock shit down, expand then fall back like you told me on my b-day."

"I ain't gon tell you not to mess wit them kats cause you gon do it any way. I just don't want you to bring any heat to the house."

"Why would I bring heat to the crib?" asked Kasey with a frown. .

"I just, . . I really don't want you on Riverside like that lil bro."

"Why bro, you always plexed up with Riverside for no reason."

"Kasey, you don't know the history of both hoods and the past our pop's plays in it. Second, . . I shot lil Chris house up a few months back."

"Why bro, what happened now?"

-FLASH BACK-

"I sat in the back of the strip club at my usual table with K-9 and d-woo. It was a early Saturday night and I decided to take a break and relax for the weekend. I passed up a few free dances from Monique and Paris because a free dance will have a nigga spendin bands without realizing what I'm doin. .

Out of know where Courtney walks up to our table looking hella fine ina black short tight dress that could hardly be called that and some sexy ass black high heels. . She joins us like she know us, looking better than half of the strippers in the club. "What's the occasion Daren?" she asked. .

"Nun, just enjoyin life," I said. . D-woo and K-9 were eyeing Courtney like a piece of mama's fried chicken. But she was definitely givin me her full attention. Bro it took all my will power to not take her slutty ass to a room. . .

"I was tellin Kasey how I used to drive fifty-plus from Money Lane to the H for some Houston nigga's I used to mess with."

"Oh yea," I said.

"Yea, I already see how you do your shit so I'm willing to put the money up to buy fifty or sixty to drive them. I just want you to make it worth my while."

I was deeply thinking about putting her in the loop because the connect been asking more of me and Rich. After a few drinks we exchanged numbers that's when she asked me, "You know lil Chris right?"

I lied and said "Naw."

She laughed then leaned over and whispered in my ear, "yes you do, you beat him up at Niesha's the first night I saw you."

"Why does it matter?"

"You know Chris fuckin Monza right?"

"For real." Asked.

"Hell yea, I was at the club and Monza was drunk poppin off at the mouth how she set you up for Christ to rob you. And Monza's cousin ain't her cousin it was lil Chris's cousin from Waco." The second I found that out I hit the door and D-woo and K-9 were right behind me, no questions asked. .

K-9 rented a dope fiend rental and drove up to Riverside. We crept down lil Chris's block. I was in the back seat and D-woo in the passenger seat. We slowly drove past his house a few times. The lights were off which meant they were sleep or nobody was home. I honestly didn't give a damn, when we hit the block again K-9 slowed, and I hopped out. I walked straight up to his front door. I beat on the door like I was the laws then I grabbed a stepping stone off the ground and broke a window. All the while d-woo was right behind me with dad's K. The lights come on and I pulled my two 45's from my back and started bustin… D-woo joined my side and let the K rip as we slowly backed up towards the car. D-woo turned and let the K spit at the cars in the drive way. While I shot the windows where the house lights had turned on.. We lit the house up for a minute and one of my straps jammed just as I was about done with the extended clips. D-woo tried to pull me to the car but I shouted 'FUCK DAT' and shuved the jammed 45 in his chest to get em off me. I don't know what came over me but I reloaded another extend and kept clappen. The car was on neutral, already a house down the street. D-woo booked-it to the car, tossed the K and 45 in the back then ran back to me.. He shook me out of my trance pulling me and yankin me till I got in the back seat. Then we mashed off...

"Damn big bro," said Kasey while putting his hands on his head..

"That's why I'm saying... I don't want you over there.."

"Lil Chris is I.G kinfolk.. I just gotta holla at I.G nem. If they trippen he'l tell me whats up.. I.G my potna bro, and I ain't got that many people I can give that title to."

Kasey moved the weights in a corner and set him and Shay's room up real nice. He had a fully stocked entertainment center across from the bed and a mini fridge on Shay's side of the bed. Daren gave Kasey 40 pounds and $500 so he could get on his feet. Kasey stashed the weed in the closet then sat on the bed and waited for Daren and Shay to return with some of her things...

Kasey's phone rang and he paused, knowing who it was...

"You the only crip I know that don't got his own phone.."

"That's cause the feds be listenin.." I.G and Kasey remained quiet until Kasey said, "Big bro told me about what happened wit lil Chris..."

"He got shot, but he's alive... I talked to my OG and he did some investigation. It turns out that Chris jacked Daren for some shit.. Ask Daren if he trying to settle the beef?"

"He is, and I'm tryin to elevate our grind to a trap squad."

"Well look, My O.G blessed me with some bread and along with the bread I been stackin I got enough to pay Daren back the B.S my cousin jacked him for, and 8,000 purchase 50 pounds... It's too much money to made to be beefin ova some shit that happened ten years ago. And just so you know I had a squabble with a few of my cousins takin up for you when all the homies met.. Now you gotta give me something to present to the homies to lock it in.. They been wantin to shoot yo mama crib up but I been the one stoppin' em."

"I thank you fa that. . My mama ain't got nothin to do with this and big bro turn zero to a hundo real quick. . This my vision for a trap squad. We sit at a round table and discuss our options. Put everything out in the open. . With that kinda bread from ya O.G I can talk to big bro about getting you bricks for $300 a pound. Plus big bro said plug wants us to move more as well as other things and I see you already got the work on lock. ."

"There's always room for improvement big dog."

I.G and Kasey laughed then it was quiet again. .

"I'm happy you home big dog, I want you to know this ship deeper than makin money. I'm tryin to dead the Riverside and Oak Ride beef. If I even hear one of my homies whisper BK . . I bust'em in the mouth. . Luckily my O.G that nigga or I know my own homies woulda been tried to cross me out."

"Let's start somethin new, . . Break the chain and eat . . .Together. . ."

"Understood."

"Tomorrow, me you Tavious, Di'lon and big bro goin to the strip club to talk and celebrate. . .I'm bout to be a father."

"Shay right, I knew I wasn't trippen. I dropped some shit over in her apartments and saw her stomach last week. . Congrats. . . But as for Di'lon. . the laws kicked his door in . . . He and Ms. Fey split the charge down the middle. . .Di'lon tried to take everything, but the law's had a snitch. . But welcome home big dog. . . See ya tomorrow."

Kasey ended the call and thought damn. . So much has changed and I was only gone for six months. I ain't finna be in hot ass trap spots. . What Ima do is put people on and have them fade the heat. . .but you never know when you have a snitch smiling in your face. . .

Shay and Daren walked in the door and Kasey could hear Shay screaming, "Kasey!" Kasey met her in the room's door and hugged her softly, making sure to cup her belly. She drowned him with kisses, tears of joy dropping form her eyes. "I missed you so much."

"I missed you too Shay. I'm home and I ain't goin nowhere."

Shay felt Kasey's body and said, "You got strong babe." While closing the room door behind her . ."You got a bed, thank god." She said with a gasp, flopping down on the soft new mattress. Kasey joined her on the bed and pulled her violet scrunchie from her hair, allowing it to flow free. .

"Your hair reminds me of those just for me perm commercials with the little girls. . . I think I want a little girl Shay."

"Well to bad, the doctor says it a boy and his name is. ."

"Kareem, . . Please let me have this one. . . and you can have the next one."

Shay's eyes watered again as she said, "you want another one. ."

"Of course, You know how much life would suck if I didn't have big bro.." Shay jumped on Kasey, kissing him like a crazed she beast.. .All the while Kasey cupped her stomach pleading, "Shay, Shay, Shay, you gone hurt'em.." But Shay was driven by lust and wildfire emotions.

"You better love me good boy, stop playin," she shouted while pulling Kasey's clothes off. Kasey fought in a playful manner yelling, "Babies make pretty ladies crazy!"

"Heeelllppp," Kasey yelled…

A few days later…

Kasey, I.G, Tavious, Daren sat at the round table in the back of the strip club enjoying the night and company of the trap squad. They drank the clubs finest and no one said a word about the granddaddy purp in the air…

Kasey stood for a speech and toast with a bottle of E&J in hand.

"I thank ya'll for this, it's a wonderful welcome home present, it's beautiful and I love this place.. But real talk…" Kasey paused swaying back and forth then continued, "This is my fam right here… Big bro, kinfolk and my best potna I.G… I know I messed up but I know I proved myself to be smarter… Thanks for the whip bro… the hona-ciblic so live…I"

"Bro you drunk, it's Honda Civic…" Everyone laughed while toasting with their bottle in the air… "Yea… that's what I said.. I want ery one to eat... and with this family we gone lee the hood beef --..."

"Sit down big dog," said I.G pulling Kasey down in his seat...

Everyone stopped and looked with open mouths when Courtney sexy ass approached the table. "Where the balla's at," she sang... sitting between Daren and Kasey... "Yo ass never fit in yo dress, is that because you want a nigga to grab it?" asked TAvious...

"If a nigga wanna get slapped.. Every trap sqwad need a bad bitch's feminine energy to put them up on game... So let's talk about expanding to another city.. Ya'll already know I been putting hella work in, in the H..."

"True enough, but the count down city is closer, and it's easy money," said Daren...

"We ain't ready for a war, and steppin foot in other nigga's territory needs preparation," added I.G...

"Why you come ruinin our night?" asked tavious..

"Nigga please... I bring in way more money than you with my eyes closed.." Courtney capped..

"She right on da cool kinfolk," laughed Kasey... Then he fell back and out of his chair..

"I'm good ya'll.." But Kasey didn't move.

"Somebody help me get lil bro home.. she gone be mad at me..." Laughed Daren

CHAPTER 12

FORGIVENESS

Daren was mo throwed then a football on super bowl Sunday, but he still held his own like a G. He pushed the lac to his and Kasey's apartment with Kasey passed out in the back seat. Courtney followed the lac in Kasey's new whip plotting her next move. After they dropped Kasey off Courtney rode in the front seat of the lac's passenger side looking good as ever. Daren drove her back to the strip club so she could get her car.

"You know I could have got my car in the morning." Courtney said.

"Somebody might try to break in yo shit, besides that. . ."

"your girl might pop up right." Daren didn't answer and when he glanced over once again he caught a glimpse of Courtney's sexy light brown thighs exposed from her rising dress.

"You like what you see? . . It ain't shit ta get a room. . .Between me and you . . On the low."

Daren was feeling hella good and his body did what his mind knew he shouldn't. It was like a flash of scenes played before Daren's eyes instantly. One moment he was on the road and the next he and Courtney were in a hotel kissing, Courtney pulling Daren's clothes off. Courtney led Daren to the hotel room's long marble double sink and skillfully dropped her thong. Her high dress gave Daren a small glimpse of her perfectly shave landing strip as she whined in a tease. Daren watched her hop on the sink, spread her legs and prop her heals up so Daren could see what he's been thinking about for so many nights. Courtney exposed her clit and rubbed it in circles with two painted fingers. Her mouth was open, eyes beckoning Daren to get a taste. He moved her hand and slowly went in. When he smelled how clean and good she smelled he dove in, tongue going to work. In less than two minutes Courtney's legs clamped down as she rode her orgasmic wave. Daren stood up and dipped his manhood in one time, real slow. Courtney's pretty lips had a tight grip like she hadn't had any in a minute. Daren sank all the way in then pulled halfway out while she rubbed her clit again. "Umm, let's see what that dick game like. . . I got that million dolla. . Shhii." Daren picked up the pace and grabbed a hand full of hair, and a heel behind his back for some tight grip. He punished Courtney furiously, making her sweet nectar drip down her ass. She screamed, "Beat that pussy up," while screaming and moaning. Daren knew his pound game was official because Courtney stared deeply in his eyes wanting more than he could give. In her eyes he could see her soul and a search for love she never found.

Out of the blue Daren saw flashes of his daughter, Crissa and Trina that made him sober up. Daren pulled out just as he came and took a step back.. He could see his self in the mirror and felt a sudden shame. Courtney hopped down from the counter with a click of her heels and said, "Let's go to the bed so I can ride the shit outta that dick…" Daren shook his head..

"Naw… this ain't right.. I'm trippin'." Courtney smacked her lips.

"It's just sex nigga, you act like we fallen in love or some-thing..."

"Put your clothes on and lets go. I can't believe I let yo sexy ass get me.. And we ain't use no rubber... I bet you woulda let me bust in you.."

Courtney rolled her eyes and watched Daren get dressed.. "Keep standing there, looking crazy if you want to.." Courtney picked her thong up and said, "I'm already dressed Daren.." Then stormed out of the hotel room...

Early in the morning Daren picked up Korita then pushed the Lac down Money Lane till they reached the highway. He had a surprise for her and even though he was tired he felt this couldn't wait.

Daren thought about what happened last night and he prom-ised to be a better man to everyone around him. Especially the women in his life. So much has happened in the past few months and now Ima father. Imani's my heart and I never thought I could love a life so much... It's a trip lil bro about to be a father too.. I hope Courtney don't feel some typea way about last night... On the real she a major part of why the trap squad brings in $70,000 a week..

"Boy, where are we goin?" Korita asked again.

"I swear you must be smoking too much weed. It's like I'm talkin to my self for the hell of it. Do you know I called Kasey the other day and he gon have the nerve to tell me hold on ma, I'll call you right back. I don't know what the hell done got into you kids... too much weed and that damn game. If ya father was here I know he'd whip some sense into ya'll..."

"Ma, stop livin in the past, and how do you smoke too much weed? Huh? And I don't even like playin the game..."

"Boy why is we headed out to the boonies for?"

"Ma will you chill and be still. All you do is worry about every-thing when everything don't need to be worried about.."

Korita sat back and watched the Texas road side of land, cows and hay. A half hour later Daren pulled the Lac up to a nice 4 bedroom home on an acre of land. "Adams hill! What are we here for baby?" Daren parked the Lac then he and Korita got out. "So much been goin on in the hood, I ain't been sleepin right with you in that house by yourself. So I paid some good money to a realtor/ real estate agent to have this house put in your name legitly. I already paid half up front, and the rest will be paid in payments, with you being promoted to a supervisor at the nursing home made perfect timing. . .The house is really already paid for, but the payments make it look good. . All you gotta do is keep working for a few years to create a paper trail then you'll have the deed to the property in no time."

Korita covered her mouth on the brink of tears whispering, "This is so nice." All she could think of was when Kay had first took her to her first house. So many promises were made for a better life now Korita truly felt that it was a possibility. Korita walked down the house's path that led to the door and Daren followed. "I know how you feel about drug money ma. And I know you're right. I'm asking for your forgiveness with this house, and I want you to know that I'm making moves to start my own real estate company."

Korita gasped as she said, "Thank the lord. I've been praying so hard for you to do something to get you and Kasey out of the streets. You both got kids which means everything don't revolve around you and him."

"I know ma, why you think I'm trying to change things. It ain't easy to just up and jump out of the game."

"I know baby." Daren pulled the keys out of his pocket and put them in his mother's hands. "You can move in as soon as you get ready."

Daren sat at the two-seater table in the back of Oak Rides I-Hop. He waited patiently after finishing his meal of chicken fried steak with country gravy, potato wedges and mac n cheese. Daren paid his tab then waited twenty more minutes for his guest to show up. He stood to leave but in the last second Trina walked in the door wearing a red velour body suit with her hair in a bun. She had white fila's on her feet with a matching purse.

"Hey boo, sorry I'm late." She said while joining Daren.

"Late, . . I'm surprised you showed up. I was already on the way out."

"So what are you trying to say?"

"You've been avoiding me T."

"No I haven't, I just been busy with school." Trina looked away as Daren reached across the table and grabbed her manicured hand.

"I thought you said you forgave me." Daren found Trina's wondering eyes and realized she was still hurt even though she said she wasn't.

"I was never mad at you because I know how you are. . .I just. . ."

Daren felt his chest pain as he said, "you expected me to be better than that. . . I'm sorry T. When my daughter was born all I could think about was you. For a lot of reasons me and CICI ain't kickin it like we should. And um. . .I guess what I'm trying to say is , if you really forgive and love me like you say you do. . . I want us to have a kid together."

Trina screamed "WHHAATT!" causing all of I-Hops customers to look their way. Trina calmed down and asked, "Are you serious?" Looking Daren in the eyes for the first time in months. "I'm for real T. The way I see it you're the one who's supposed to have my child anyway… I just fucked up. Plus I love lil bro and life would have been weak growing up without'em…"

"Daren I don't know… What about school and everything."

"You ain't gotta go to school right now right now T. And you can go back after you have the baby. You ain't gotta work, go to school or nothing… I got you T."

"I'm not tryin to depend on you Daren."

"So you really don't forgive me then."

"I do forgive you, I just don't know if I'm ready to be a mother.. And then what about all the bitches you be fuckin."

"What bitches?" Asked Daren with a frown.

"You think I'm stupid. That's why you always keep me away from your friends. On top of that how can I depend on you with your crazy lifestyle?"

Daren thought about Courtney and his beef with Lil Chris then changed the subject. "Are you hungry?"

"Not really, I ate lunch on the run when I left school."

"Knowing you was coming here to have lunch with me. That's the typea shit I be talking bout. Fuck it, let me show you something and if the answers still no then I'll leave you alone T."

Daren had a 2 bedroom house in the outskirts of Money Lane that only he knew about. Daren's house was out of the hood, but not as far as Korita's to be considered Adam's Hill. Daren set it up like this so he could get to Korita's or Crissa's in 20 minutes if he mashed the gas.

The whole ride Trina kept eyeing Daren with a million thoughts running through her mind. Was he serious, and should I really sacrifice my future to have a baby with him. He already broke my heart once… How can I trust him to leave the game alone and live a normal life.. I can't forget about the baby mama drama that's bound to rise. But on the flip side he keeps me looking good and I never want for nothing. His tongue game is on point and his stroke game is something serious… Maybe I should.. People make mistakes and I do love him..

Daren pulled into the house's drive way and asked, "What's on your mind?"

"I was thinking about how much we've been through… Who's house is this? If it's one of your so called friends place I was just playing.. I don't want to meet any body.."

"This is my house Trina. You'd know if you answered my calls and now all of a sudden you never at home.."

Trina followed Daren into the house surprised to see Daren was on his grown man shit. There was a fifty-five gallon fish tank in the living room that had too many angel fish to count. In the corners of the living room stood African tribal statues. Bookshelves filled with black history could be seen here and there. In the center of the living room was a black leather wrap around sectional couch before a giant entertainment center. Full body length pictures of Malcom X, Nelson Mandela, Noble Drew Ali and Clarence 13 X hung on the walls.

"Damn daddy, this house is hella fly."

Daren followed Trina into the kitchen, speaking to her while she rummaged through the fully stocked place she loved to spend her time.

"I'm tryin to give you the finer things in life, keep you safe as well as write my wrongs." Daren took Trina's hand and pulled her to his room.

Daren pushed open his room door showing Trina nothing but darkness until he went in lit the jasmine scented candles. Trina saw red rose petals that led from the door all the way to the King size bed. On the side of the bed was a stand with a tray neatly set up with whipped cream, a bowl of sliced papaya and strawberries. There was a bucket of ice with a bottle of moet and two champagne glasses.

Daren and Trina met at the foot of the bed and waited for her reaction. She looked deeply in his eyes while slowly taking off her velour body suit and kicking off her shoes. Trina's heart began to race because she knew Daren liked to put the tongue game down before anything. Daren took it slow and sat Trina's naked body at the foot of the bed. He took her socks off and massaged her feet, every so often kissing her inner thigh to tease her. Trina laid back with deep sigh, drifting to another world. Daren pulled out a small black box and set it on Trina's chest. Trina grabbed the box moaning, "What's this?" When she saw the ring she sat up with a jolt, eyes wide.

"Don't play dumb Trina, be my wife and have a family with me. Forgiveness is the key to a healthy relationship."

Trina put the ring on her finger and watched it glisten by candlelight. "Oh my god how long have I waited for this." Trina's eyes watered as she leaped into Daren's arms, kissing him longer and harder than she ever had in their whole relationship. Daren caught his breath and laughed. "I'll take that as a yes." Trina sat back on the bed, pulling Daren on top of her.

"Kiss me and touch me all over. I want deep slow love till I pass out."

Daren started with Trina's lips and worked his way down thinking; This is how making a baby is supposed to be. Thank god she forgave me. .

Crissa sat on the porch of her mother's house crying her eyes out. A hour ago she made the hardest decision she ever had to make in her life. "But I had to!" she cried… I can't take care of my daughter and mother at the same time…" Crissa listened to Korita on the phone then told her. "I guess Daren didn't tell you she's brain dead. He's so inconsiderate when it comes to me…" Crissa listened then replied, "I don't want to be a burden to you. But I can't afford this house and I hate asking Daren for money… speaking of the devil.. I'll call you back…"

Crissa hung up her new cell phone and set it next to Imani's baby monitor. Daren pulled up in his new Nissan Maxima, beatin John Be's song Angel. Daren hopped out looking fly ina red and black SouthPole outfit with some fresh black air max. Daren was on cloud nine but his smile faded when he saw Crissa's hurt. He rushed to her side asking, "What's wrong BM?"

"I pulled the plug on my mom. I can't handle the stress of work, Imani and keeping up with this house. I was calling you to help but the medical company came and took the medical equipment and hospital bed form the living room."

"Why are you out side CC?" Asked Daren looking at the baby monitor on the porch.

"I just can't stand to be in that house right now.. Too many memories.. I love her so much that I kept her hooked to those machines for me, knowing her condition was never going to get better... selfish right?"

Daren didn't know what to say so he just held Crissa close.

"Do you think God will ever forgive me?" She whispered.

"I wish I knew if God was loving, forgiving or vengeful and judgmental like the pastor say. All I know is the mother of my child deserves more. Maybe it's time for a change CC."

"Like what, baby daddy?"

"I got my mama a big house in Adam's Hill. I did it hoping you'd move in with her so she can help you raise Imani. It's dangerous here CC, you know what I do. This way you'll have some free time to figure out what you want to do with your life."

"You don't really care about me Daren."

"What type of shit is that CC, you the mother of my child... Bottom line I want you and Imani out of Riverside."

"Fine Daren, fine... Now leave me alone.. please." Crissa continued to cry her heart out so Daren stood to let her mourn. He went in the house on a search for Imani and his joy immediately returned.

Tavious drove Tiffany's Honda down Money Lane with nine pounds in a duffle bag in the back seat. After chilling with Tiff and Janette he was drunk and high as a kite at the same time. Still he knew he needed to drop some of these bricks because he hadn't moved shit sence Kasey blessed his game a week ago. Tavious was on the way to drop off his bricks to his potna lil Kee-thow on the northwestern outskirts of Money Lane. Lil Kee-thow's money was always good and he came through in a clutch because Tavious really needed the bread. Lil Kee-thow's parents had a nice three-bedroom house and sence Tavious had to deliver he charged $425 a pound.

Tavious exited the highway and stopped at the stop sign. Out of nowhere a black suburban and a white Dodge van pulled up to a stop on both sides of him. Tavious started to mash the gas for a high speed chase, but a black Mercury Sable pulled up in front of him. Jump out boys in all black hopped out the undercover cars and surrounded Tavious with guns drawn. Not in his right mind Tavious had a .45 under his seat and four grams of white girl in his lap he'd been snorting the whole ride.

Tavious could only put his hands up like the laws ordered. All he could think was damn, . . .Jammed up by the feds. What the fuck I do. . This ain't even my whip. . Tavious watched the agents close in and open his car doors by reaching in the windows because he had them rolled down. . His weed or sack of dope was visible but the agent in the passenger seat only grabbed the keys out of the ignition.

"Just from what I see we got enough for a federal indictment. . .Mr. ah. . Tavious Gibson. Why don't you come with us."

Tavious was taken to FBI headquarters and placed in an interrogation room. An hour later an agent walked in with a straight face and took a seat across from Tavious. "We both know what you had but that's small compared to what you can give us." Another agent entered the room and placed an open file with a picture of Rich on the table.

"I don't know who that is. Obviously he a blood and Ima crip."

The first agent said, "Well our C.I say's you do heavy business with some of his people. . ." The second agent said, "It's simple Mr. Gibson. . give us something solid and all this will magically go away."

"I don't know nothin about them kats, but I'll give you somebody movin big heroin."

"We already know about G-baby. . " said the second agent. The first agent snapped, shouting, "We're not going to play good cop bad cop or listen to you try and slither your way out of this. The next word that come out of the mouth better be information we want. Or you might as well get ready for a federal jumpsuit."

"Daren… he works for dude in the picture…"?

The words came out of Tavious mouth so fast he didn't realize he said them. The second agent left the room then returned 3 minutes later with another file and photo. "Another one of our C.I's mentioned him before but we don't have much to go on… Is this him?"

Tavious hung his head then whispered "Yea…"

"Speak up," shouted the first agent…

"Nigga fuck you!" shouted Tavious suddenly standing bold…

The first agent leadped over the table and choked Tavious to the ground… Tavious was cuffed so he couldn't put up much of a fight. Eventually the second agent broke the tussle up and helped Tavious back to his seat. "If you don't want me to help you move pass this then I'll walk," said the second agent. Tavious dropped his head again and thought; Forgive me kinfolk… Tavious nodded.

"Good, you're free to go, for now.. My name is Agent Buckner and I'll be in touch." Then both agents left the room…

CHAPTER 13

THE GOOD LIFE

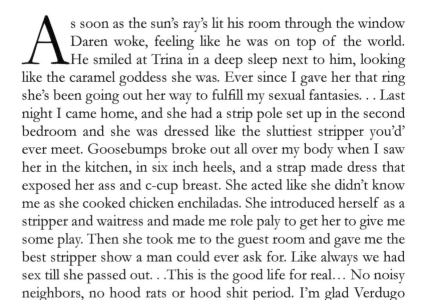

As soon as the sun's ray's lit his room through the window Daren woke, feeling like he was on top of the world. He smiled at Trina in a deep sleep next to him, looking like the caramel goddess she was. Ever since I gave her that ring she's been going out her way to fulfill my sexual fantasies. . . Last night I came home, and she had a strip pole set up in the second bedroom and she was dressed like the sluttiest stripper you'd' ever meet. Goosebumps broke out all over my body when I saw her in the kitchen, in six inch heels, and a strap made dress that exposed her ass and c-cup breast. She acted like she didn't know me as she cooked chicken enchiladas. She introduced herself as a stripper and waitress and made me role paly to get her to give me some play. Then she took me to the guest room and gave me the best stripper show a man could ever ask for. Like always we had sex till she passed out. . .This is the good life for real… No noisy neighbors, no hood rats or hood shit period. I'm glad Verdugo gave me that push to elevate my hustle. Now the door to get out the game is in my reach.

Daren laid there till eight waiting for Trina to get up, but she was still in a deep sleep. He couldn't be mad because he's been punishing Trina at night with the stroke game. He wanted a morning quicky but didn't want to wake her.

Daren got out of bed, grabbed his phone from the nightstand and then made his way to the bathroom while checking his missed calls. After he got out the shower he picked out a burgundy and black fubu jersey, and burgundy jeans from the cleaners and black low top Nikes from his walk in closet. Trina still hadn't woken so he took his weed tray from his nightstand kicked back in the living room. Daren sat in the middle of his sectional couch rolling a blunt of cush while watching Belly.

ZZZT! ZZZT! ZZZT!,, "Bro, I thought we agreed to enjoy life a little!"

"Yea, . . we just chillin at the trap though. . .You comin through."

"Maybe later, I'm bout to pull up on ma and check on Imani first . . Why? What's up?"

"Same ol same ol, we running low on everything. . .How long you gone be?"

"I don't know. Courtney over there?"

"Naw, . . I spoke to her last night. She said she moved all her shit already to and she'd be here later. . . Y'all both always say that and never come."

"Well I gotta come for shit show today. . .Call me when Courtney get there a-ight."

"Aright big bro bet."

Daren drove down the path of Korita's acre and stopped in her driveway with a loud skirrt! He hopped out and saw Korita on her same old porch chair smoking a cigarette, enjoying a cup of coffee.

"Hey son, good morning."

"Morning ma," Daren replied, taking a seat next to her.

"This is rare, since when do you be up this early?"

"I know ma, it's something new I'm tryin. I wanna make it a point to get over here every morning and check on ya'll… Ma…"

"What baby?"

"Why you still smoking cigarettes if you ain't stressed. We living good now."

"I worry about—" Korita paused then remembered what Daren said about worrying about everything. "Where the baby at?"

"In her crib asleep, and don't you go wake her up boy! I mean it…"

"Koo ma," Daren said, then his kissed Korita on the cheek and ran in the house.

Daren walked in Crissa's room to find Imani laying in her crib, kicking her feet with a bright smile. Daren picked her up and he smiled when she started babbling in baby gibberish. Daren kissed her while walking into the din in search for Crissa. He found her at the kitchen bar with a bottle of Jack Daniels sipping out of a glass tumbler. Daren sat on the bar stool next to Crissa with the look of… WHY?

"Why is mommy drinking when we living good?"

"Crissa snapped back, "Money, big houses and cars doesn't make life good Daren."

"Well it damn sho don't make it bad, so what is it CC?"

Daren handed Imani to Crissa and took the bottle and glass to the kitchen. When Daren came back Crissa gave Daren back Imani saying, "I could have sworn you're Imani's daddy."

"Why we always gotta go through this CC?"

"You're right, you know what Daren… I need some time to myself."

"No problem, move your stuff into the empty room. My mama got the baby for however long you need."

"You don't understand, I need to be away from everyone."

Daren watched Crissa grab her purse off the bar and head to the front of the house. Daren followed her trying to control his anger with Imani in his arms. "What the fuck is wrong with you? You act like you can sit down and talk to me." Crissa ignored Daren and walked out side.

"Watch you mouth Daren." Demanded Korita.

"Ain't nothing to talk about Daren, I need time to myself..."

Daren stopped in the yard and watched the mother of his child go.

"You could at least take the car I gave you..."

"I don't want it," Crissa shouted.

When Crissa walked out of Korita's fenced acre she reached in her purse, quickly finding her lighter and box of Kool's. She lit one and thought, 'Fuck Daren, he thinks he can just move me in a nice house and throw money and a car in my face and everything is supposed to be fine. Trina gets treated like a queen and I'm the one that pushed out his first kid. Actin like my daddy n shit, he barely spends time with me, never takes me out. Hell he don't even fuck me anymore...I guess I really am the bitch on the side. I knew I shoulda got the abortion when I had the chance...

Back at Korita's Daren just stood there watching Crissa vanish in the distance.. Daren glanced back at his mother with a frown. "What's wrong with that girl ma. She got everything she could want and some?"

Korita sighed deeply, "Stop looking at what she's got and think about what she's goin through baby. Her whole world was turned upside down. She just lost her mother, and now she has a baby that depends on her."

"She act like Imani don't got me too ma."

"Of course Imani has you Daren, why don't you see wha this girl is going through. She's grieving and she needs more than material things." What am I supposed to do ma?"

"Let's be real about the situation baby. You're not trying to be with her, are you?"

When Daren didn't answer Korita said, "You have to be considerate of her feelings. Now give me that baby and go talk to her."

❖   ❖   ❖

A week later . .

Daren purchased a cruise trip for him, Korita, Kasey, GG and Shay, Imani. Of course Shay insisted that Courtney come to keep her company. The ship set sail from Miami down along the coast of Cuba and finally to Nassau where the ship would dock, and they would spend three days and nights at a beautiful resort.

After four days of sailing and taking in all the sights along the way they finally arrived in Nassau's beach resort and pulled their luggage into the three bedroom bungalows Daren rented. The bungalows shared a spacious open air living room one hundred yards off the beach. Just outside the bungalow was a large inground barbeque pit with plenty of palm trees for shade and three net hammocks tied to them. Glossy wooden tables and chairs surround the barbeque pit giving a nice view of the crystal clear ocean.

Daren and Kasey stood at the pit so they could lay down seasoned barbeque chicken breast and turkey legs. Korita, Trina, Shay and Courtney sat by a nearby table talking while GG lay on a hammock next to them with Imani asleep on her chest.

"Umph rea honey, this is a long way away from Money Lane," GG said in a low voice, trying not to wake Imani.

"I know mama, this is so beautiful and just look at my boy's I'm so glad Daren is finally going legit. I want to make this a yearly family tradition, with all my grandbabies." GG whispered, "Amen to that, speaking of babies.. Trina, when you gon give Imani a brother or sister?"

"Since we're on the subject, I missed my period," said Trina while wiggling her finger. Shay, Courtney, Korita and Trina screamed in high pitch yells. Imani woke and started screaming right along with them. Daren looked up form the firey pit asking, "What is wrong with ya'll?" Kasey followed Daren to their table on investigation mode. Daren grabbed Imani from GG and quickly calmed her down. Korita motioned for Daren to come close. "Sit down baby, when were you going to tell us about your engagement and my grandbaby?"

Daren joined Korita, looking the joyful ladies in their eyes.

"I thought it was our dinner surprise but ah-"

Trina cut Daren off and said, "It just slipped out, sorry babe."

Kasey put his hands in the pockets of his polo jeans and kicked up some sand.

"Damn bro, why you ain't tell me nothing.. You used to tell me everything."

"I was gon tell you Kasey, but I got a lot on my mind with goin legit, CC and Imani." Daren left to take Imani inside because even though Courtney was smiling he could feel her anger and envy.

Korita clapped saying, "He is going to be such a good father. You better be takin notes Kasey." Shay sat rubbing her pregnant belly, fighting her sleep.

"I'm hungry Kasey, is the food almost done."

"Kaream turned you into the hungry woman," joked Kasey.

GG said, "You'd be hungry too if you were eating for two."

"yea… I can't wait till my lil man touch down," Kasey said proudly.

GG asked, "With Daren looking into real estate what are you going to do Kasey?"

Kasey shrugged his shoulders, "What eva big bro need me to do."

Korita smacked her lips, "That's all good and well Kasey but what about you and your plans…"

"I ain't got no plans ma…"

Daren came back hearing the fuss shaking his head. "Let's not ruin our vacation. I want ya'll to know I got Kasey a good job set up, so can we just leave it alone.."

"I'm ya'll's mama, I can be concerned about ya'll's wellbeing."

"And it's highly appreciated ma, but I paid a lot of money for this.. Please don't ruin it.."

Daren put his arm around Kasey's shoulder and pulled him back to the pit.. As they lay meat Daren said, "Shake the bad mood bro. You know how they get. Tell me some strip club stories.."

Kasey's face lit up as he went in, "Bro let me tell you about Bolivia…You know ever since you took me to the strip club my first week out I been hooked. All I wanted to do was lock in wit a stripper but wasn't havin any luck. Remember dat night I called you to see if you wanted to pull up wit us?"

"Yea, I was busy bro, . . Get to the story."

"So me and Tavious was at our normal table blowin purp. I was in heaven bro, so many half naked women in high heels and pretty made up faces. I was shy and nervous this being my second time to the strip club and all. Dat's when Tavious told me "cuzzo, take some bread to one of the stages and give a few dollars." . . "I was so turnt that I grabbed my whole band from my pocket and flew to the stage. A stripper named Bolivia danced. . She was bad big bro. I neva seen a exotic woman with curves like dat. Right off the back I knew I had to hit it. I watched her climb to the top of the pole like super woman den spin down and around while she was upside down. She had on pick glossy four-inch heels and a pink net top and thong. What she wore showed so much I didn't see the point in her wearing anything at all."

"Bro would you get to the point."

"Yea, yea, . . So Bolivia slowed her spin, landing perfectly on the floor and her side. She rolled on her knees while scanning the crowd. All the while she bounced her juicy ass up and down to the music. Bolivia made eye contact wit me and I must have had SUCKER stamped on my forehead. Like a fool I held my bread in front of me with both hands. Bolivia's bright smile turned seductive as she crawled to me with her tongue out. When she got close to me she said, "I'm Bolivia." I just stood there stuck when she put her face close to mine, tossed her long black hair over my head and shoulders while humming in my ear. I don't know why but I loved her mixed smell of sweat, perfume and makeup."

"You smell like grapes," she giggled in my ear. . .

"It's perp." I replied, then Bolivia knelt on her knees and pulled her thong to the side. I put a ten dollar bill on her waistline and what she did next surprised the hell outa me. I really got scared on da coo. . She leaned back then raised her legs in the air. . -CLOW- . . She clapped her heels then opened her legs while luring me in with a teasing smile. When I leaned in over the stage as much as I could Bolivia balanced on her heals and back moving her barely covered sex in my face. Everybody was screamin and I could smell her through all of the flashy lights and chaos. Bolivia stood asking, "Let me dance for you when I get off stage." All I could do was nod as I watched her dance to the other side of the stage. From that moment on all I wanted to do was get some cuddy from a stripper."

"You really actin dramatic bro, did you fuck her or not?" asked Daren. .

"Just chill bro, let me tell you.. I got back to the table with Tavious and told him. Bolivia wana let a young G hit kinfolk, watch."

Tavious laughed, "Don't fall in love so quickly kinfolk. They strippers. Plus a dance is $20 for a two minute lap dance."

"I ain't tripping kinfolk, I'm feeling good an I'm still gone try."

I waited for Bolivia blowin purp, trying not to drink to much cause you know I'll be outa there so quick. Then right on time Bolivia came out of the back and headed straight for our table. She was confident and eva so sexy as she looked me in the eye's asking, "Do you want a dance, I'll take my time."

"Hell yea." Bolivia grabbed my hand and pulled me to the back of the club. The back was lit by low light. She lead me to one of the sectioned off booths with cushioned seats. She sat me down in the middle of the booth and stood with one leg between mine. She whined to the music keeping eye contact all the while. "So what do you do?" She asked.

"I sell big weed wit my kinfolk nem."

"So you're a balla." Bolivia turned around and sat in my lap with a grind. She leaned back grabbing the back of my neck with both hands, still grinding. I couldn't help myself bro, I let my hands caress Bolivia's thighs and waist thinking it was coo.

"I wish you could.. But you can't touch me.. The rules." She said. She stood, turned facing me and straddled my right leg. I was the hardest I even been and we locked eyes when she felt my manhood. She kindly adjust my manhood on the side of the leg then angled her sex right on it… She grind and moaned in my ear, "I wish I could make you cum so bad."

"What would it coast?"

Bolivia's breath was heavy and I could tell she was feelin me.

"Do you really wanna know?"

"I do, so stop playing and tell aG how much it's gon cost for a lil fun."

Bolivia laughed in my ear then leaned back with a serious look in my eyes.

"I got that good good, I'ma high priced slut too."

"So what you sayin, I'm not a balla but I'm not broke neither.."

"I tell you what, give me a hundred dollar tip and I'll let you try it. After that I'll tell you my price."

Before I knew what I was doing I put a hundred dollar bill in her thong. She caught my hand and lead it to her wet slit. She let me finger her one time and said "That's for you to take home." She looked around keeping an eye on security as she freed my manhood. She stroked me a few times, rubbed the precum on my pants while letting me know, "I'm on the pill so don't worry.."

"She played it off coo like she'd done this many times. She put her wetness on my manhood then sank down real nice and slow. It was so good and so quick I didn't know what to say at first. She pulled her wetness off of me and straightened her thong still dancing to the music. Dang das some good for real, so what's up wit it?"

"Two grand ain't nothin to a boss." She stopped dancing as she spoke with a newfound seriousness.

"What, you for real?"

Bolivia rolled her eyes actin boogie all of a sudden. . .She stood over me with her hand out tom bout, "$20 dollars for the dance! Would you like another?"

I just shook my head and paid her. When I went back to our table with the look of defeat and blue balls Tavious was dying laughing.

"She played me like a trick kinfolk."

"I told you cuzzo, but don't even worry bout it. Next week we can go to Wild Zebra's in the outskirts of town. They have five dollar dances on Saturday nights. One of the girls that work there is homegirls with my bitch Tiff. Her name's Monique, she bought bud from you a couple a times. . Know who I'm talkin bout?"

"I don't but who cares. . . It's goin down. . You shoulda been told me bout Wild Zebras."

"We was supposed to go this week but we came here. . This the good life for real bro. I think that's what I wana do. . Open a strip club. It's the only thing I can see myself doing."

"You jus wana fuck all the strippers bro. That's not good business."

"Not all bro, just a few like my side bitches. . .Now I was thinkin. . ."

Daren half listened to Kasey's view for his strip club and watched Trina talk to Shay and Courtney. She talked mostly to Courtney and Daren could tell that Courtney was luring Trina in. . .Little did Trina know Courtney was a fool. Daren thought about how much he cherished this life with Trina and his daughter, and he wished he could get Crissa on the same page. But the reality of the situation was two women wouldn't let him be in love with them at the same time. Even though Trina's not like that, the jealousy factor always comes into play. . .

Daren thought about the new trap house and it suddenly dawned on him. . This trap shit getting out of control. I don't feel comfortable being over there with all that extra shit. I.G and Tavious starting to do way too much. . . I.G coppin two keys of powder every drop and cooking one up in the trap. They move the cooked key in the Manor by fifty packs and I know Kasey be getting broke off for lettin'em do it. Kasey got mad love for them dudes too. . It is what is. . I just gotta keep my distance. . .

❖   ❖   ❖

Later that night…

Daren and Trina just finished soaking in their room's large Jacuzzi while taking turns sipping on a ice cold bottle of Moet. Daren fed Trina iced strawberries out of the bungalows fruit basket then lay her naked body down in the middle of the bed.

"AHH! You're so good to me," Trina moaned..

Daren rubbed Trina's back down with lavender and vanilla scented oil. He made sure to get every part on the back of her body, making sure to take extra care of her ass, neck, spine with his strong firm hands. Trina asked, "Are you sure you don't want to go dancing with Courtney and Kasey…"

"Naw… This all the clubbing I need right here."

"What do you think about Courtney, she cute right?"

"Hell yeah, why do you ask?" Daren said, already knowing where Trina was going with this. "I just wanna fulfill your fantasies so you keep it real with me. This way our marriage will last forever."

Trina turned around so Daren could do the front of her body. She also wanted to see Daren's facial expression.

"You know I'm down for whateva but let's find someone else. Shay and Courtney are cousins… Kasey was telling me about this Bolivian stripper. She's pricey but you don't see exotic Bolivian strippers everyday."

"Ok babe, now focus really good on my sensitive areas."

Daren went back to work on Trina's body. Trina moaned as she asked "Who taught you how to work that tongue like that babe. I get wet just thinking about it."

"I never told you before?"

"No, and I really wanna know."

"My second girlfriend used to give me head all the time at the dollar movies. One night I snuck in her room for more than some head and that's when she parked me. She told I couldn't have any head or nun unless I learned how to make her cum really good.."

"Oh really.." said Trina, feeling her heat rise..

Daren was massaging her inner thigh close to her womanhood and Trina wanted him to touch her there sometime soon.

Daren laughed, still working on Trina's inner thigh. "Yeah, I'll never forget how she said it. –You ain't getting none unless you eat my pussy good first-… So I did what she said. I wasn't that good at first, but she taught me all the right spots to lick, how much pressure to add, and how much ladies love the circling motion around the clit.."

Trina was so worked up that when Daren went down on her she came with the first few tongue strokes. Trina moaned in ecstasy, mashing Daren's face to her sex.. Trina's legs locked Daren's head in and he smiled thinking… The good life…

CHAPTER 14

MY LAST DROP

The plane ride home was boring but at least it was a straight shot Kasey thought. When he and Shay got home to their apartment they immediately took showers and got ready for bed. Daren was never here so Kasey took over the apartment's rent because Shay spent more time here than anyone. Shay moved her's and Kasey's things into Daren's room because it was slightly bigger.

Kasey sat on the bed rolling up while Shay stood at the dresser's mirror eyeing him. "What is it prego?" asked Kasey.

"I just can't believe Daren is marrying Trina." Shay said brushing her hair and readying her head wrap. When Kasey didn't reply she asked, "Did you hear me babe?"

"We ain't even eighteen yet Shay. We too young to be thinking bout that."

"I was just sayin babe."

"Me too beautiful. ."

Kasey took a deep inhale of his dro and said, "It's good to be home, back to my regular good ol dodo."

"Boy you is so crazy." Shay laughed. . She turned around with a serious look, feeling her emotions go haywire. . She sat on the bed next to Kasey with her swollen stomach sticking out of her night gown.

"Kasey . . .You love me right?"

Kasey finished rolling his blunt, giving Shay the why you actin silly look. "Of course Shay, what kinda question is that?"

Shay rubbed her stomach as she said, "I just wanna know if you would ever marry me. I wanna be a family someday. I don't want to just be your accidental baby mama." Kasey knew not to light his blunt because Shay would throw up from the smoke. "I'm not sayin that I won't marry you Shay. I'm sayin not yet. Right now I'm focusin on stackin for this baby you bout to pop out. Let a couple of years pass before we start thinkin in that direction." Kasey Kissed Shay then she lay down with a smile. .

Kasey went to the living room and lit his blunt while he turned the TV on. He sat on the couch and Korita's words started bothering him again. . What am I gon do till I get my strip club. Big bro said this his last drop too. I really ain't got no bread saved so if he slide back I still gotta do me till then. . I guess Ima have ta pull up on Rich myself.

Daren rented a white van to meet Verdugo for his last drop. Kasey, D-woo and K-9 were in the back strapped and ready for protection.. Just in case.. Courtney was in the passenger seat, dressed in a all black spandex long sleeve shirt and pants with some black heeled boots. Courtney had her money in a bag at her feet. Her usual $250,000 to cop 100 pounds. Daren thought how crazy the energy was between them because as soon as Courtney was away from Trina her phoney girlfriend act was gone.

Daren thought to himself; I'm investing 300 thousand to start my real estate company. That leaves me with enough to cop 300 pounds with Courtney's bread.. I still haven't thought about what I'ma do about the plug. I know they gone be fucked up.. Maybe I should introduce the plug to Kasey or Courtney... Naw.. Not Kasey.. That'll make him think I want him to stay in the game. If I do that Ma gone be hella heated.. Damn.

Daren drove west down Money Lane for about 3 miles until Money Lane curved, turning into Pearl Street. Pearly Street was full of warehouses and car lots. Daren pulled into the warehouse of the address Verdugo gave him with a nervous feeling. He kept telling his self this is my last drop, this is my last drop.. .Daren parked in front of the warehouses garage door and began to call Verdugo. Before Daren could make the call two men pulled the garage doors open by chains from the inside. One of the men motioned Daren in with fast hurry up movements. Daren pulled in and parked in the open empty space of the warehouse.. Daren hopped out looking for Verdugo but found only Hispanic men with automatic rifles strapped to their backs. They wore Hectors Tire Shop grey mechanic uniforms as a cover.

One of the men approached Daren and shook his hand.

"I am Ruben, Verdugo's not here. But I have your 300 pounds and two keys…"

The garage doors closed just as a forklift came from the back of the warehouse. The forklift dropped the packaged bricks off in front of Daren then returned from where it came..

"The money young brother," said Ruben in his Hispanic accent..

Daren looked back into the van and Courtney and Kasey got out, each with two bags of money. They sat the money in front of Ruben then got back in the van, just like Daren told them to do…

There was an uncomfortable silence as three men counted the money with Ruben watching over. Once everything was account-ed for a table like scale was brought out for Daren to weigh his purchase. But this time the bricks were in big compressed blocks of ten and eleven. Daren weighed the blocks one by one while

D-woo, K-9 and Kasey loaded them.. Finally they were back on the road.

It was a Friday night and Niesha's was jumpin more than it ever jumped before. Now that Daren was floodin Money Lane with player prices more people were in position to bring Daren money. Niesha's was the moment before the finish line. Where most of Daren's out of town clientele came to cop at least five or more bricks a piece.

All week Daren stayed in the wind using the van for cover. He got his last drop on Tuesday, and it was almost gone tonight. Except for the forty pounds Daren left in the stash at the trap house, which was Korita's old house. Kel called early this morning asking for twenty. When Daren told him this was his last drop Kel begged Daren to hold twenty for him and lookout with another plug if it comes his way. Kel hadn't called so Daren left twenty back at the crib outa loyalty because he could have sold them already. The other twenty was for Kasey so Kasey could stack some bread to hold him over during their transition out of the game. The problem was Kasey was having a hard time holding on to the money he made. When it came time to re-up Kasey always had a story of why he didn't have all the money . . "I got rent, car problems, phone bills, . . let me make it bro," Kasey would whine. Daren told Kasey to stop spending so fast. Just the other day Kasey bought a pound of dro in competition with Daren and called it his smoke sack. . .

Niesha's was live as usual thanks to Daren's phone and Johnnyboy's people. The regulars came in and left after they mingled to make it look good.

Courtney, Shay, Terra, Niesha, Ms. Nancy, Daren, Kasey, I.G and Johnnyboy sat around the kitchen table blowin a new strain of dro Daren got his hands on from Austin. He said his potna Cool Aid home grew it and he called it fruity pebbles. It looked just like budded fruity pebbles except it had crystals all over the buds. Daren gave Ms. Nancy an ounce of his rare dro then told Aron to chill and roll his whole pound of fruity pebbles up and just blow. . .Shay wasn't feeling good, so she took Kasey's car back to their apartment once the smoke got too thick. Kasey wasn't paying her any attention anyway. He was too busy following Johnnyboy around making sales.

Terra passed a blunt to Niesha asking everyone random questions to make conversation. For some reason I.G and Niesha was low key beefin, but Terra knew that Niesha had a crush on I.G since high school.

"What school y'all think is better, . . Riverside Hastings or Park Village. . ?"

"For shit show Hastings," blurted I.G. .

"All school's is whack," said Kasey counting money in his lap and on the table.

"I think Oak Ride Park Village was alright," said Daren.

"Way better than Hastings, . . It's all ghetto and it stank," joked Niesha. .

"How you know, you went to Hastings for like a month, you a whole park village-" Niesha cut I.G off saying, "For your info I made it through half of freshman year. I got kicked out for beatin' up your ex... What was her name?"

"Laqwasha, she almost got on yo ass though," said I.G.

"Ugly ass bitch, know you could do better," capped Niesha..

"UOO, if you don't ge tyo knock kneed, turtle neck looking.."

"I. G, you look like a burnt Kermet the Frog."

Everyone bust out laughing but Kasey. Daren shook his head watching Kasey count his money with a serious look of determination.

"Bro, take that to the van. Stop being so flashy." Daren tossed Kasey the keys to the van. Kasey caught the keys and wrapped his money in the bottom of his shirt then dipped to the garage.

Kasey sat in the passenger seat of the van and counted his money all over again. It was still $7,890. Kasey thought I should have way more bread than this. If big bro done I ain't gone have no choice but to pull up on Rich. I been flipped the same bread for no reason. I know I fucked up too.. I can tell big bro done from the way he said it.. "This my last drop bro, you betta get ya money."

Courtney walked in the garage looking good as always. She joined Kasey, standing in the open passenger door of the van. When she saw Kasey's aggravation she crossed her arm's with a devious smile on her face..

"What," said Kasey.

"I was just thinking we could help each other.. That's all.."

"Naw, I'm good.." Kasey began stuffin his bread in his pockets..

"You don't look good.. I've been thinking since Daren's fallin back maybe you and I could keep things going.."

Kasey nodded thinking it could be a possibility. Courtney did have the bread..

"But you gotta stack some bread nigga.. I only fuck with boss nigga's"

"I know I been tripped, the strip club got me. It's like a drug I can't shake.."

Courtney locked the door that lead into the house then returned to Kasey's side.. "I'll help you shake it, if you'll let me. All you gotta do is get Daren's phone and the plug." Courtney dropped down and started unbuckling Kasey's belt. Kasey spoke in a stutter, "Hhh he, he, prolly won't give it to me.."

Kasey shook out of his trance and buckled his pants. "Back up.."

Courtney did and Kasey made his way to the door.

"Get that plug Kasey, or you gon be a broke ass nigga just like Tavious.."

Kasey left the garage without a word.

Since Daren was down to his last forty bricks he decided to step in the bathroom and call Big V. He answered on the first ring. .

"You're getting faster as well as purchasing more with each drop. My friends are looking forward to this long term relationship. In fact they would like you to come to Mexico to meet them personally."

"Tell them I'm forever grateful, but I'm out V. . I'm converting to real estate." Verdugo didn't answer but Daren could hear his heavy breathing over the phone. "But I got a homegirl, . . She's been puttin up the bread for a hundred every time I cop from you."

Verdugo sighed, "Real estate, . . Sorry to hear that. I must speak to Rich on the matter. But tell me about this homegirl."

"Her name's Courtney, she my brother's baby mama cousin. She ahh. . From Houston and she bout her bread. She drives back and forth from Money Lane to the H moving a 100 a night, each time she touch down. I been givin her good prices and I know she could put up the number's you want."

Daren listened to Verdugo's plea for Daren to stay in the game. . But Daren remained firm in his choice.

After Verdugo hung up Daren called K-9. .

"What's poppin."

"Shit, I'm making preparations to fall back and I got this million dollar phone I'm trying to get off. . I don't know if you and D-woo wana go half or. ."

"Ima holla at em, if we don't wana go in Ima cop it myself. . What you askin?"

"Five grand, . . And Ima show y'all how I do. I know y'all ain't feelin Riverside, . . But it'll be simple to move everything to Oakride- -."

Daren Glanced at his phone. . "Let me hit-chu back so we can meet. Rich callen."

"O.G, was good."

"I needa favor young dough."

Daren could tell from the sound of rich's voice it was going to be some bullshit. "I just talked to big V and they not happy but it is what it is. . As for me and you we go back, . . way back till that night when I hid your father's K. . .One last drop, . . I need you to go in with me. . . 800 or so, . . half and half. ."

"Why do you need me?"

"I took a major loss, one of my car lots on Pearl Street got hit. It can't be tracked back to me, but the loss almost took me out the game. . Between me and you somebody snitchen."

Daren thought, all the more reason I'm trying to get out the game.

"Why shouldn't be your reply after all I've done for you young dough."

"When, . . and where Rich."

"Tomorrow after noon, my place."

Daren hung up then returned to the kitchen table.

Kasey was back in his seat with a mean mug and I.G was trying ot cheer him up. "What's up big dog…" Kasey shook his head and started rolling up..

"I know what will cheer you up, we going to the strip club… on me," said I.G making eye contact with Kasey… Kasey's eyes went wide with a forced smile..

Kasey laid on his back in a deep sleep, with his mouth wide open. Shay woke up early in the morning and lie propped up on her elbow watching Kasey sleep by the morning sun. Around 10am she grabbed the remote form the night stand and turned the TV on with the volume on mute.. She read the captions of women's stories who gave birth on oxygen till Kasey sat up around 12:50..

Kasey stumbled to the restroom, brushed his teeth then flopped down on the bed. Shay just shook her head. "The strip club again?"

Kasey rubbed his temples as he said, "Your cousin tried to holla at me last night.."

"I figured she would sooner or later. She thinks Daren's going to give you his phone... She's money hungry and wants to be a balla nigga's side chick.."

"What the heck is a balla nigga's side chick..."

"You know, someone to get money with and have sex with no strings attached.."

"She crazy dan a mug."

"I know, she always try's to fuck my connects if they got big money and she always tells me which means you said no."

"So you was testin me. How do you feel about me going to the strip club?"

When Shay didn't answer quickly Kasey asked, "Better yet, would you rather me cheat on you, or keep it one hundred and tell you I'm feeling another female?"

Shay sat up looking Kasey in the eye... "Be honest with me and I'll do my best to keep our sexual relationship on point.."

"How Shay?"

"Trina was telling me and Courtney how to keep your man and how she plans to keep Daren even though he had Imani while they were together. She was saying how most men will want to have sex with other women during a long term relationship so its best to be honest and open with each other.."

Kasey sat up looking Shay in the eye. "So if I like, lets say a stripper and I wanna have sex with her you'll pull her for us?"

"I'd be open to it. And it won't be a all the time thing either Kasey..."

"When I find her I'm sho gon let you know..." Kasey moved next to Shay and rubber her stomach while kissing her neck...

"I think I wanna be with you forever.."

"So we're going to get married?" asked Shay happily.

"We just might, Soon as I get my bread right...

Kasey convinced Daren to turn Korita's old house into the trap house. Against Daren's better judgement he did just to keep

Kasey out of Riverside and the Manor. The living room's couches had been moved out and replaced with a glass round table, a tv and stereo. The kitchen's refrigerator was stocked with snacks and plenty of liquor. Korita's room was left the same just in case she wanted to stop by and rest after work, which she never did. .

Daren was in his old room with the door closed and locked. He had the broken bed up against the wall and the floorboard pulled exposing his forty pounds. At the door he had a duffle bag of money so he could re-up with Rich.

Daren paused thinking; I should have stupid bread right about now. Buyin cars, houses and keepin up with Kasey's B.s really killen my pockets. Kasey spend money faster than he can make it. He lucky he my lil bro or I would have buried him a long time ago. He owe me $18,000 but I guess I could let it go for a gift for his newborn on the way. . . Naw, . . I want him to pay me first to learn some responsibility. Then I'll let him have it. I'm glad this my last drop. . I need this house for my real estate move to jump. . . I can tell ma don't really like this place anyway. Too many hurtful memories.

Daren took the forty pounds out of the stash and made two separate bags of twenty. Next he moved the floorboard and bed back making sure everything was straight.

Daren walked into the living room to find I.G, Tavious and Kasey at the round able. I.G baby sipped his crown royal and cranberry juice. Tavious and Kasey threw back shots of E&J while passing a blunt of fruity pebbles back and forth.

"Whas up wit it O.G?" I.G said watching Daren take a seat at the table with his bags.

"The game won't let me go, but I gotta trick up my sleeve for they ass." Daren put one of the bags of twenty pounds in front of Kasey and waited for his money. .

"About time big bro, dangg."

"About time my ass, 300 a pound if you ain't got all my bread Kasey."

Kasey dug in his pockets and gave Daren all he had. "I only got four grand bro."

"That's the shit I'm talking about. . . I know you had at least eight grand last night. . Damn Kasey. . . And two more grand on top of what you already owe me.

Tavious passed the blunt to Daren while asking Kasey, "Front me ten pounds cuzzo."

"Hell naw, I owe big bro too much money. And my lil mans on the way."

"Cuzzo, you know I'm good for it. Don't I always pay you?"

Kasey huffed, "I gotchu five, and I want 375 a pound by to-night kinfolk. After dis, no mo fronts."

"I should be telling you that same thing Kasey."

"Alright big bro, alright.." Daren hit the blunt real hard eyeing Kasey. I.G pulled out 6 grand and placed it on the table.. "I got the bread for 20 right now if you got it."

"Really the last 20 sold to my potna Kel. But after that I'm going to get my last drop. All you gon need is 20."

"I'ma need like 50 or 60 once I make my rounds."

"Just chill and be still. But after this, I'm done ya'll… for real for real… I like I.G, he bout his bread. Tavious and lil bro, ya'll bullshittin. Too much tricken at them strip clubs."

"Don't start naggin, acting like Ma bro…"

"I guess you think re-up money grow on trees. Don't think I won't get on yo ass Kasey. Stop playing wit my money.."

"I got you big bro. I'm done with the strip club till I get my own strip club…"

"Sounds good." Daren hit the blunt a few times then passed it to I.G…

Daren grabbed his two bags and stood just as the door bell rang.. "It's me, Courtney.." Everyone calmed down returning to what they were doing. Daren let Courtney in trying not to fall under her spell. She wore a long sleeve blouse that matched her red monkey jean skirt with some open toe heels..

"Can I talk to you in the kitchen?" she said, walking to the back not giving Daren much of a choice. Daren locked the door then followed, thinking; what could this girl want now. Daren met Courtney by the fridge, trying not to make eye contact with her. Which was pretty hard because she smelled and looked so good. "I'ma boss bitch, and you a boss nigga right…"

"Right."

"I have no problem taking things over with Kasey after this drop.."

"I already put a word in for you, but me and Kasey done…"

"I know it's just that, I'm moving 100 every time I drive to the H…"

"AND?"

"It' seems like all I do is drive now. I feel like I took all the risk for you to get out the game…"

"Your reward is well worth the risk. I charge you 250 a pound and I know all doing is dropping 30, 40 here and there to niggas you got wrapped around your fingers. I know you taxin at least 375. You making free money off my connect."

Courtney gave Daren the evil eye while tapping her heel on the kitchen floor.

"What do you want from me Courtney?"

Courtney whispered, "Why can't I just be your side bitch and run this operation while you run your legit business?"

"I'm getting married and I already got too much female drama."

"You can't say I haven't kept it G with you and Trina and you know she was askin questions.. The risk I'm takin for you ain't enough for you to dick me down every no and then."

"You keep throwin that in my face. You know what. I'm finna lock you in with the plug. You aint even gotta drive tonight. Just relax your sexy body and lets see if I can get a truck sent in your direction."

"Fine, call me when you're tired of fuckin wifey… and you will." Courtney stormed out of the house and yelled, "Bye Kasey, I.G. Fuck you Tavious.."

CHAPTER 15

A CRAZY STORY

————————∘⟨✑⟩∘————————

Daren leaned back on the counter shaking his head at the thought of Courtney. It didn't seem like a bad idea, but he owed it to Trina to do right by her. Daren looked around the kitchen and saw the dirty Pyrex's, scales and trash left over from I.G and Tavious's cooking up the keys of coke. Daren sighed thinking; I'll die before I go to jail behind these fools. . Daren's phone rang in his pocket and he just stood there. The ringing stopped then it rang again two minutes later. .

"Hello."

"Get ya money together and pull up young dough," said Rich.

"Big V ready already?"

"He say he in route but I'm doing this as a emergency drop for me. I just want all the money ready so everything will go smooth. Just pull up and chill."

Daren shook his head but said "alright" then hung up the phone. Daren ran to the door with his two bags in hand, "Trap

Daren parked his van in Rich's driveway and sat there. His only thoughts were; my hustle game so hard the game won't let me go. This shit crazy. . .Daren glanced at his bag of money in the back of the van then got out trying to shake his negative energy. K-9, D-woo and the rest of the homies sat on plastic crates spread out around the porch.

"What it be like dough?" said D-woo trying to pass Daren a blunt.

"Shit, slow booggie. . I'm good whoo." Daren dapped everyone up then made his way to the front door. Daren knocked once and Vicky answered the door a second later like she'd been waiting. "Come in baby," she said with a faint smile, but Daren could tell she was frustrated.

Daren walked in to see Rich on his couch with stacks of money everywhere. Rich spoke in his smooth calm tone giving orders on his phone while Vicky and Janice sat at the round table counting stacks of money looking like they didn't want to. Daren made eye contact with Rich, mouthing, "Was up."

"Hold up young dough."

"Ima just wait outside. Till you ready fa me to count mine."

Rich nodded then continued his conversation. Vicky huffed then let Daren back out. On his way out he could hear Rich yellin, "Y'all betta straighten ya attitudes. . . I do too much fa y'all outa kindness. . ."

Daren had a seat on one of the empty milk crates by the door. A blunt and a can of O.E came his way. K-9 pulled up a crate next to Daren as the rest of the homies moved in.

"Run a crazy story dough... Somethin funny, I know you done been through some shit." Daren search his memories then laughed to himself...

"A-ight, I got one. This is how I first got on my feet when I found my father's money. On everything my father had $970 in his stash. I don't know how I remembered. It was like a dream when I seen him in the stash because he would always wake me on accident to get it. When I got old enough I soaked up some game then hopped off the porch. With the little bread I had I was coppin 50 packs of work from Juan Lu in the mannor. Ya'll know Juan Lu, the Puertorican cat. He like 40 somethin, he drive the orange Dodge Ram and he be everywhere it jump." D-woo, K-9 and the homies nodded in remembrance..

"I had just cleaned up in the manor, flipping 2 packs real quick. After that I copped two more packs and ran down the street to the block buster. I bought some Funyans, a Sprite and some gars then headed back to the manor. My main goal was to help my mother out because we ain't have shit to eat and the lights was off. Before I could get out the stores parking lot a big black heavy set dude approached me. I immediately thought the dude was the law because he wore a white t-shirt, some black jeans and white off brand sneakers…

"Hey youngsta, letme holla at cha…" He flagged me down..

I guess I stuck out with gars in hand wearing a Nike jumpsuit with some decent air max on my feet.

"Where the weed at youngsta?" he asked.

I was more than green back then so I said hell yea like it was nothing. I ain't gon lie, I was on my roach nigga shit. I had about nine grams left in my smoke sack I copped from Rich yesterday. I was trying to pop dude for 25 then go grab another half.

"You got it on you right now?" dude asked.

I told him I didn't, remembering I had work on me and I didn't know this cat, nor have I ever seen him around. I could tell he saw my hesitation because he told me. "I'm good people youngsta, I ain't no cop. I stay in the fairway apartments, #27. Bring some weed through and I'll burn one wit-cha."

I watched dude leave and walk into his apartments trying to figure this cat out. I mashed my chips thinking if I should serve dude or not. I had work on me and ya'll know how hot it is in the manor. You really gotta be ready to serve friends and run like a track star. I drank my Sprite in a long gulp then made my way over there. I could use a lil AC break and if it look funny I'll just dip... That's what I thought anyway.

I stuffed my gars in my pocket as I knocked. "It's open youngsta." I opened the door, went in and saw dude leaned back in his recliner in his living room. "Take a load off youngsta. They call me Yella Stone."

"I'm young dough." I said as I sat on one side of the long couch.

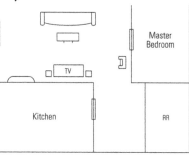

Yella Stone Apt.

To my surprise dude's apartment was nice and real welcoming. Across from where I sat was decent entertainment system, with a big ass tv. Next to the tv was a open bar that led into the kitchen. The bar was lined with the finest bottles, and it had a silver tray of upside down glasses. Dude's apartment was small so from where I sat I could see into his room if I looked to my left. All I could make out was his tv and the foot of his bed.

Yella Stone dropped a crisp twenty dolla bill on the table and waited. In a fluid motion I pocketed the money and tossed him the skimpy sack. He opened it, took a whiff. "Oowe! Wee! This some good bud youngsta."

I stood to leave but dude tossed the sack back on the table. "Roll one up."

It was free so I said fuck it and sat back down. The AC was ice cold, and the Manor never sleeps. "It's a weed tray under the couch young dough."

I reached down and found it more towards the middle of the couch, then I started breaking bud down in my lap. Yella Stone saw the small amount of bud I was breakin down and shook his head. "Roll up the fatty young dough."

So I did just that. When I finished rolling I tried to pass it, but he tossed me his lighter. I lit the blunt, took a few puffs then passed it. Yella Stone took a long hard drag then passed it back to me, holdin in all the smoke for a long while. I laughed as he slumped forward looking like he was silently hiccupping trying to keep the weed smoke in. I thought dude was about to die till he finally blew the cloud of smoke out. . .I took a few more puffs then tried to pass the weed, but he shook his head, "You know where to get some work at young dough?. . I got a home girl that like to party. She good money to youngsta."

I was feelin dude vibe, so I said, "fuck it, call her up."

Yella Stone ran into his room and came back with his roll of cord and house phone. Before he flopped back down in his recliner he was callen her.

"Sherry, I got a youngsta here that got some fire ass bud. He say he know where to get some party materials too! . . Umm humm, . . Hurry up, I'm not sure how long he gone be here. . ."

"Youngsta, she asking if its' straight drop?"

"I'm not sure, but I ain't never had not complaints."

"He say it's good, just hurry up and see what he tom bout." Yella stone hung up the phone and I smoked half the blunt by myself.

"Roll up another one if you want to youngsta."

I had a mild buzz from takin the blunt to the dome solo dolo so I sat the sack and weed tray on the coffee table in front of me. About ten minutes later Sherry let herself in locking the doors three locks behind her. I was expecting to see some fiend out smoker from the manor but Sherry was fine. She had on a black tights with a matching tube top and some red flip flops showing off her cherry red painted toe nails. She had shoulder length golden brown hair and cherry red freckles on her pretty face. The first thing that came to my mind was how I never fucked a white girl and it was crazy because she had the body of a black woman.

Sherry sat next to me acting real touchy feely as she spoke. "Hi, my name is Sherry.. Umm, this isn't a all the time thing. I just like to party every now and then. I usually get some from the manor but its always bullshit work, on top of that the rocks are always too small… Sooo… Umm.. I guess let me get a twenty so I can try it out. If its good I wanna spend some money with you."

My jaw dropped when I saw her pull a wad of money out of her top. One of her big ass titties almost popped out but she caught it. I couldn't believe such an attractive woman smoked.

"Where the bathroom at?" Yella Stone pointed to the door across form the kitchen door. When I shut the bathroom door behind me I pulled my sack of work out to check it out. I moved the fattest rock to the opposite end of the bag and tore the corner. I tied my sack back up and put it in my pocket then headed back. I gave Sherry her work as I took my seat and her eyes opened wide.. "What is it?" I asked..

"You must get this from Juan Lu, it's straight drop.."

"I don't know what you talkin bout…" I lied..

Sherry explained, "We used to mess with Juan but we had a fall out about a month ago. Ever since then we've had a lot of trouble with the manor." Before I could say anything Sherry had already took off to the bedroom. Not a minute later I could hear her smoking and coughing. The next thing I knew she was at the bar throwin shots back, screaming and tossing her head around like she was a wild sorority girl… "WHEW!" she yelled with her back to us. I guess she pulled her money out and counted then put it back on her way to sit with me.

"That's some good shit, I'm positive its Juan Lu's, he's the only one in Money Lane with work like that." She put $100 in my hand looking me in the eye, talking really fast. "I hope you're not gonna go anywhere because I'm gonna spend a lot of money with you. I have a lot of friends that are big spenders just so you know.."

I counted the money then found myself back in the bathroom with my sack of work in hand. I busted a couple of rocks down with my thumb nail to give her a decent hundred and dumped the work in some toilet paper. I returned to my seat handing Sherry her dope and her eyes lit up like it was Christmas.

She stood and on her way to the bedroom she put a piece of work in Yella Stone's hand. I leaned forward watching her stash the dope with a shake of my head. Then I realized why they called dude Yella Stone.

Sherry made her way back to the bar and fixed herself another drink. She looked back at me asking, "would you like something to drink or do you wanna watch a movie? We got pay-per-view!"

"I'm good." When I stood with the intention to leave Sherry pleaded, "Don't leave hun, I told you I was gonna spend some money. All you gotta do is sit here, relax and get paid." I didn't even get a chance to say no because Sherry handed me a drink and kindly forced me to sit back down.

"Roll up another blunt youngsta, take a load off. I promise Sherry gon bring you mo bread than you make at the Manor with less hassle."

I said to myself, fuck it. I made a quick $140 and if she by another 100 that will be all my work. Even though it was at least a pinky size blunt left in the ash tray I started rollin another blunt. It was his weed anyway.

Yella Stone stood and said, "put somethin on his mind baby," as he made his way to the bedroom. Sherry grabbed the remote from the coffee table and started scrolling through the pay-per-view movies. I couldn't believe when she ordered a girl on girl porno flick. I had my head down rollin up in the weed tray but I ain't gon lie, I kept glancing up at the TV. What she did next surprised the hell outa me because I was eighteen and had never been in this situation before.

"Dough, tell me you served tha hoe?" said D-woo.

The homies started talking about what they would have done feeling amped up about the story.

"Just chill, let me tell y'all. Y'all gon laugh y'all ass off."

Sherry slammed back a couple more shots at the bar then got loose as hell. She started swaying, whining and dancing across the living room. As I lit the blunt I glanced to my left and I could see Yella Stone's legs dangling off the foot of his high bed. If we leaned forward we would lock eyes. This some crazy ass shit I thought to myself, but I just went with the flow. I watched Sherry fold her top down and it had a hard time cupping her breast from underneath. I took a couple gulps of my drink, tasting gin and orange juice. Sherry leaned forward saying, "That's right, drink up so we can have some fun." I sat back trying to watch both Sherry and the TV, but she was blocking my view. I leaned to the side trying to see what was going on because we ain't never had no type of cable at home. It was a yella and chocolate chick about to do sixty-nine and that shit had me ready to serve Sherry, but dude was still here. .

Sherry moved the coffee table out of the way and stood directly in front of me. She rolled her top down to her waist letting her titties jiggle in my face. After that she turned around, bent over and slowly started rolling her tights down while bouncing her ass. I'm telling ya'll, this white girl had a sista ass and I wanted to hit. But Rich told me so many stories about how you not supposed to fuck smokers. But she wasn't your typical smoker on the block. I couldn't help myself, I starting rubbing one of her ass cheeks and as soon as she felt my hand she grabbed both ass cheeks then rolled her thong down. She grabbed her ass and opened her goodies for me to see. I stuck a finger in for a smell test and she had the good womanly smell. She didn't have no stretch marks, sores and her shaved pussy was really pretty. I stuck two fingers in and her body shook in pleasure.

"Yes daddy," she moaned. She managed to roll her tights and thong down to her ankles. My touch must have gave her the green light because she turned around, dropped to her knees in front of me. Sherry aggressively grabbed my belt buckle and undid it and my zipper. Once she freed my manhood she got on some real live hard core porn shit. She started slurping all loud and slapping her face with my manhood. I kinda jerked from her roughness and I thought she was going to die when she deep throated my manhood because she was choking and her eyes watered as we made eye contact. She moaned and sucked me so good I came in less than three minutes. As I bust my nut she kept on suckin, drinking every drop..

This white hoe was nasty then a bitch but I liked that shit and I was ready now. She stood and grabbed a condom from the oriental pottery on the coffee table, then dropped back down to her knees. She sucked me back to life and put the condom on my man hood.

"You live Sherry," I said…

"Thanks, now show me what you can do big daddy."

Sherry turned around and straddled me reverse cowgirl. She started bouncing up and down and screaming like I was killin her. But on the real I wasn't doing shit. I leaned forward a little to grab some titties and saw Yella Stone watching us and smiling. I sat back because I really wasn't feelin dude there. But I was already in so I got mine.

I froze from the best nut ever and hugged Sherry's back so she'd stop bouncing and screaming with her crazy ass. Sherry jump up half naked and ran in the room, shutting the door behind her.

"That's some crazy ass shit dough. I woulda man handled dat hoe," said D-woo.

That's not the crazy part.. Peep.. I went to the restroom to clean my self up and fix my clothes. I sat back down at my spot on the couch thinkin how crazy this day turned out.. Wait till I tell lil bro…

I finished my drink, and I could hear Sherry screamin over loud pounding smacks like Yella Stone was putting some major work in. I looked around as I lit the blunt really tryin to fight my buzz. I was feelin hella good and I happened to look behind me and saw some pictures. . Pictures of Yella Stone and Sherry in Army uniform with their platoon. The next line of pictures was a wedding. Yella Stone's and Sherry's wedding. . .I couldn't believe it.

I could hear Yella Stone in the room yellin, "Dirty slut, fuck'em good next time." As Dude pounded away she cried, "OKKKAAAYY DAAADDYYY!"

"Hell naw," I said as I stood. I was so discombobulated that I stumbled and ran into the door with a loud boom. Before I could get all three locks undone Sherry ran out of the room with a sheet wrapped around her body. Her face was sweaty, and her hair was all over the place. She met me at the door begging, "Don't leave, please. What's wrong?"

"What's wrong." I said looking at their wedding picture. "I'm not really down with all this."

Sherry ran her fingers through her hair to straighten it. "Oh that, that's nothing. . Stone and I are swingers. I told you we like to party. Look, just give me your number so I can call you if I need something. . Better yet, give me all you got right now."

I dug in my pocket and pulled out my sack of dope. "Give me a hundred for the rest of this."

Sherry went back to the couch and gathered her money from the floor. "Sorry I'm usually not like this. . .It's just, . . We haven't had any good dope in a while." She gave me the money and I took her number down instead, then dipped.

"Did you ever go back over there?" asked K-9.

Hell yea, they put me on feet spending six to seven hundred a week. They really the reason why I was able to buy my first ten bricks from Rich. The only bad thing was they became too needy, always needing fronts once they run out of bread till they get their next government check. On top of that Yella Stone always wants to watch me fuck his wife and I wasn't feelin that. They crossed the line when they tried to have a threesome with sherry tied up.

"Tell us another story dough." Said D-woo.

"Let me tell you bout my second bitch. . "

Daren began his second story, and a grey Dodge van came rollin up. Everyone was so in tune with Daren and faded that nobody paid attention to the van's sliding door open. Two crips with blue bandanas on their faces began firing at the house with an AR-15 and a SKS. At the same time another masked person jumped out the van and ran up to Daren's van. Oak Ride bloods barely had a chance to clap back. Bodies hit the floor while the two crips in the van continued spraying the house up. The other broke Daren's van's driver window, hopped in and quickly hot wired it. SKKIIRRTT… the van back out of the drive way.

The two vans pulled up to lil Chris house and pulled into his garage. Everyone moved quick taking the bags out of Daren van and the guns out of the blue van. Then both vans reverses out of the garage to be disposed of evidence… Lil Chris, and five other homies stood in a circle not expecting to see money..

"We musta caught em' before they got the drop.. Gotta love Tavious dope fiend loose lip ass," said G-baby..

Lil Chris rolled close to the bag on his wheel chair to get a better look…

"If I.G find out he gon be heated…" said one of the crips…

"You worried about I.G… OG said not to mess with Oak Ride. You betta hope he don't find out.." stressed lil Chris.

G-baby said, "He won't, you paralyzed form the waist down. How I see it you need your cut more than any of us. After we bust this shit down.. I'm noving to the H. As long as none of us say nothing we good cus."

CHAPTER 16

BURY MY BROTHER

Kasey, I.G and Tavious sat around the round table, each with a stripper from Wild Zebra's in their lap. The twenty pounds Daren just fronted Kasey were piled in the middle of the table like trophies. One of the bricks was split open and half poured on the table. Everyone was randomly grabbing weed to roll solo dolo blunts. Bottles were being passed around and the radio had the party jumpin.

Monique leaned back and whispered in Kasey's ear, "When are you gonna spend the night with me again. I won't even charge you."

"Whenever I get a chance. I really been on grind mode."

Tavious and Paris sat smoking and drinking until Paris got up screaming. . "OOO, this my song." Tavious hit his weed real hard while moving his head up and down and side to side to the dancing motion of Paris ass shakin in his face. Tavious blew out the thick cloud of smoke then caught his breath.

"Well fella's, I thank that's my que to exit. If you need me I'll be in the bathroom." Tavious and Paris danced all the way into Kasey's old room.

"That's what I'm talkin bout kinnn-folk," cheered Kasey. .

Monique passed her blunt back to Kasey, then grabbed the bottle of remy and took a big gulp. All the while she danced and grinded on Kasey, letting him put a hand up her skinny skirt. Back that ass up by juvenile started playing and Honey Bunz started doing what the song said in I.G's face. I.G just sat back enjoying the show like the G that he was.

Monique had a strong buzz, but she kept on drinking. She took another gulp from the bottle, set it back on the table then straddled Kasey.

"When you gon get out the game?" she asked, still grinding to the music. Honey Bunz smacked her lips saying, "Girl I hate when you get too drunk. You get all emotional n shit. We just tryin to have a good time before we gotta go to work."

Kasey replied, "It's coo, big bro gon help me get a strip club soon. Maybe y'all can come work for me."

"Does being a manager make as much money as stripping?"

"I don't know, but you can strip and manage the club for all I care. That's how live Ima be."

"I'm down, and I'll bring you a lot of strippers."

"Why you ask about me gettin out the game? On da coo money really good. I'm only gettin out the game cause big bro goin legit. But Ima still mess wit Rich on the low and keep I.G nem straight."

Monique took the blunt from Kasey and said, "It's just cause I like chillin with you and your situation reminds me of my brothers. My brother used to ride around with guns shootin up shit, pushin work, robbin. I'm mean my younger brother was with the shit for rea. In the end it all came back to bite him in the ass. He robbed and shot too many people. The next thing I know I'm burying my brother."

"I'm sorry to hear that, Life's a trip ain't it."

"Don't worry about it, it happened a few years ago…"

Honey Bunz smacked her lips. "Can we change the subject… Please!"

Monique wiped her tears away then smiled, "I know I be in the strip club with my ass and titties out. But I just be selling these dudes a dream so I can pay my bills. I really want to get away from this life.."

"I know what chu mean but it is what it is. I wish I could do something to help your situation."

"You can, let's go in the other room. I just want to feel good to take the pain away." Monique pulled Kasey to the room saying "I'll be more than your manager.. I'll be what eva you want me to be…"

Kasey and Monique hit the bed kissing and pulling each other's clothes off. Kasey said between kisses, "I hope you not bull-shitting.. But you know I got a baby mama."

"And, what that got to do wit us?"

"I'm just saying.. You deep and coo as a fan. Once I get straight I'd like you to meet my BM cause she promised me I could have a threesome… and my birthday comin up too.."

"Boy I could set you up a threesome right now, if you want…" Monique got on all fours and Kasey could see her juicy wet sex under her short shirt. Kasey's phone rang.

"Hold up, let me get that." Monique smacker her teeth while bouncing her exposed ass at Kasey.

"Call them back in a minute.." Kasey couldn't fight it so he dove in without protection. With an extra boost from the drank Kasey forcefully put the pound game down on Monique because she couldn't help but scream and run. Kasey phone rang again and he stopped, thinking, I should prolly get that. People don't just call my phone back to back unless its important.

"Hello… what.. Hell naw… What hospital… I'm on the way…"

❖   ❖   ❖

Kasey mashed the gas to the hospital praying... I hope big bro is ok... Kasey parked as close as he could then ran into the emergency room entrance. Before he got to the nurses desk he shouted "Richard Fryson's room!"

"Down the hall to the left, first door.." Kasey didn't say anything to his family in the lobby he just ran to the room as fast as he could. He stopped in the room door not wanting to believe his eyes.

Rich and D-woo were on bedrest. D-woo had bandages on his shoulder, arms and one of his legs. Rich's chest and stomach was bandaged and both of them were connect to every monitor you could think of . but Rich looked to be in worse condition than D-woo because he had a breathing tube up his nose.

Kasey approached slowly then dropped to his knees in front of Rich's bed. Kasey cried, "What happened? . . Where's big bro?"

Rich cleared his throat to speak but could hardly get his words out. D-woo's breathing was hard and his words were full of anger. "They gone Kasey. We the only two that made it."

Kasey dropped his head in Rich's bed to hide his tears, sobs, pain. . . "Ima kill who eva did dis!" screamed Kasey. . .

Rich spoke in a raspy barely audible voice, "Let it go Kasey, you don't want that on your heart."

"I know my hands bloody. I also know just because you a killa don't mean you don't deserve forgiveness. As for me, I have none. . They dead OG, I swear, I swear they dead."

Rich coughed then whispered, "Never ending cycle, break the chain. . . A mean."

Rich couldn't finish so D-wo said, "A mean hustle don't mean shit if you can't enjoy it. . Your words are always wise O.G but you stuck in bed wit a shit bag. I'm outa here tomorrow and I'll spray every house on Riverside if I have to."

Rich started to say something, but he went into a coughing fit then all of his machines went hay wire.

The doctor, nurses and C.N.A's all rushed into the room. Kasey hugged Rich crying, "He need help, . . what's wrong wit'em?"

"Sir we know, please move so we can help him." A nurse had to pry Kasey off of Rich. . Kasey half fought her crying, "It's not supposed to be like dis. . .Hurry up and help'em." One of the stronger male C.N.A's picked Kasey up and carried him out into the lobby. . .Kasey could hear, "we're loosing him." Followed by a loud electric jolt. . ."Clear!". .

Korita held Imani sitting in a numb silence in the lobby. She was in so much shock that she couldn't cry. Kasey walked slowly to his family and Shay, Trina, GG, Tavious, Domo, and even I.G surrounded him looking for answers. .

Shay hugged Kasey and they cried together. .

"Big Bro gone, . . " is all Kasey could manage to say through is pain. .

I.G stood on Kasey's side with a hand on his shoulder. . . "It ain't no body in my set, on Trey 7. . When I find out who it was they dead Kasey. . You got my word." Kasey nodded and let his tears fall.

A minute later the doctor approached with a look of failure on his face. "Is this the family of Mr. Fryson?" . . Kasey looked up asking, "Is Rich ok?"

The doctor shook his head grimly. "He didn't make it. He went into cardiac arrest and um… we weren't able to revive him.."

The choir sang life is pain as the congregation began filling in the church. Crissa, Korita and GG sat on the crying silently. Behind them sat Shay, Kasey and then Trina. The rest of the family and friends were there. And no one said a word about the bloods behind Kasey, and the Crips on the front row other side with I.G. Crissa held Imani, patting her on her chest while Korita and GG sat in a strong embrace. Kasey sat next to Shay with no emotion, staring off into space… Shay did more crying than anyone because she knew how much Kasey loved Daren. A few of Daren's friends had even showed up. Nancy, Niesha, Johnnyboy and his younger brother came to pay their respects. Even Smoker

Joe showed up, cleaned up and decently dressed. Courtney stood in the back crying not sure why her tears fell. The music stopped as the preacher gave Daren's eulogy.

"Daren Gibson was a kind hearted loving person, who often tried to take the weight of the world on his shoulders. We will forever love him for that bravery and let us find joy that his soul has returned to God's loving embrace…"

Kasey blocked out the preacher thinking.. they don't even know big bro like that.. this shit crazy.. Now what ma I suppose to do. All that money gone except the lil I scraped up . and that wasn't enough to pay for this funeral. Thanks to D-woo and I.G I was able to bury my brother.. Me and Shay most likely about to lose big bro's apartment in the fairways.. It's too expensive anyway. Now where am I gon stay. I ain't trying to stay with ma all the way in the boondocks. Ma prolly gon need her old house to get big bros company rolling…I could sell my car… Kasey shook his head thinking, dat's weak den a bitch. But I gotta do something. I ain't even got no plug to get on the grind. I lost my big bro and I lost everything.. But when I think about it I never really had anything. It all went as fast as it came.

Crissa held Imani then gave her to Korita before her fussing fit turned it into a full blown yell. Crissa glanced back at Trina and gave her an ugly look. Crissa though; BITCH, I don't see what Daren saw in her. Her ass ain't even as fat as mine. And I know that ain't no mothafucking wedding ring on her finger. I see through that school girl shit she was just with him for the money. I can't believe Daren chose that over me when I'm the one who went through nine months of doctors' visits, waking up sick and shit, then he be acting like my daddy. I was so stupid to love somebody who didn't have it on their mind to love me back and Korita with her fake ass, she play her role so good. Like she care for me. I know she just let me stay with her because of Imani. Now his black ass dead and I'm stuck with his baby. I told him I wasn't ready to be a mother.. And who is this bitch crying in the back.. Probably another one of Daren's side hoes.

Trina's eyes were pouring rain as she twirled her wedding ring around her finger. Trina felt even more pain when she looked at Daren's pearl and gold coffin in the front of the church. She kept asking herself how could the love of her life be the one getting buried today? Trina felt the envious eyes of Criss and immediately wanted to beat her up. Out of respect for Daren Trina looked down thinking; I know she's jealous of me, but my pain is deeper than hers. At least Daren got to witness Imani be born and spend a couple of months with her. My child will never get to meet his father . . EVER!!

So now what should I do? Get back in school before I get too big and lazy. . ? I got rid of my apartment and moved into Daren's house like a dumb ass. . How in the world am I going to pay for that with no job. Daren paid for everything, and I know I can't depend on Kasey. . Daren already told me how Kasey blows his money because he doesn't have to work for it.

Trina glanced up and Crissa made another ugly face at her. Trina slipped back in her thoughts trying to figure out why this woman hates her so much. If anything I should be mad cause Daren was cheating on me with her in the first place. Oh god my heart is so shattered. And I know the real Daren from being his best friend before a sexual relationship. I know if he could, he would make it work with both of us. Obviously she's childish. I don't know why I'm entertaining thoughts of her. I need to get my mind right so I can take care of me and this baby.

Korita held Imani tight whispering, "My baby, my baby, my baby." I told him not to get involved with them streets. I had to do this with K and now him. I pray for Kasey so hard, but I know I ain't got no hope with his hardheaded ass. Now I got two grandbabies without a father and its so hard being a single mother.

I.G, Kasey, Tavious and D-woo in his wheelchair lingered at Daren's burial plot after everyone left. Daren's coffin hadn't been lowered into the ground yet, and Kasey couldn't leave because his body wouldn't let him. Kasey stood with a blunt of dro lit, not giving a fuck about the cops. He wiped his nose then pulled hard on the blunt till he went into a coughing fit. Once he caught his breath he said, "Y'all don't gotta wait fa me. I just gotta see'em bury big bro."

D-woo pulled out a blunt from his pocket and lit it. "It's supposed to be me in that coffin. With all the fuck shit I done I'm still here. . .Daren saw the grey van at the last minute and pushed me. . .He tried to bust back but got wet up instead. . ."

I.G thought, grey van. . .Only one person I know gotta grey van. is G-baby. . .they use it spray shit and jack niggas. . .but only a foo would go against O.G word . ."

Courtney walked through the grass focusing to keep her balance in her black stilettos. She held her dress up with one hand and a open bottle of E&J in the other. When she joined the circle no one said a word, but the embrace of her presence was overstood.

Courtney took a sip form the half empty bottle then walked sluggishly to the edge of Daren's open grave. She squat down lookin in allowing her tears to fall.. ."Families usually don't stay for the casket to be buried. My grandmother used to say its disrespectful to leave a loved ones open grave like this.." A short moment of silence passed as she took another drink from her bottle. "I don't believe in superstition because life is what you make it. But if that's the case why do we live a life of struggle and pain?" Courtney laughed as she cried. "It's crazy how we're oppressed but instead of coming together to fight the oppressors we kill each other. I know my hustle game too hard but they could never pin-point my moves.."

"Das why we stay in the wind," said D-woo.

"Courtney who you talking bout?" asked I.G.

"The man and the ones at the bottom of food chain."

Kasey sucked up his tears and said, "I gotta figure out a way to take care of every body like big bro was. Ma ain't got nobody to rent big bro's houses so da trap squad ain't over... I.G, if you really my potna I need you to find out who did this. You already know whas on my mind.."

I.G and Kasey locked B's and C's as if it was understood.

"When the time comes I want in," said D-woo. The way D-woo's cold emotionless voice sounded Tavious knew he wasn't playing..

Courtney stood as a strong breeze blew her dress and hair...

"I'ma lay low for a while but callas soon as you get on, K Kasey."

Courtney took another sip then poured some liquor on Daren's coffin.. Then she stumbled her way to Kasey and gave him the bottle. I.G and Kasey tried to help steady her but she shouted "I'm OK!"... then made her way towards her car...

Kasey took a swig of drink then hit his blunt. He looked back and forth at the trap squad wondering why everybody was still here.

"Like I said, Ya'll aint gotta wait fa me.. I'm not leaving till they-"

"We heard you big dog, till they bury your brother.." said I.G. Kasey finally passed the blunt to I.G then took a seat.. then everyone sat down except Tavious... "I'm gone ya'll." Then Tavious made his way home with his head down...

EPILOGUE

For the next few days Kasey just lie in bed with Shay. He would watch her sleep, eat, shower and do it all over again. He barely slept and when he finally did doze off he woke maybe a hour later feeling his pain and hurt all over again. Kasey dozed off and Shay woke up next to him happy that he was finally sleep. Shay got out of bed running to the restroom feeling like she was about to pee on herself. When she returned Kasey was awake, lying on his back with his hands behind his head, staring at the ceiling. Shay climbed back in bed and cuddled close to him.

"You feelin better?"

Kasey's breath was shakey as he explained, "I guess I am. . I just don't know what I'm gona do. Shit ain't the same without big bro. I'll probly bust the rest of my weed down in sacks but I'm not used to making $10 here and $20 there, when bro had me movin weight. Now that Rich and bro gone it's gon be dry real soon."

"Just find another plug Kasey."

"You make it sound so easy, the plug was only fuckin with big bro and Rich for what eva reasons. In all the times big bro reed-up I saw dude like twice." Shay kissed Kasey's lips then looked deeply in his eyes. "Babe, it's all good. I'm sure you'll figure out a way to make money. Now stop stressing and love on me. . .Please."

"We ain't gon be in this apartment for long, and you due in a month. I ain't got no bread saved and I jus. . " Kasey paused because he was getting worked up. Shay laughed, hugging him tightly. "You're so cute when you're mad."

Kasey held Shay's stomach yelling, "Babe chill you gone smuch my lil man!"

Shay sat up laughing, then stopped quickly. . "Don't make me laugh babe, you know Kareem puts pressure on my bladder. I almost peed on myself."

"My bad, I keep forgettin you like a ticken time bomb."

"But seriously Kasey, my grama already brought Kareem a lot of stuff. I'm mean a bunch. Onesies, diapers, wipes, bottles and all that. So you don't' have to worry so much."

"I'm worried cause that's her. I ain't bought my son shit."

"All I'm sayin is you have some time still. Maybe you should focus on the positive and not the negative."

"Yea, well. . .I do have big bro's phone. I just need the plug. But before I can mess with the plug I need some money. . .I mean like some miracle money. . Some pop out of the blue rob Santa Clause money."

Shay started laughing then stopped and held her stomach giving Kasey the evil eyes. . . "Is that the hungry face?" asked Kasey. . .

"I'm craving chicken fried rice and egg rolls, wit lots of lemon sauce."

"Get the phone and order it Shay."

Part two coming soon. . .

ELEMENTALS, RISE OF THE HELL FIRE STORM (BOOK 1).

BY DAMIAN L. JOHNSON

In the year 2030, a cluster of astral diamonds came to earth from the depths of the universe and gave all life on earth elemental spirit power. But this great gift cost the human race everything they had built so far.

Fifty-one years later, Dante Saint will attempt to rebuild a fallen rebellion his parents had formed seventeen years ago. The Hell Fire Rebellion was formed to overthrow a powerful force lord of the world's richest city, 7-nations. This is the last city of pure humans as well as the city that controls the world's resources.

With the last of his family and a fiery storm of elemental power, Dante will try to bring equality to the world, but the deaths of his parents and his hell fire clan wright heavy on his heart. Dante must look deep within and use the power of elemental ascension to do the impossible.

Ascension – the art of mastering mind, body and spirit by absorbing new levels of elemental power; an awakened one can unlock the power of the higher mind and walk the earth as the highest potential. Will Dante do it?

Story told by Karma's Dream. . .

If you're a fantasy reader you're going to love the Elementals World. It's full of family relationships, knowledge and wisdom and it's a journey that never ends.

Find it at amazon.com

Book 2 coming soon. . .

The Everyone Movement

With the release of this series and elementals, I strive to create the most powerful movement known to man. The Everyone Movement is a collection of movements with the same goal in mind. That goal is world peace. The everyone movement will act as an umbrella, focused on bringing the worlds most positive creative minds, businesses or non-profit organizations together.

MISSION

I truly grew up the son of a hood legend, thinking I had no other choice but to sell drugs in his absence. If only there was some sort of platform or world-wide organization such as this one to save me from the hard knocks of life, or show me there was another way I would have been open to it.

The Everyone Movement will be the leading force that brings humanity out of ignorance and darkness. Help us find a better way to live and cope with reality. I search and strive for a unified loving people who will break down the barriers of the poverty, disease, death and the overwhelming pain felt on this Earth. When I look at life, I realize everyone is worth it, everyone has a purpose or talent. Everyone is royalty. Join us to manifest our king and queendoms. Together a heaven on earth is in reach...

If you interested or wish to join the movement:
Facebook; Damian Johnson (The Everyone Movement)
Instagram; Damian.L.Johnson1989

ABOUT THE AUTHOR

Damian L. Johnson graduated from St. Phillips College but now attends Southwest Junior College. Damian is the author of several upcoming books such as Project Cosmic Consciousness, Spirit Warriors, Trap Queen series, The Royal Family series and more to come. Damian has a passion for writing and would love to write and connect with people who find joy in his books. You can write to him at: damian.l.johnson1989@gmail.com

CPSIA information can be obtained
at www.ICGtesting.com
Printed in the USA
LVHW081757021222
734478LV00006B/639